Aerial

Flying High Duet Book 1

Manuela Rouget

Copyright © 2021 Manuela Rouget All rights reserved

This is a work of fiction. Names, characters, places and incidents either are products of the author's imagination or are used fictitiously. Any resemblance to actual events or locales or persons, living or dead, is entirely coincidental.

No part of this book may be reproduced, or stored in a retrieval system, or transmitted in any form or by any means, electronic, mechanical, photocopying, recording or otherwise, without express written permission of the author.

Editing by Zainab at Heart Full of Reads Editing
Cover design by Taylor Dawn at Sweet 15 Designs
Interior Formatting by Manuela Rouget

*To all the circus artists, pros and amateurs alike.
Even if you haven't performed in a while, you haven't been forgotten. We still want to see you on stage. We still watch your videos.
We still obsess over you.
Sometimes even enough to write a book.*

Content Note

This is an adult book, intended for readers 18+. Sex is described graphically, along with MMMF orgy scenes.

Please note that Loup and Fauve are in an open relationship at the beginning of the book, and they will both have sex with people that aren't their official partner. They do not, however, consider it cheating.

Sport-related injuries are mentioned a lot, but not graphically described. There are also mentions of STIs in the beginning of the book.

Most performances described in this story are inspired by real circus acts, but some aren't, and I don't even know if they're possible. To find out which are which, head to my reader group on Facebook, *Manu's Circus Monkeys.*

In any case, don't try them at home.

Chapter 1

Fauve

I MADE IT.
That's all I could think as I approached the massive glass building. In the past year, I had managed to convince my parents to fund this, get the paperwork done for my French business school to grant me a gap year, applied, and got accepted at one of the best circus schools in the world. I made it.

The National Institute of Circus Arts of Montréal, Canada—aka NICAM—was an imposing edifice. It had that modern, clean feel to it, almost like a skyscraper, but without being high enough to deserve the name. It was difficult to decide if it was pleasing to look at or not.

My parents gave me a year. A year, fully funded, to prove to them I had what it took to realise my dreams and make a career out of my passion. I was almost certain they were just waiting for me to fail, and for my "rebellious phase"—their words, not mine—to end. Then again, they never thought my application would get a second glance from the admissions committee, let alone pass and be accepted.

I was on the right path, and failure was not an option.

Being an acrobat was a childhood dream that turned into a high school hobby and, later, an adult passion. I started gymnastics when I was six, then moved on to circus in my early teens, only stopping in 2020 because of the pandemic. That's when my parents decided that an artistic career was no career at all, and made me go to business school to get a degree instead of pursuing my dream. Because of that, I'd wasted three years of my life studying something I had no interest in, but no more. I had just turned twenty-two during the summer, and this year was mine.

I understood my parents' point of view, of course. During the months when the sickness plagued the world, so many incredible circus companies had gone bankrupt due to confinement measures and lack of audience, but it was over now. The world's population was vaccinated and craving live shows like never before. I could make it. I had made it.

I checked my phone while walking towards the entrance. Two new messages.

Loup: Have a great first day, Plume!

Mom: Hoping to hear great news from you soon. Tell me later how your first day went.

As I read my mother's text, pursing my lips while looking at the screen, the device vibrated again.

Thibault: Smile, Pussycat, you look like someone murdered your puppy!

I raised my eyes, looking for my new flatmate's broad shoulders and perpetually tousled dark hair. We had met online a month ago, when I'd first started looking for an apartment in dedicated websites. We'd hit it off, so I did a video chat interview, and ended up moving in last week.

I quickly typed in a text when I couldn't find him.

Fauve: Where are you?

In his second year, Thibault studied in the three-year program that aimed at training complete and polyvalent professional artists with solid theoretical, physical, and creative abilities. I envied him a lot because I only had a year to stay in Montréal before I had to go back to France to be the perfect daughter. Due to the time constraint, the standard three-year program wasn't a possibility for me. I had to settle for the intensive one.

Bright green eyes narrowed in on me, and a handful of seconds later, I felt a strong arm around my shoulders. Being a trapezist carrying his flyer daily, Thibault was much bigger than me, his biceps around my shoulders almost as wide as my thigh. He also had no clue of what the words "personal space" meant. I awkwardly disengaged myself from under his arm. We'd only met last week, and this type of physical intimacy was not *at all* warranted. Yet. Thibault was positively yummy, and I wanted a bite.

"Are you nervous?" he asked.

"Not really. I was just reading a text from my mom. She's subtly telling me that she hopes this day goes horribly wrong, so I would come back home. Hence the long face."

"Oh, I see. I take it my joke went unnoticed then. Did you get it? Pussycat, nickname for Fauve, and pussies can't exactly have puppies?" he explained with a shit-eating grin.

Amongst others—like the ones causing my present predicament—my parents had this great idea to name me Fauve—a big cat in French—exposing me since childhood to several jokes of more or less good taste. I'd known Thibault for less than a week, and he was already enjoying himself.

"You are so not going to be calling me Pussycat for a whole year."

"Or what?" he teased.

"I'll think of something. Remember, we're going to be living together."

"How could I forget?" He chuckled, giving me a hungry once-over that left very little doubt to his intentions. "Okay, so not Pussycat, then. How about Kitty? Kitten? Puss? Chaton? Or do you prefer Tigress? Panther? Lioness? Feline?" He nudged me in the side as he listed my options.

"No, no, no, no, no, no, no, and no. Or I'll find something equally ridiculous for you."

"Game on, Puss. Welcome to NICAM!" He disappeared in the crowd of students that had formed as he said it, nimbly avoiding them until my eyes lost him. He moved with the grace of a dancer, which I guess he kind of was. For the second time in thirty minutes, I rolled my eyes.

I was left staring at my phone, alone amongst the unfamiliar faces, trying to figure out how to answer my boyfriend and mommy dearest. Loup's text was easy and cute; a 'thank you' with a kiss emoji did the trick. After writing three different drafts and erasing every single one of them, I decided to let my mom stew for a while instead of answering right away.

Along with the other students, I made my way to the main hall where the Dean was preparing for her speech on a dais.

Donna Loewenberg was one of the legendary founders of the Cirque des Etoiles, famous for propelling circus arts into the 21st century, thanks to their daring acts, million-dollar productions, and technological approach of performing arts. She was a mythical athlete and a businesswoman, the first aerialist to ever put a trampoline under an aerial silk and use it in her routine. I'd seen photos of the burn marks she got on her entire body rehearsing that act; they'd been both awe-inspiring and horrible.

After retiring as an artist, she'd also contributed to founding NICAM, providing her company with an endless stream of talented young performers. The woman was a living legend.

Her grey mane was pulled back in a severe bun. I knew from her videos that it fell below her shoulders. Her piercing blue eyes scanned the mass of students like a hawk, nestled above sharp cheekbones. A grey pantsuit completed her look. The only piece of her outfit suggesting that she was from a more creative background than pure business was her bright pink shirt.

She looked smart, and her reputation suggested she was actually a lot smarter than she looked. That was one of the reasons she'd always been an idol of mine.

She tapped the microphone on the podium to check its volume, arranged her notes on the stand, and finally started talking.

"Hello, everyone. I will not be falsely modest and assume that all of you know me. I'm Donna Loewenberg, and I expect most of you to be familiar with my background. If that's not the case, well, I'll have to inform you that you got lost, and the University of Montréal is next door." Students chuckled at that. She waited for the noise to die down to continue. "No strays? Good. Ladies and gentlemen, welcome to our intensive ten-month program for professional circus performers. Let me first congratulate you on your admission. Every year, we receive more and more applications, resulting the selection process to be extremely cutthroat and competitive. You are our fifty lucky newest students. Congratulations to you all!" We applauded, and once again, she waited for the room to quiet. "However, you know the selection period is not over. One of the specificities of this program is that, just like in a reality TV show, only the best get to stay until the end of the school year. Four times this year, we'll rank you based on your grades for both theoretical, practical, and creative subjects. Then, you'll do an evaluation performance in front of the class, and it will be graded, too. The average between those two grades will be used to rank you, and only the top half of the class will stay.

"By the beginning of November, there'll be selected twenty-five students attending the program; and once we near the end of January, only the thirteen best will stay. We'll conclude the program with six candidates for the last three months, who'll be competing for a spot as a resident artist in one of the permanent productions of the Cirque des Etoiles.

"Take every single subject seriously; that is the secret of a long-lasting and productive career as a circus performer. Nowadays, being good at your specialty is not enough. You have to be a complete, polyvalent, adaptable artist in order to succeed."

She looked around as she said these last words, her gaze challenging, scrutinising all of us. My competitors seemed to be coming from all around the world, even though English was the predominant language.

Her speech was well rounded. She probably was used to giving it, too, since every year a new class of the intensive program started, followed two or three days later with one of the three-year program. These guys had vastly different schedules, though, so I knew I wouldn't see them much. Except for Thibault, that was.

The crowd was very different from what I was used to. In business school, all my classmates had the same looks, outfits, and haircuts. The courses didn't nurture one's individuality at all. Here, people had more piercings than I could count, platinum blonde or psychedelic rainbow hair, and tattoos. I even saw a student with what looked like a Chihuahua perched on his shoulder; and another guy had long-ass, pastel fake nails and lashes. Everyone's originality was pouring through their pores.

I kind of loved it.

On the dais, Donna Loewenberg continued her speech. "Well, now that the unpleasant part of my monologue is over, let's get down to the logistics. Your schedule will be divided between mornings and afternoons, the early hours being reserved for more general subjects such as personal finance, circus history, anatomy, gymnastics, muscle building, dance, makeup, and music, whereas the afternoons will be reserved for the practice of your specialty. The ones NICAM can offer tutoring include but aren't limited to acrobatic, hand to hand, wheels, balancing on objects, juggling, magic, aerials, trampoline, and I can probably bring in artists from the Cirque des Etoiles to tutor you if it isn't enough.

"You're welcome to have as many specialties as you like, but be careful with your time management. Days only have twenty-four hours, and I don't care if you're being audacious and trying out new things; a boring, sloppy act is still a boring, sloppy act, and I hate them. Be smart, bold, and know your limits; that's the best advice I can give you.

"About injuries, if you hurt yourself doing something stupid, you're out. You're not here to be stupid; being a stupid performer will get you killed, and I do not want your death on my conscience. If your injury happens because, well, injuries happen, and sometimes it's just bad luck, NICAM's medical team will help you recover as quickly as possible. If you're unable to come back to your pre-injury level within three weeks, you'll be out of the program as well, but with a spot reserved for next year. This school is not a democracy, and I'll be the only judge of whether the circumstance of your accident falls in the stupid category or not."

I could not afford to hurt myself. I planned on being smart, nevertheless, my parents wouldn't allow me to come back next year. This was my only shot, and getting the job at the Cirque was the golden outcome.

"I guess I've said it all now except this: I look forward to getting to know each and every one of you. Remember, be smart, bold, and know your limits! You're dismissed for the day!" Dean Loewenberg finally concluded her speech.

"Want a beer?" I heard Cody, my second flatmate, yelling through my door.

"Sure!" I yelled back. I promptly said bye to my boyfriend and his moms—it was getting pretty late in Europe anyway—closed my laptop, and stood to walk to the living room. Cody, Thibault, and Logan were sprawled on the couch, barely leaving me any space, watching an episode of *The Office*.

I was still surprised at how supportive of my career Loup's parents were, even if they had encouraged me, bringing me to and from classes and competitions since the minute I became friends with their son, and had been doing it for years.

My two flatmates and their friend sat side-by-side on our sofa, arguing like an old couple. Logan was the one whose room I had inherited, and even if he didn't live at our apartment anymore, he still spent some time here. The first thing anyone would notice about him was his tattoos. Every single centimetre of his visible skin was covered in ink. His hair was cropped short, and he even had some unfinished designs on his skull. He had scared me a bit at first, before I realised he was the goofiest of the three, always cracking jokes and trying to make me feel at home.

"You know, I really don't get it," Thibault complained, waving at the TV. "This guy is an asshole, and he's not even funny. How can you watch this stupid show?"

I don't think he was expecting an answer, but Cody replied anyway, "It's funnier if you work in an office, and besides, it gets better, trust me." He winked at me, his storm-grey eye briefly closing behind his thick, nerdy scale glasses. He always wore them, saying he was blind without them, but I was curious to see how he would look.

Cody was as hot as Thibault but in a different way. Even having known him for a week, it was apparent he was a bit of a nerd. He studied engineering and loved all things technological. A keen intelligence always lit up his grey eyes, and his lips were perpetually twisted up in a half-smile as if he was the only witness to a never-ending joke.

His colourful outfits were always tastefully put together, and his hair combed to the side. He cultivated a stubble on his cheeks, making it look effortless while monopolising our only bathroom for at least forty-five minutes each morning.

Reaching for the remote, he switched off the TV, and handed me a beer that was waiting for me on the coffee table.

"Thanks."

I gestured for them to make space and sat on the couch next to Logan. When he realised we were all out of breathing space, Thibault slid down on the floor next to me, putting his back to my shin.

"So," Cody started as I took a sip of my beer, "tell us more about that mysterious boyfriend you were talking to just now." He grinned maliciously, watching me intently and studying my reactions. Thibault lifted his eyes towards me, observing me upside down, Spiderman style. Again, an appropriate comparison.

"He used to be my friend in school, then became my Adagio partner back when we started, as teens, really, and it... evolved, I guess? We started dating about five years ago and kept training together as well. He actually applied for NICAM, too, but didn't get in. His name's Loup."

"What's Adagio?" Logan asked. I opened my mouth, but before words could come out of it, Thibault chimed in, "Circus stuff. Like hand-to-hand pyramids, but with only two people. It's pretty tough, loads of core strength, and the artists have to be super flexible, too."

Curiosity sparkled in Logan's chocolate eyes while Cody's attentive mind caught onto another part of my explanation.

"So, I take it you're not going to see him until June? That's a long time. Will you guys be okay?" He tried to sound concerned, but his eyes glimmered with mischief.

"Loup's going to join me as soon as he gets his visa. He's applying for one of those Working Holiday ones, and they're pretty easy to get. They're only valid for one year—they make you go back at the end—but since that's how long NICAM's program lasts, it's kind of perfect.

"He's only just started the process, so he should arrive around January. Until then, we've decided to have an open relationship. We're way too young to waste four months waiting for each other. Besides, I trust him; we'll be fine." Saying the 'open relationship' part of the sentence without blushing—from both shame and excitement—was more complicated than I thought it would be. We had made that decision together, and I didn't regret it. It was quite the opposite; I looked forward to enjoying myself without Loup, possibly discovering new things I'd like or dislike, then sharing my adventures with him. Willingness to experience was one of the qualities we shared, and I was sure the ensuing conversations would be fun.

"So, let's talk hypothetically for one second; if I were to kiss you right now, and you kissed me back, that wouldn't be an issue, would it?" I suddenly felt thankful that Cody was sitting on the other side of the couch with Logan between us. I kind of wanted to know what that kiss would taste like, how my fingers would feel messing with his perfectly-combed chestnut hair, and his stubble against my skin.

"I think you just broke her," Thibault teased, watching my blush intensify when I noticed how long I'd stayed silent. I flipped them both off, and they chuckled. "What happens when your boyfriend arrives?"

"When he arrives, we'll be exclusive again," I explained. "It's temporary, nothing more."

Cody's eyes were fixed on my lips. "Well, that sounds fun." He shook his head, frowning, and added, "And what did your parents say when you were accepted? Did they throw you a party? I mean, getting accepted at NICAM is a pretty big deal."

I winced. "Honestly, they weren't thrilled. My parents don't want me to become a professional artist, and that's why I was only able to apply for the intensive program. I showed them the brochure, explained I could take a year away from school, then go back and finish. They were so sure I wouldn't get in that they said if I did, they'd help me.

"So now they're paying for everything, but I've had to promise to finish college after this year is over. If I don't get the job at Cirque des Etoiles, that is. If I get hired, all bets are off; they know nothing will make me go back. That's why I have to be the best. I don't want to go back."

There was a moment of silence, then Logan asked, "How did you meet Loup, if your parents hate the thought of you being a circus artist so much?"

I shrugged. "In high school. I had quit gymnastics, but was still great at it. He figured it out in a PE class and convinced me that circus was for me.

"And my parents don't exactly hate circus, they love watching shows, and my mom is a total gymnastics nerd. They just think I don't have it in me, and I'll end up miserable in the end. I think I broke my mom's heart when I quit that team. She was never an athlete, so she projected those hopes in me, you know?" I rubbed my nose. "We were never close, but we were closer when I still went to practices. She totally thinks circus is not as prestigious, though. She's quite snobbish, never misses an occasion to look down on me."

"Wow, that sucks," Thibault said. "Even being supported by your relatives, being good at what we do isn't easy."

"Loup's parents helped me a lot. That never fully compensated for my parents being jerks, but I couldn't have done it without them."

It felt strange to explain my shitty parents' behaviour to almost strangers. But Cody, Thibault, and Logan were good listeners, and with the year I had ahead of me, I desperately wanted them to be my friends.

So it felt good, too.

Chapter 2

Fauve

FUCK FUCK FUCK FUCK.
I totally fucked that up. It was only Tuesday morning, and I was already sitting on someone's face and making friends. Not.

In my defence, the girl I'd been partnered up with by our teacher was a juggler, and she had almost as much balance as I had dexterity with balls. Or clubs. Or rings. Juggling ones.

So, instead of helping me rise off the floor and onto her shoulders, she managed to lose her balance while I maintained my precarious one, fall on her butt, and with me on her shoulder ... well, you get the picture.

Let's just say that I was suddenly grateful we were both fully dressed.

It was not the first time someone dropped me, but it was probably the least dignified amongst all my recent falls. It was not about the landing position—I'd found myself in much more compromising situations—it was the fact that usually, when I fell, I fell doing something hard.

Not standing on someone's shoulders. This, I could do with my eyes closed, while on one foot and doing a split.

Juggler Girl—Nathalie, I'd learned earlier—stormed out of the room, her rainbow hair swinging behind her. How childish. If you end up with your face up someone's butt because you're bad at something, at least be an adult about it. And if it's because you're good at something, well... then you should definitely be an adult about it.

In a corner of the room, two eerily similar brown-haired girls—sisters, probably—were laughing at the situation. From what they were doing, I was certain Adagio was their speciality too, and they were probably mocking our beginner's mistake. As soon as Loup arrived, I'd show them what I was about.

"Hey, are you okay?" another girl from our class—Mary Sue, maybe?—asked me softly.

I realised at that moment no one had worried about my possible injuries. Not that I was hurt, but knowing people were at least pretending to be worried about me would be nice. Everyone, except Mary Sue, was still focused on their partner and their pyramid.

It was our first collective class of the day and the first since the beginning of all classes where I could have shined. Acrobatics. It wasn't a specialty class, though, so the level was pretty low. Even so, it was clear that—apart from some rare exceptions—the magicians, the clowns, and the jugglers weren't in their elements.

"I'm fine, thanks. I think by now, I'm used to it," I answered. "Adagio is what I do, and as a flyer, I kinda get dropped all the time. Pretty ironic, right?"

"Yeah, we should change the name from flyer to human crash test; that would be more accurate. My specialty is the Cyr wheel." She smirked evilly. "You know the correct word is 'top,' though, right? A flyer is when you do aerial stuff."

My cheeks flushed. Here most people understood French, but classes were in English. "There's no way I'm calling myself a top. It'll stay 'flyer' even if I'm never getting up on an aerial silk again." I changed the subject before getting the chance to embarrass myself further. "Is Cyr wheel the huge hula hoop you're supposed to do cartwheels in?" I asked. I had tried that once, ended up face-planted after flopping ridiculously on the floor like a dead fish, then courageously decided it wasn't for me. She nodded. "That's pretty awesome!" I exclaimed. "How do you not throw up?" It was an actual question; that thing spun ridiculously fast because if you spun slowly, you face-planted. Trust me, I was kind of an expert.

"The most well-known trick is to look at something that's not spinning, like your hand, your foot, or the wheel. But the truth is that you get used to it. And I almost threw up the first time. Another time, I fell in the audience because I couldn't walk straight." She winked at me before asking, "So, if I understand our situation well, your partner stormed off, and I never had one, to begin with. Wanna pair up with me? I think we have enough of a weight difference for me to be your base, and since hand-to-hand is your thing, you can climb on me and get us a good grade. I promise I'll teach you how not to throw up when you're on spinning things in return."

"Deal," I answered without hesitating. She seemed fun, and Cyr wheel really was an impressive specialty. She should at least be strong, a decent dancer, and have a great sense of balance.

At that moment, I also realised I really wanted a girlfriend who shared my interests.

I had a pretty tight group of friends back at home, but we had met in college for the most part, and none of them were artists. They didn't know the exhilaration of training for months, followed by the fear of ruining it all in under ten minutes. The careful choices of costume and the makeup applications. The adrenaline of entering a stage, of being blinded by the spotlight. The utter exhaustion that accompanied a standing ovation.

Those feelings were all drugs, and I was definitely an addict. I would like to have a friend to get high with.

"Also, call me Mary," she commented. "My parents wanted to call me Mary, with Sue as a second first name. But my father was so overwhelmed when he got to the register office after my birth he forgot to write a comma between the two. Those are pretty important, you know?"

Yeah, I liked her.

On Wednesday, Mary and I started sitting together in all of our classes. Surprising us both, Nathalie decided to sit on my other side while we listened to our teacher for the hour explain how to recreate one of the most iconic makeup looks of the Cirque des Etoiles.

The juggler focused on her notes at first, and, for a moment, I lost myself in the multi-coloured curtain that was her hair, creating a separation between us. It wasn't pastel or subdued, no. The colours were vivid, bold, alternated in horizontal stripes that created a psychedelic effect. I couldn't decide if I liked it or not.

When the teacher stopped talking and announced it was time for us to experiment on our own faces, Nathalie finally opened her mouth to speak.

"I wanted to apologize for yesterday," she whispered. "I got frustrated; I shouldn't have stormed off like that. It was one of our first classes, and I already made a fool of myself. Since I partly grew up in a circus, I thought I would be better at acrobatics, but it seems my muscle memory has failed me. So, I'm sorry."

I understood her; she really had made a fool of herself, but more because of the way she left rather than the fall itself. I didn't say this last part out loud, though.

"No problem, it happens." I extended an olive branch. I wasn't here to make enemies, after all. "I can help you get better at acrobatics if you'd like. And you're a juggler, right? You could help me train, too!"

She smiled, and nodded in approval. "I'd like that."

The rest of the week passed in a blur, and for better or for worse, I didn't sit on anybody else's face. My fall during the acrobatics class had already allowed me to make two friends; I wasn't going to push it by repeating the experience.

Our schedule was intense, class after class, following themselves relentlessly.

For now, there were no clear favourites in our promotion. It was only the first week, so everyone shone in their specialty and pretty much sucked at everything else.

It turned out Nathalie was indeed a fantastic juggler. She had based her whole routine around juggling balls with LEDs in them, and made a show of switching off the light before starting. That gave the impression that her six luminescent balls were levitating, moving so fast they almost created continuous trajectories of multi-coloured light. By that point, I was sure all my classmates were aliens with no stomach at all, because that routine and all the spinning colours, really made me nauseous. She had taken to coaching Mary and me in her art, and we trained in between classes, only a few minutes at a time, but Nat assured me it was enough to learn.

Only Mary didn't get to show off her skills, except in our dance lessons, where she was clearly the best. Even without her wheel, watching her gracefully spin made me dizzy. Again.

I got home on Friday night with my body feeling like it had been hit by a bus and then trampled by a herd of elephants. Only my dignity kept me upright as I painfully climbed up the stairs to my apartment. By the time I opened the door to my room, I was sure I was dying, and if I laid down, I would never wake up.

No, I'm not a drama queen.

I took a long soothing shower, grimacing every time I had to lift my arms, legs, crunch my abs, or move in general. I was tired, but I didn't feel like spending my first official Friday night in Montréal sleeping like a baby, so instead of jumping into bed like my body wanted me to, I headed towards the living room, where I was pretty sure I was hearing the boys' voices.

I plopped my ass down on the couch, next to Thibault, our thighs coming into contact, and gestured for him to move. He was occupying an entire three-seater sofa all on his own, so I didn't think requiring breathing space made me a bitch. Not that I was going to ask his opinion anytime soon. Cody was slouched on the beanbag occupying a corner of the room.

I frowned at him when he didn't move, and he smirked. "Don't worry, Puss, you won't have to endure my presence for long. I'm leaving in a bit."

"You're leaving? Where are you going?" I asked, genuinely curious.

"I work at a cabaret on Friday nights. I have this rope number I do there, then with Stephanie—I think you know her, she's in my year—we choreographed an aerial chandelier routine. It's pretty fun, and the pay is okay, so I do it every week. Come watch me one day if you feel like seeing something impressive." He winked at me. "Well, I really need to get going. Logan's not here, so I'll have to do my own makeup today, and it always takes me ages. See you later, Cody!"

I watched him leave, dumbstruck.

"What the fuck is an aerial chandelier?" I blurted.

"From the videos he showed me, it looks like a giant chandelier suspended from the ceiling, and he performs on it as if it were a trapeze or any other aerial apparatus," Cody explained. "With the cabaret lights, it works really well, and it's pretty awesome."

"So, that's yet another torture instrument suspended several metres above the floor? Does Thibault ever spend any time on the fucking ground?"

"He can't. Not my story to tell, though, so you'll need to ask him." Cody changed the subject abruptly. "Also, we wanted to go out and have a drink after his show is over. Are you in? You can't spend your first Friday in Montréal holed up in an apartment."

"Sure, when does he finish? If it's late, you'll have to make me stay awake. I'm beat."

"We can go early and wait for him there. How about we head out in about an hour?" he offered.

"Perfect. I'll go get ready."

Cody and I left for the bar he'd picked out at nine. I hadn't asked where we were headed to, and I should have, because it turned out to be a karaoke bar. And I was definitely not a singer.

I considered relying on liquid courage to loosen up before feeling ridiculous at the sole idea of surrendering to stage fright. I was a circus artist, goddammit. Close to a professional one, even. I was going to get on that stage and sing as loudly and off-key as I could, without relying on alcohol to numb my senses.

I pulled up my metaphorical big girl panties and gestured for Cody to hand me the songbook.

I hadn't eaten dinner yet, so I ended up having a beer with french fries and a burger while waiting for our turn—Cody having insisted on singing with me.

The song I'd picked was "My Heart Will Go On" by Celine Dion. Since I was going to be ridiculous anyway, I might as well go all in and enjoy screaming into a microphone like an idiot. Now that I thought about it, it actually sounded awesome.

The bar was packed and the queue to sing was so long that Thibault joined us before we could get on stage for the first time. The remains of his stage makeup turned his already bright green eyes into a surreal shade, and I physically felt his gaze on me the moment he entered the bar.

I wasn't particularly well dressed, but I'd made an effort, especially if you considered he had almost only seen me in gym clothes and the occasional pair of jeans. The dark green long-sleeved lace bodysuit I had on made my waist-length red hair sparkle like flames in contrast, shining in the dim lighting. My dark brown eyes were underlined with kohl and—unlike his—looked darker than their natural colour. The short black skirt I was wearing exposed my legs. After the week I endured, they were covered in bruises and burns, but I didn't care. I was proud of each and every one of the marks on my pale skin. I got into NICAM, and now I was busting my ass training to stay.

Tennis shoes completed the look to be comfortable as we walked the paved streets.

Thibault's eyes lingered on my exposed skin, and I saw both desire and respect glimmer in his gaze. He knew the amount of hard work, tries, falls, and retries it took to get to that point.

Cody's eyes followed his friend's, and he seemed only then to notice the bruises. He opened his mouth, but Thibault spoke before a single sound could come out.

"It's normal, man. Remember how hurt I get whenever I start training more intensely? Don't get protective because she's a girl. The only thing that's likely to happen if you do that is her slapping you while I hold you down."

"Maybe I'm going to start being protective over the both of you; that way, I'm not discriminating," Cody retorted. He then continued more softly, "Your bodies are your work instruments, you have to take care of them. I ..."

Unfortunately, I never heard the end of his sentence since we were then called to sing on stage. 'Unfortunately' because I was one hundred per cent preparing myself to ask him whether he was volunteering to help me take care of my body. Yum.

I took my beer with me to the stage—never leave your drinks unwatched, ladies—and sashayed to the podium, rolling my hips more than usual since I knew that Thibault and Cody were following me.

As I had planned, we sang at least thirty decibels too loud for it to be comfortable for the other patrons, and so off-key that glasses started to shatter.

I'm just kidding; I'm not a drama queen, remember?

We came back to our booth, Cody sitting first, followed closely by Thibault and me. To sit together on the same side was a tight fit, but Thibault tucked me under his massive biceps, and Cody pulled my leg over his knee, and somehow, we managed.

Cody's hand traced circles on the inside of my thigh while Thibault nuzzled my neck. I was getting more aroused by the minute and wondered if they knew the effect they had on me. It became apparent they did when Cody started hinting at us all sleeping in the same bed, and my answers grew increasingly confused.

"Thibault, how do you feel about going back home? I think our Fauvette here needs a bed."

"I agree. We should go tuck her in; this first week must have been exhausting."

So, to home we went.

Even if at that exact second, sleep was the last thing on my mind.

Chapter 3

Fauve

"I THINK I MIGHT have a shot with both of my flatmates," I suddenly blurted out.

I had slept late this morning and lounged in the living room, watching Netflix with Logan the whole afternoon. Cody and Thibault joined us then, leaving periodically. The situation was slightly awkward, but not as much as I thought it would be. I was suddenly thankful for my exhaustion that had prevented things from going any further. Not that I wouldn't have liked it, but this Saturday might have been uncomfortable.

In the middle of the afternoon, I took advantage of my lack of motivation for anything productive to call Loup. We'd been talking for a good half-hour, and I couldn't keep the words from coming out of my mouth anymore. Loup was both my best friend and my boyfriend. Talking with him would help me sort out the situation I was in.

It wasn't here yet, but I could feel a headache coming.

"Both? What do you mean, both? I thought you had three flatmates," Loup questioned.

"I'm telling you I might have sex with my flatmates, possibly both at the same time, and you're surprised by our apartment's logistics?" Typical Loup. Raised by two incredible moms, he lived in his own matriarchal world, with its own rules, and was one of the most open-minded people I knew. That was why I'd fallen in love with him, and I loved him more every day.

"I have so many questions now, Plume. You have to explain the flat logistics first. Then, I want to know which flatmates want to sleep with you. I need pictures and detailed descriptions, maybe their Facebook profiles, too. You can't be heartbroken when I get there, so I might even give them a call, make sure they treat you well.

"Also, what are you going to do about it? Are you into them?"

I smiled at the camera. My boyfriend was too cute for his own good.

"Okay, so the third one is not living with us anymore; he used to rent my room and ended up moving out 'cause the company he'd just started went bankrupt. Now, he's a tattoo artist's apprentice and sleeps on our couch sometimes, when he feels like it. He's still got the keys, though.

"The ones I think might wanna sleep with me are Cody and Thibault, you know, the engineer and the trapezist? I'm not sure if it was them dropping hints or if I misinterpreted, but I think they've had threesomes together before." My cheeks were slowly but surely heating, and it was getting more and more difficult to meet Loup's eyes in the camera.

"'Threesomes' as in *threesomes*, plural?" he questioned, emphasizing the 's.' "Are they bi?" His eyebrow was raised, turquoise eyes glimmering with mischief.

"I don't know," I whined. "It didn't come up. They're both shameless flirts, although in different ways. Both hot, too."

"What did they say, exactly?"

"Mmmh, we were drinking together, Cody was to my right and Thibault to my left, and they were both very touchy-feely—but not jealous—and then I started to have trouble talking because I was distracted, then I complained, and Cody started being almost flirty with Thibault, saying they had to make an effort 'cause I couldn't be the first lady to not be comfortable between them," I blurted without stopping to take a breath, almost leaving no space between the words and blushing scarlet red at the memory.

"Okay, and what happened then?" Loup was leaning towards the camera now, pupils dilated. My cheeks felt as if they were on fire, and heat slowly descended the sides of my neck, too. I hadn't done anything wrong, and Loup definitely didn't look angry—more divided between curious and aroused, really—but telling my boyfriend about other guys seemed wrong, taboo somehow. I powered through my discomfort. I was a strong, independent woman, and I had to trust him to ask only the questions he really wanted answered. Before I could speak, he got impatient. "Come on, Plume, whatever happened, it's okay. I just want to know what has you so flustered."

I took a deep breath.

"I'm not one hundred per cent comfortable talking to you about it, I think. I know I should be, but... I don't know. It kinda feels wrong."

He seemed to be thinking for a moment, as if looking for what to say, the turquoise depth of his eyes unreadable, a tanned hand scratching his blonde hair. He was classically handsome; light hair, light eyes, golden skin, and a devilish grin that made my panties melt every time I saw it. Said grin was slowly appearing on his face. He'd just had an idea.

"Now, now, I can't have you feeling like talking to me about anything feels wrong; it's just not acceptable. You know you can tell me anything, anytime. Right?" he insisted. I stared at him, speechless for a few seconds. I did know, but society didn't function that way. Sleeping with several men in a short amount of time would give me a label of 'SLUT', and it was quite challenging to get rid of. "Do you have my present nearby?" he continued. Again, I nodded. "Good, get ready on your computer; I'll call you back from mine. We'll need our hands free for this." He winked at me, then ended the call.

The same day I got accepted into NICAM and he didn't, Loup bought me an absurdly expensive connected sex toy, which claimed to make you feel as if both partners were in the same room. I had the male side, looking like a traditional rabbit sex toy, and he could use an app on his phone to control its movements and vibrations—even thousands of kilometres away.

I was still dubious about it. I had taken it out of its box only once to check that it worked and clean it. Talking—even in the vague-ass terms I'd used—to Loup about Cody and Thibault touching me at the club had made me all hot and bothered, though, and it emboldened me. Feeling dirty as hell, I locked the door, undressed, and switched on my computer, placing it on my bed between my spread legs so the camera had an unhindered view of how aroused I actually was.

I opened the package, sleek and black, enclosed fancily with a magnet like some kind of luxury jewel, and took the device in my hand. I hoped the battery hadn't run out, otherwise the situation would become ridiculous quickly. I pressed the button, and it started vibrating. Hurray! The battery had resisted sitting untouched in the box. I switched it off again, waiting for my boyfriend to connect.

The toy wasn't too big, a pretty bright purple, and soft and warm in my hand. I was now dying to know how it felt pressing on my clit, or better yet, inside me. That thought almost got me started without waiting for Loup to join in. Almost.

Messenger started ringing with an incoming call on my computer, interrupting the toy's journey towards my aching core. I answered the call, revealing an uninterrupted view of Loup's muscled thighs and erect cock. He'd already started massaging his length, proving for a fact that he wasn't bothered by me talking about other men.

"Hey, Plume, now you're going to tell me what happened with the two of them. In detail. Otherwise, I'll use the very convenient app I just downloaded to switch off dear Nora in your hand. Touch yourself, make yourself feel good as I watch and control your pleasure, and tell me *everything*."

I started breathing heavily, truly aroused now, but a little bit embarrassed by what I was about to do. I was a virgin as far as phone sex went, and I suddenly wished we had practiced before in less unusual circumstances.

The toy—Nora—started to vibrate at its maximum intensity. My right hand went to pinch my nipple, almost of its own accord, while the left one guided the purple piece of silicone to my clit. I gasped when they came in contact, pleasure spreading throughout my whole body like an electric current. I flicked my nipple harder. If we kept going like this, I would come in less than three minutes and without telling Loup anything about what had gone on the night before.

As if hearing my thoughts, he lowered the vibrations to a minimum. I groaned in disappointment; I was already so close.

"Use your words, Plume, tell me everything. If I like your story, I'll make you come again and again until you scream so loud your entire building knows what I'm doing to you."

I opened my eyes. I didn't even remember closing them, but it appeared I wasn't in control of my face—or my body, for that matter—any longer. My inhibitions taken away by my almost orgasm, I started talking.

"We went to a bar on Friday night, a karaoke one. At first, it was just innocent and fun, then it... changed.

"They took me back home, touching me the entire way back. The touches were never sexual, but they weren't innocent either. Always high on the thigh, or on the neck, or the crook of my elbows. Highly sensitive places. By the time we got home, my skin felt like it was on fire, my body ached for them. My panties from that night are destroyed, it was that hot."

The toy came back to full power suddenly, and I opened my eyes, that I didn't remember closing—again. On the screen, a bead of pre-cum had appeared on Loup's cock. His movements had grown more urgent, more desperate, and I knew he was as close as I was, his dick twitching under his ministrations. I was dying to lick it, feel it in my hand and on my tongue, taste the salt in his arousal and in his sweat.

"Once we got home," I continued, "Thibault knelt in front of me and almost lifted me from the ground with his hands under my thighs. I think he's even stronger than you, he moved me around so easily. Cody stood behind me, and started playing with my nipples while kissing and biting my neck."

"Oh, dirty girl. Did you like having their undivided attention?" Loup breathed out. "I bet you're getting wet just at the thought of it. Spread those legs and show me how wet you are. I want to see, show me how he played with your pretty nipples."

My boyfriend's dirty mouth was making me even more aroused than I'd been the night before. I didn't think I could be more turned-on without combusting. I obeyed, though, and the vibrations of the toy intensified, Loup's movements becoming hectic on the screen.

I started fucking myself with the toy, slowly inserting inch after inch of it into my aching core, rotating it slowly so that it would hit all the right spots. My hips bucked, making the penetration deeper, more acute.

"Thibault made me come with his tongue twice before even looking up. Cody's hands were on me as I climaxed. Fuck, it felt so good." The words were failing me, I was unable to convey the ecstasy that my body had been subjected to, the night before. "He didn't stop, though. He started fingering me, first with one finger, then with a second one. As he did so, he looked at Cody and asked, 'Care for a taste?' I thought they were going to switch sides, or that he'd make him suck his fingers, but Thibault simply got on his feet, his hand wedged inside me, and kissed Cody, open-mouthed, with tongues and everything." Lost in my tale, I almost didn't see Loup's cock twitch as hot cum exploded on his abs. A smile crept upon my lips. My boyfriend was as bi as they came. Of course, the whole situation was going to do it for him. "Loup, want to stop? You just finished, you don't have to listen to me anym—"

He cut me off by starting a new rhythm on the app, controlling the sex toy. The vibrations started increasing to an almost painful level, maintaining it for a handful of seconds before decreasing, until it stopped. The cycle repeated every ten seconds or so. I copied the new rhythm in my movements, pushing the toy deep inside me when the vibrations were stronger, and taking it out in between.

"No way we're stopping right now. I made you a promise, and you're not screaming yet." Having his undivided attention, Nora's movements started to emulate a hand's, bending in a way I didn't know it could, as if I had fingers crooking inside me, pressing hard against my front wall. It sent pleasure sparking through my entire body, my nipples throbbing painfully. "After they kissed, what happened?" He was completely focused on me now, his cock laying soft on the top of his thigh.

"Thibault got back on his knees, and grabbed Cody's arm, pulling his hand until it got between my legs, too. Thibault went back to licking me, crooking his finger" —it felt like Nora was repeating that exact same gesture as I described the scene to Loup—"and supporting my weight with his other hand. My legs had given out one orgasm earlier. He looked at Cody, and honestly, Loup, they know each other so well they communicate without words. It was so hot. Cody used his hand that was between my legs to put one—or maybe two—fingers inside me too. I was wet, and I kept feeling their fingers touching and caressing each other in me. It was so erotic, I wish you'd been there." The last part of that sentence had slipped without me realising it.

"Oh, I wish I'd been there too. I could have taken Thibault's place and sucked on your clit. Or maybe fondled your magnificent breasts while they made you come. Or even helped them and put a finger in there. Or kissed you until you were breathless, and then kissed you some more." Even on another continent, Loup knew how to play my body and mind, and I came so hard I saw stars. A quiet scream escaped my lips as I fucked myself with the toy through my orgasm. "Tell me what happened next," he ordered without even waiting for my climax to come to an end.

"Cody put the fingers that were in my pussy in my ass. I came again when he did it, it was all too much. I never knew four hands on me could feel so good."

"So, you liked some ass play, Plume. I can't wait to get there, discover what we could do together. Can you imagine this type of thing between us? Maybe I could make you come without even touching your clit." He paused for a moment, predatory eyes fixed on the screen, studying my every reaction. "What happened after that?"

"Nothing. They made me lie down on my bed, and left after tucking me in."

"Did they kiss you good night, at least?" he inquired.

"They did. Cody leaned in first, to devour my mouth, and I almost pulled him in bed with me. Then, Thibault just kissed me on the forehead."

"Oh, so they want you to want more. And tell me, do you? Do you want them both to take you at the same time, to pound inside you relentlessly until you can't remember your own name? To make you come so many times you can't walk, or even function without help? Do you want to feel stuffed by their cocks, one in your pussy and one in your tight asshole?"

Loup punctuated every question with an increase in the toy's vibration. He was controlling my pleasure like never before, almost as if he had the remote control directly plugged to my nervous system.

My orgasm built and hit me with the force of a freight train, a scream I couldn't smother escaping my lips. I clamped around the toy, my other hand rubbing my clit until I got so sensitive, I couldn't take it anymore. I pulled Nora out, my release glistening on the purple silicone, leaving a wet stain on my sheets.

"You know what, Plume? I'm pretty sure they would like that, too."

Chapter 4

Fauve

I WOKE UP WITH the worst emotional hangover ever. Even worse than after an important presentation, or the entire Christmas week. In two days, the pleasure threshold I'd managed to reach before had been multiplied threefold—at least. I felt like I had known emotional heights that I would never be able to climb again, and suddenly going cold turkey was making me feel both angry and sad.

The memories, the tales, the touches, the orgasms, and even the men were mixing in my head so much that it felt like I'd been part of a foursome the previous night, whereas I'd just spent my time, alone, masturbating in my room. My body was conscious of that fact, but my head—which had already felt unbridled lust and arousal at the hand of those three men—was fighting it, clinging on to the fact that they were with me, at least in spirit. The contrast between the two made me want to curl up in bed under a mountain of blankets, eat loads of chocolate, and watch the Rabbia show of Cirque des Etoiles on YouTube for the nine-hundredth time.

Since it was a Sunday, that's exactly what I did. Minus the chocolate, because I was avoiding my flatmates and all the sweet goodness I owned was stored in the kitchen, out of my reach. I needed time to get used to the fact that I'd almost had sex with them two nights ago and masturbated—with my boyfriend—to the thought of that moment yesterday.

The worst thing about it all? I wasn't regretting any of it. If anything, I wanted more. So much more.

That thought also contributed to my shitty mood, since the events of the previous days made me feel both too much and not enough.

Was it wrong to let Loup know exactly what had transpired between me, Thibault, and Cody? After all, it wasn't only my intimacy I'd shared with him. What would my flatmates think of it? Not that I planned on telling them. Did I? Would they feel betrayed? Or worse, assaulted in some way? Would they be disgusted to know Loup had orgasmed to the thought of them kissing? Would I? What was the difference between what I'd done with my boyfriend and a guy sharing pictures of his naked girlfriend with his friend? Neither Cody nor Thibault had been consenting to what we'd done, since it'd happened without their knowledge. The fact that they were men didn't change they might feel that their intimacy and trust had been violated. How would I feel if I were in their place?

That last question actually managed to calm me and slow down my spiralling a little bit. If I were in their place, I would probably not feel betrayed. They knew I had a boyfriend, and they knew I hid nothing from him. So, if roles were reversed, I would probably expect them to tell their girlfriends about our threesome-that-wasn't-a-threesome. And to that tale, there were only two possible reactions: angry jealousy or hot desire. Since my flatmates knew Loup wasn't of the jealous kind... maybe they would expect us to have a little phone sex over it? Or was it a stretch?

My newfound calmness allowed me to pay more attention to the show on the screen. It still astounded me, even if I knew it by heart. The sheer creativity involved to create something like it, and the talent and physical abilities to back it up were truly amazing. It was my dream, displayed in front of my eyes, my objective. I couldn't let my preoccupations over boys lead me astray. It was too important.

Feeling resolute and less panicked, I focused on the show. I wasn't even close to ready to get out of bed—let alone my room—but I was determined to get there. Or at least forget and repress everything that had happened this weekend until I was able to function around Thibault and Cody. Ideally, I would be adult enough to talk to them about it, but maybe that could be a tomorrow kind of an issue.

I woke up with a start, having dozed off hypnotized by the end credits, when the side of my bed dipped.

"Wake up, girl, wallowing time is over. I don't know what's up with you guys today, but this flat is awfully silent, and I'm done waiting for someone to keep me company. Which tea do you want? You have to pick so I can go get the others. I brought Earl Grey, a mint-flavoured one, and an herbal infusion my mom makes out of plants she grows in her backyard."

Wait, what? I unglued my sleepy eyes to be faced with a large, tattooed hand with thin fingers splayed out on my pillow, right next to my face. It took me a minute to take in the words as well as the voice uttering them.

"No, Logan, I'm not coming out of my room right now," I said while turning on my side to face away from him. "Leave me alone, please? What are Sundays good for, apart from wallowing, anyway?"

The asshole then had the audacity to pull my blanket away from me and take off running. "Get up, you'll sleep tonight. We're doing a flatmate teatime, I even brought cookies!" he exclaimed before running out of the room.

Cody

Logan couldn't take a hint. I'd known him forever, and loved him like a brother, but subtly reading people's tells just wasn't something he was good at. It was obvious Fauve had no interest at all in being in our living room. She was chewing her full bottom lip while her hands twisted anxiously in her lap.

Watching her uncomfortable in our presence, after our deed, was entertaining as hell. Since she was a lot more flexible than most people, her fingers bent back at impossible angles, and she even managed to crack her toes by pushing her pointed feet against the hardwood floor. It was weird, unique, and I liked it.

I liked to watch her move, for the exact same reason. She didn't do anything like everyone else. When she picked her stuff up from the floor, she never bent her knees. It just wasn't necessary, since she was almost flexible enough to touch the ground with her elbows. When she reached for ingredients or utensils in the kitchen, you never knew in what positions her back would end up. And when she stretched, even sitting on our couch, her whole body turned into a festival of surprisingly elegant weirdness.

Fauve took a sip of her tea, and put her mug back on the coffee table. She then proceeded to crack her neck, applying pressure on the side of her face with her palms. This... this was my limit, right there. I grabbed her hands and gathered them in mine, keeping my movements slow and appeasing, trying to prevent her from fidgeting. It didn't work; her knee started dancing again.

What I wanted to know was, why? She had seemed relatively at ease yesterday, and we'd been together the night before. What had happened last night, that had her so jittery now? Had talking to Loup made her regret what we did on Friday? The thought was very concerning. Did it mean our make-out session was a one-time thing?

We were all in the living room when her phone rang from the incoming call, but I heard the moans and muffled sounds coming from her room, much later. I wasn't spying on her, I just needed to go to the bathroom and had to pass her door to do so. She hadn't been as discreet as she was trying to be, and I assumed she was talking with her boyfriend. My cock had instantly turned rock hard, remembering the soft noises she made as she came apart in my arms on Friday.

But what did a—okay, very heated—conversation with Loup have to do with anything?

"So, how did you guys meet?" she awkwardly asked, her eyes resolutely fixed on the coffee table. She had freed her hands from mine to hold onto her tea as if it were a lifeline, and my eyes met Thibault's. My trapezist best friend was seated on the other side of the couch, and had, just like me, picked up on Fauve's body language. At least his puzzled look told me that much.

"Cody and Logan's parents met because they went to the same nanny. They were like two years old, right?" Thibault looked at Logan first, and then at me, checking the accuracy of the story, as he did every single time. It was just part of the experience, at this point. "My parents met theirs when I was in elementary school. They hit it off, and so did we. We've been inseparable ever since, even if we've ended up taking wildly different paths."

Fauve managed to relax slightly while Thibault was talking, sipping on her tea as I watched her shoulders loosen up. She had a strong body, too muscled and thin, to be within the contemporary conception of beauty. Yet, again, I liked it.

Thibault finished his tea, put his mug on the coffee table and stood up, saying he had a rehearsal to get to. My best friend had no idea what the word "rest" meant. Having freed his hands too, Logan grabbed his notepad, laid down on the sofa and started sketching on it, resting his head in Fauve's lap.

"Oh, take your mug back to the kitchen, will you?" I scolded him. Thibault was one hundred per cent an artist, and he often forgot that dishes didn't wash themselves. With an apologetic smile, he obliged.

Taking advantage of the newfound quiet, my French flatmate angled her pretty face towards me, and with a wavering voice that did not sound like her at all, said, "Cody, this is going to be awkward, I know it, but I wanted to talk to you about something, and I think I might as well rip the Band-Aid off." So, it sounded like I was about to learn what had her fidgeting so much after all. "With the whole open relationship thing, I've been meaning to do an STI check-up as soon as I got settled, but I don't really know how it works here. In France, there are specialized hospital wards where you can go without having an appointment. Do you know if it's the same in Canada? Maybe you guys could come with me, just in case they ask me stuff I don't understand."

"Um, yeah. Maybe?" I hesitated. What did I say to that? "But why do you need a check-up, anyway? You and Loup have been together for years, right?" The words left my mouth without giving me time to consider how prying they were.

It didn't seem to upset her, and she explained, "Well, that's the only way of being certain. I know I haven't slept with anyone else, but..." Her voice trailed off, and she started avoiding my eyes again. I didn't press on, taking off my glasses to clean them, the familiar gesture settling me during this weird conversation.

"Okay, fine, I'll come with you," I said after adjusting them back on my nose.

"I need to go too, we can make it a group date," Logan chimed in happily, barely lifting his eyes from his notebook. "I'm overdue for a check-up anyway."

"And... uh," she hesitated, "do you think Thibault could come, too?"

I narrowed my eyes at her. This conversation was getting weirder. Suddenly, what she was trying to do dawned on me, and I exclaimed, "Fauvette, are you trying to trick us into getting checked up for STIs?" My smile turned mischievous, while she started twisting her fingers in her lap again. Her way of bringing the subject up had been both smart and mature. Slightly manipulative, too, but it was for a good reason.

It also meant she was considering having bare, full-blown sex with me—us. I readjusted my pants to prevent my hardening cock from becoming completely apparent through the fabric of my jeans.

"No!" she protested. "It's not a trick, it's just—"

"Tsk, tsk, Fauvette. It's all good. I'll ask Thibault when he can make it and we'll go all together, like very good friends." I winked, watching an adorable blush climb up her neck and on her cheeks.

This year was going to be fun; I could feel it already.

MANUELA ROUGET

Fauve

The next few weeks fell into a more relaxed rhythm, after that intense first one.

Mary Sue, Nathalie, and I became quite the inseparable trio, getting along better than I could ever have imagined.

Mary's unwavering self-confidence never ceased to amaze me, while her sarcasm amused me to no end. Unlike me, her parents approved of her career. Originally from Eastern Europe, they were gymnasts that had immigrated to the UK before she was born. They taught gymnastics to kids in a small town close to London, and she was only unable to attend the three-year NICAM program because of the associated costs. She was twenty years old—younger than me by eighteen months, even if her mature behaviour fooled most people—and I quickly started considering her as a little sister. If our build and colouring weren't so different, we could have been.

Mary's physique betrayed her parents' origins. With her big glacier blue eyes, pale skin, and straight, almost platinum blonde hair, she could have easily been a contestant in a pageant and won. She was also taller than most women in our class and had the delicate features of a beauty queen. Only her muscles and calloused hands made her athletic career known. Just like everyone in our class, the girl went through gruesome physical training on a daily basis, and she was built.

Nathalie was crazy smart and quick on her feet. After all, as a juggler, she had to be. She was a year older than me, having taken the time to get a degree in Marketing from the University of Montréal, before applying for the program we were in.

Her little sister, Keira, lived with her in a flat her parents rented while touring North America with their circus company. I was slightly jealous of her upbringing, creative and free. Both Roy sisters were jugglers, and Nat's plan for her first evaluation presentation involved the two of them together on stage. I couldn't wait, my friend on her own was already a sight to behold, and she said her sister was close to her level. I couldn't wait to see what they would come up with together.

We spent most of the time at NICAM together. After partnering up during the Acrobatics class—more or less successfully—we also did in Makeup and Dance, and even when classes didn't actually require partners, we would still help each other by giving the other pointers and constructive criticism. Nat also made Mary and I practice our juggling every morning.

At home, too, we fell into a more comfortable routine. I had learned not to come out of my room too early, since the pull-up bar installed in the corridor was on the way to both the kitchen and the bathroom, and Thibault worked out bare-chested in the morning. After coming out and almost drooling all over him, I had started waking up half an hour later.

I'd discovered that I loved watching TV shows with Cody and Logan. For some reason, the heating system in our living room had a problem, and nestling between their warm bodies on our sofa after a day of strenuous exercises became a moment that I regularly looked forward to.

We planned to go to the hospital for our check-up next week, and I patted myself on the back for how responsible bringing up the STI subject had been. I was already feeling like shit that Sunday, so why not take advantage of it and take care of an unpleasant conversation? Two birds, one stone.

Plus, I wasn't oblivious to the way Thibault and Cody looked at me, it was going to come up at some point. And while the other rules we had put in place with Loup about our open relationship were negotiable, the we-do-not-get-sick one was a hard limit. I had felt a bit guilty implying that my boyfriend might have cheated on me—I knew he'd never do that—but Cody had seen straight through me anyway, so I figured it wasn't that bad.

I was also discovering that Logan had mostly been away that first week for my benefit. I was starting a new life in a new place, after all, and he thought that having someone, especially the roommate I was replacing, crashing in my living room while I was still trying to find my bearings, might be overwhelming.

Now that he knew we got along, he was spending more and more time at our place. By the third week of our cohabitation, I had walked in on him lounging in his underwear in the living room more than once. When I questioned his absence of clothing, he'd pointed to the multiple still healing, sometimes upside-down tattoos on his arms, legs, and lower torso, and said in a matter-of-fact voice, "My boss only gives me the simple, boring designs to do on customers. He says I have to get better for him to give me more complex assignments. But how am I supposed to get better if I don't do anything challenging? I swear if I have to draw one more infinity symbol, I'm going to plant the tattoo gun in my eye instead." He'd then taken a few deep breaths and continued, "Of course, you can train on fruits and everything, but once I draw a design I like on a non-living canvas, I like to make it on someone's skin so that I see how it really looks, how it heals, that sort of thing. Since I'm just starting and I don't have that many volunteers, I tattoo myself a lot."

"So, are you the one who drew all of your tattoos?" I asked, impressed.

"Most of them, yes. Obviously, I didn't do my back, or my right arm. But the rest are all mine. Some of them are terrible, I know," he said with an embarrassed smile, "but I'm getting better, and I'm pretty proud of my most recent pieces." He pointed to a geometric, upside-down dragon tattoo drawn in shades of grey on his right thigh. "I'm still retouching this one, but I like the art a lot. That's why it's upside down, actually. I like to look at it without having to stand in front of a mirror."

He was right, the artwork was amazing. With pointillism and thin lines, the drawing was both unique and lifelike. I took it all in, only now paying attention to how hot his ink-covered body was. There was visibly a lot of unfinished work on it, bigger pieces that would require several sessions to complete, but I liked seeing the process, the work he put in before reaching an amazing end result. He let me ogle him a while longer then, totally misreading the intentions behind my perusal, and teased, "Hey, if you like my work so much, maybe you could give me a theme, and I'll create a piece for you."

"No offence, Logan, these look great on you, but I'm never, ever, not in a million years, getting a tattoo."

Chapter 5

Cody

WE ARRIVED AT THE clinic in the early afternoon. Halloween was coming up, and walking in the decorated streets with a gawking Fauve had been fun. Apparently, the holiday wasn't as important in France as it was in Canada, and watching her experience things for the first time was quickly becoming one of my favourite activities. I had to figure out more stuff she had never done before so it could happen more often. The thought brought a lot of hot scenes to the forefront of my brain. Would she like my ideas?

My excitement died down as soon as we arrived at the hospital, though, and all my creative sex scenarios were replaced by thoughts of all the times I should have been more careful in my sex life. I mean, I attended all the sex education classes on protection and contraception, and even aced the exams. I just hadn't applied those lessons to my life as much as I should have. Since Thibault had participated in some of the times when condoms were forgotten, he was probably beating himself up over not being careful as much as I was.

I wasn't exactly an optimistic person; it was one of the reasons I was the top student in my class. I was great at imagining what could go wrong, how it could go wrong, and how to fix it. It made me especially good at engineering.

At that moment, though, it meant that I was already imagining how to explain to both my parents and Thibault's that we were HIV seropositive because of a hot threesome, including the both of us and a blonde with very large breasts.

TMI? Probably.

My preoccupation must have been apparent, because Fauve caught my hand and Thibault's and held them tightly, pulling us inside the hospital as if she thought we were going to bail. My eyes met my best friend's, and he looked even more scared than I did, so I understood her concern. Logan followed us whistling as if he didn't have a care in the world. He also got check-ups a lot more often than we did, and was responsible in the bedroom. That probably helped him be more relaxed.

I understood my fear was stupid, if I were to catch an STI because of unprotected sex, it was better to know it early on. My anxiety was bordering on nausea anyway.

Logan went ahead of us and showed us where the waiting room was. We sat, Thibault and I quiet while Fauve and Logan were chatting carelessly. I envied them, as much as I liked fucking bareback, it was never going to happen again, unless the person could prove they were clean. There was no way I was going through this level of useless stress again.

Fortunately, the wait was short, and two nurses entered the room asking who was going first. Fauve simultaneously poked me and Thibault in the ribs, and we stood up without a word.

After leading me to a small room, the nurse asked me a series of questions, and declared she needed to draw blood because my homemade tattoos were a hepatitis C risk. I knew Logan was crazy rigorous with his material and disinfection of tattooing areas, so I wasn't concerned by it at all, but extended my arm anyway.

Ten minutes later, I was out of the room, with a sample number and an appointment to get my results the following week. I met Thibault in the waiting room, Fauve and Logan having left for their exam. He had a manila envelope under his arm. He probably didn't need the blood test, lucky bastard.

"So?" I inquired.

"All clean." He beamed, his shoulder muscles visibly uncoiling.

I exhaled deeply. If Thibault was clean, the chances I was, too, were high.

Fauve and Logan joined us as I finally allowed myself to relax. A bit.

"Hey," she said, holding a carbon copy of Thibault's envelope to her chest, "how did it go?" Then her gaze navigated between Logan and me. "You don't have your results?"

"No," I answered, "it takes a week to analyse blood samples for hepatitis and the rest, we'll have to come back."

"Hepatitis?" She frowned in confusion.

"You can get it through tattoo material, but I'm not worried. Logan never uses the same needles twice, and is super thorough in his disinfecting."

"Of course, I am," my friend protested. "I care about my customers!"

Fauve gave me a very slow once-over, as if trying to see through my clothes. All my ink was hidden, though, making her focus turn laser sharp.

"You have tattoos?" she asked, trying—and failing—to sound unaffected. I smirked.

"Oh yes, Fauvette, I think I had over twenty the last time I counted. I'm Logan's favourite test subject." I winked, smug as fuck. My smile grew bigger as I watched a blush appear on her cheeks. Logan and Thibault chuckled at my obvious flirting.

"Where?" she asked again, her voice pitched low as she played with a strand of her hair.

I wrapped my arm around her shoulders, starting to walk us towards the exit. "Oh, in places where they're easy to hide with work clothes. So mainly legs, back, shoulders. My most recent is on my lower abs, maybe I'll show you someday," I said cheekily.

She turned scarlet red, which made us all laugh.

"Come on, let's go home," she demanded, walking away from us.

I ogled her tight ass for a moment before following in her footsteps, Logan and Thibault flanking me, still laughing.

Fauve

As October advanced, the competitiveness in our classes increased exponentially, the first evaluation presentation—and with it the threat of being kicked out—creeping up on us.

Mary and I threw ourselves into rehearsals. We had decided to join forces, the teachers having given us complete creative freedom, and we'd figured coming up with something more original and daring, would be easier together.

I video chatted with Loup, too. He knew exactly what I was capable of and usually had good ideas. I talked to him almost every

Saturday, and he knew everything that was going on in my life, both at NICAM and outside of it. I had needed an extra call from him to help me and Mary put our act together. The three of us had brainstormed for almost two hours before coming up with a plan for our performance. My bestie and I had thought of performing together for a while, but now needed a concrete idea, and talking to Loup had helped.

Nathalie had started rehearsing with her sister, so we saw her less even if we still practiced our juggling together every morning. She was so busy the rest of the day that we went from spending every school minute together, to only seeing each other before eight in the morning.

As planned, Logan and Cody went back to the hospital, and both their results came back clean. It had changed the atmosphere in the apartment, all touches becoming charged, electric almost. Considering the rehearsals and associated exhaustion, we hadn't had time to do anything about the desire that saturated the air—to my growing frustration. Cody announcing that he was covered in tattoos had made my curiosity—and lust—go off the charts, and I was just dying to see them.

The three weeks before the performance were an emotional roller coaster. I spent some moments feeling fine, then the next minute, I started to freak right the fuck out. I couldn't get eliminated in the first round. It was just not a scenario I had considered.

Two weeks before D-day, the device we'd made for our presentation arrived, and our real training began. Cody helped us make the plans for it and find a manufacturer that could have it done in under a week. It was nothing too complex, so it wasn't too much of a challenge either.

Our idea for our performance was bold, neither one of us knowing if what we wanted to do was possible. We'd never seen anything like it, which was both a very good thing—the teachers would be surprised as hell—or a very bad thing. Like, impossibly bad.

We trained and planned and rehearsed until late every day, only stopping when utter exhaustion and a bit of desperation overwhelmed us. Not counting the day of the show, we still had ten full days to go until the performance, so all things considered, we weren't late *per se*. But we were still in that phase of the rehearsals, where it looked like everything was going to go wrong, and nothing would ever come together.

That night, I was so upset when I got home that Cody—having stayed up waiting for me to know if the device he'd helped us make was working—spooned me in my bed, caressing my hair as I fell asleep.

I slept well for a few hours until my body awoke me at five thirty in the morning—an entire half-hour before my alarm was scheduled. Nerves buzzing with adrenaline, I jumped out of bed, scrambled three eggs, and devoured them with buttered bread before heading to NICAM. There were going to be some long days in my immediate future.

I had stretched for one full hour, and rehearsed for four when we first left the corner of the gymnasium Mary and I had claimed as our own. One of our classes of the week was on the other side of the building, and we had to get going if we didn't want to be late.

We had considered skipping, but honestly, we needed a break. Look at me, considering an aerial arts class a break. Stress was making me completely insane.

We got to a light-coloured room, bathed in autumn light passing through windows that covered an entire side of the wall. I hoped they were at least double-glazed, otherwise imagine the heating bill in winter.

The room was nice, though, with its high ceilings, light-coloured mattresses on the floor, and industrial setting; it managed to look refined and inviting at the same time, a blank canvas oozing creation. A variety of aerial apparatuses were dangling from the ceiling, most of which I already knew, at least by sight, if not by name. I felt comfortable, serene, and my days truly needed more serenity right now.

"Hello, everyone. Please, please, come in."

I turned slowly when I recognised the voice, a smile growing on my face. Thibault had just come through a door to our right and was smiling back at me. He waved at Mary and came to stand in the middle of the students, his right hand rising to ruffle his dark hair.

"Some of you might know me. I'm a second-year student at NICAM, and one of the best aerialists in the professional program." He flashed us all a cocky grin, his green eyes sparkling. I swear the room was suddenly flooded with oestrogen and wondered if I was the only one suffocating. "Since there are no aerialists of any kind—or at least, not yet—in your class, you've been divided into smaller groups for your first class. That's why we, as students, are teaching. Because it's only an initiation, I will have no problem guaranteeing your safety." He managed to flex his enormous biceps while saying it, and students swooned. I rolled my eyes. He really was incorrigible.

He divided us between the most standard equipment; trapeze, aerial silk, and aerial hoop, and showed us a series of simple exercises to do while he walked around and gave us pointers.

When he came at my side, I was suspended upside down, trying to convince my hands that it was okay to let go, even if only the very sensitive back of my knees were in contact with the trapeze bar. I remembered being able to stay in that position when I was a kid, but for some reason, everything in me now screamed that I couldn't hang on and was going to fall. How stupid. I was a lot stronger than when I was a kid. Body awareness really was a curious thing sometimes.

"Hey everyone, stop and look at me for a second," Thibault started. I began to get off the trapeze, but he interrupted me, "No, Fauve, not you. I need you for a quick demonstration. Keep doing exactly what you're doing.

"Look here, in this position, some people feel more confident than others," he said it very matter-of-factly, and I was agreeably surprised. My flirty, teasing flatmate seemed to take his teacher role seriously. "A simple way to help is to place a hand on the ankles of the aerialist, at least, when the device is low enough. It will make it completely impossible for them to fall, and at the same time, alleviate a little bit of the weight." He encased both my ankles in his big, calloused hand, and pressed down a little. "Go ahead, Fauve, let go. I won't let you fall." Feeling a little more secure, I did and even shook my arms under me to relax my hands. It really wasn't difficult after all.

Crunching my abs, I reached back for the bar and unhooked my legs to get back on the floor.

"Thanks," I said, beaming at Thibault.

"Anytime, Fauve, just let me know if you need my help again."

Seeing Thibault teach was... nice. Before actually witnessing it, I would have sworn he would be one of those teachers who took advantage of their position to steal inappropriate contact, or just tease awkwardly. But he had the opposite attitude, completely focused on his task, professional, in his element, genuinely happy to share his passion and distributing kind gestures and proud encouragement to everyone.

It was well known that confidence was sexy, but watching my aerial arts teacher stroll through the room as if he owned it, I was discovering that paired with a respectful and kind attitude, it was irresistible.

He hadn't called me by my nickname once, but wasn't cold either. He was treating me and behaving like a caring teacher would.

When the period ended, I left the classroom much more flustered than if he had been his usual teasing self with wandering hands.

Serious Thibault was a real turn-on. Who would have known?

Chapter 6

Fauve

IF I CONTINUED PACING like this, I was going to wear a hole in the floor of the backstage area. This, I was sure of. But I couldn't help myself. Adrenaline was riding me hard, and no amount of stretching or controlled breathing helped me in any way.

Mary and I weren't ready for this performance. We had been too ambitious in the planning of our act, and with only a couple of weeks to rehearse, our routine unfolded perfectly about only one time out of four. We risked our spot in the second phase of the program, sure, but we also risked a serious injury. Even if we had modified our initial idea to simplify the act, nothing we did was without risks.

Three weeks ago, we asked for Cody's help to create a three-metre high Cyr wheel; the objective being that I stand on Mary's shoulders then perform the act as an acrobatic duo, both twirling inside the wheel.

It didn't work, at all, and I realised how insane an idea it was. So, we'd adapted and modified the act, using the giant prop more like a décor element than actual circus apparatus. It was aesthetically pleasing, but I was worried the difficulty level of our performance was way too low to pass this exam.

As I watched the performances before our own, I was sceptical of it. We would not make it.

The other students had kept their cards close to their chest, that much was apparent. The level had risen drastically tonight, as opposed to during our classes. Perfectly executed and daring acts were in succession while I peeped through the heavy red velvet curtain.

Nathalie and her sister, Keira, had put together a juggling in the dark act, using seven LED rings instead of the balls she usually favoured. As always, watching the colourful trajectories made me nauseous, so I didn't watch the entire performance; going back and forth between the backstage seats, the bathroom to check my makeup, and the curtain to check up on the act. The petty part of my brain was praying for one of the rings to fall, while the nice, supporting part scolded it for not wishing the best for a fellow artist and friend.

After the juggling act, came a comical magic one. Between training and discovering Montréal, I hadn't had the chance to fraternise with all the members of my class. The two girls on stage, Stacy and Clarissa, were part of the ones I had never talked to. They were amazing, though, going through their quick-change routine flawlessly, the outfits snapping on their bodies without anyone understanding how they had stepped out of one and into the other. And they were funny, with their Barbie doll attitude and overly rigid motions.

By the time it was our turn to perform, my stomach tightened and my breath fell short. I felt like puking. Mary and I held hands, took three deep breaths, and she said for the millionth time, "Relax, girl. Stop freaking out, we've got this."

Just like all the other times, it didn't help—at all—and I tried to dry my sweaty hands on my red mini dress.

We made our way to the centre of the stage, and just like every time I performed, I felt my artist persona coming out, drawn out by the applause, the lights, and the terrifying second of silence before the music started.

This was where I belonged.

The first notes of "Far Away" by Sophie Maurin started playing, and Fauve Laurent ceased to exist, replaced by a confident acrobat who could do anything.

I helped Mary up onto my shoulders. I wasn't used to being a base, and my body wasn't adapted to it, but only she could control the giant Cyr wheel well enough to give it its first impulse. She couldn't do it from the floor, either, since it was huge.

Mary took the steel ring in both of her hands and sent it rolling. It started making circles around us, giving a lazy rhythm to our routine, echoing the music. When she aced it, the wheel spun for the entirety of our routine, acting like a surreal metronome.

Her mission accomplished, Mary jumped down in an extended backflip so graciously she appeared suspended in the air for a moment.

That first part was always the tricky one—if I didn't stay immobile and my body toned enough—Mary didn't have the necessary support to get the wheel in motion. We had lost hours getting her on my shoulders, only for her to fall down the moment she bore the weight of the giant steel prop. I sported two enormous, raw, purple bruises on each side of my neck, just above my clavicles. For this reason, padding had been added to my costume mini dress.

This time, for the first time of the day, it went perfectly. A part of me almost started a celebration right then, but it was quickly smothered by the focused part of my brain.

The rest of our act was all things that I was used to doing. It was different from usual because I was partnering up with Mary and not Loup, and my new bestie and I didn't share the same connection I had with my long-time boyfriend. At home, when the Duo Animal—our stage name—was performing, panties flew, and the audience caught on fire.

This time, as she had said in our first class, I was climbing all over her, doing splits and backbends and handstands to get us a good grade while she supported me.

Overall, it wasn't a poor performance, but I was far from proud of it.

Failure left a bitter taste in my mouth.

I was coming back home, still mulling over the depressing announcement I had just heard. Even after a good half hour, it didn't bode well with me. Looking up at the little lights on the metro plan, I remembered the events of this insanely stressful verdict day.

We had been left to our own devices all day on Friday. In the morning, we were supposed to have an aerials class again, since it was the only class that wasn't taught by the deliberating teachers. However, after a few minutes of warm-up, it was apparent that no one in the class paid any attention to what Thibault said. He dismissed us with a verbal kick in the butt. According to him, "Being suspended several metres above the ground while thinking about something else was a short path to an early grave." He might be right on that one, but everyone was too worried to care. Which proved that he was, in fact, definitely right. Falling headfirst towards your death should unquestionably be a source of preoccupation.

I couldn't go back home, though. I didn't want to be left alone and bite my fingernails in the dark, which was exactly what I would do if I went back. So, I stayed at NICAM. The place had a very distinct smell, a mixture of sweat with rosin and magnesia, the two powders acrobats and aerialists used daily to respectively stick or slip on the apparatus. I hated rosin; it was almost impossible to get off once you had put some on and increased the probability of burn in case of a fall. It also massively decreased the risk of falling, but my brain failed to understand that part.

I breathed in the smell several times, in case it was the last.

Then, I caught myself doing this sappy shit and went to grab a coffee. I was almost certain our performance wasn't enough for us to stay in the program, but I needed someone to say it to truly start grieving. At this point, I was a big lump of anxiety shaped like a human being.

I spent some time creating an Excel table, simulating all my test results in all the subjects, then the grades I would have to get at the performance to pass, and that calmed me down a little. Then, I started doing the same for all my classmates, but since I didn't know any of their grades, it was a shot in the dark, all based on hunches and my opinions. It relaxed me, the familiarity of playing with the software helped in unknotting the giant ball of nerves that was my body.

Numbers were easy, reassuring, and it was one of the reasons why my parents didn't understand why I disliked Business School so much; I wasn't bad at it. The thing was, it was so boring it felt like my soul was dying a little every minute I spent in class.

Being an artist was hard in the sense that it was all about what others thought of you. Art wasn't countable, measurable, or classifiable. Numbers added up or didn't, and the answer was almost always irrefutable. Art had interpretations, periods, movements, and what was worthless at one time could be worth millions a century later.

With the performing arts, add the challenge of their ephemerality, and I was suddenly in an intense conversation with myself on whether my existence would leave a mark on earth, or if I would just dissolve into nothingness and be forgotten.

Yeah, I needed that verdict. I needed it badly.

After several hours that felt like months, the time to gather in the hall came, and an unusually silent crowd started to assemble in front of the ever-standing dais. Minutes passed and after what seemed like ages, the teachers climbed the steps to the podium, the dean following them this time. None of them seemed happy, and the students quietened more, stopping all unnecessary movements and ruffling.

Dean Lowenberg needed to get on with it, otherwise someone was going to pass out from holding their breath for too long.

"Hello, everyone. We've known each other for two months now, so you know I'm not the type to beat around the bush. I'm going to call out your names in ranking order until twenty-five names are called. Then, everyone I haven't called will know that, unfortunately, they have to leave.

"It may seem like I'm torturing you by announcing your rank in front of your classmates, but we want you to know who to look at for example, and how to progress. Your detailed grade report will be sent to you by email.

"And without further ado, our best student this bimester is..." Someone I'd never even heard of. If I ended up staying, which was very unlikely, I needed to become more aware of the competition, get my head in the game, because I was becoming ridiculous.

Nathalie ranked fifth, and both Mary and I cheered hysterically when her name was announced.

The quick-changing Barbies ranked eighth and ninth.

The Adagio girls who'd mocked me ranked thirteenth and fourteenth.

I dared to hope when Mary ranked twentieth, but she was an incredible dancer, and a decent acrobat, so her grades in those two subjects must have helped.

Only five names were left; if my name wasn't one of them, I was going home, back to France, back to business school and my judgemental mother.

There were worse fates, for sure.

The verdict came, and all the adrenaline left my body, replaced by bone-deep exhaustion.

"Ranking twenty-fifth," Dean Loewenberg continued, "and our last student to pass on to the next phase of the program, Fauve Laurent!"

Twenty-fifth. I had ranked twenty-fifth. I was still in the program, but felt defeated, anyway. That had been a close call. *Way* too close.

Mary and Nathalie cheered as loud as I had for them, but my ears weren't registering the sounds anymore; it all felt muffled, distant.

"Hey, girl!" Mary shrieked, pulling me into her arms and wrapping me in a tight hug. "We made it! We're in for another phase!" I extricated myself from her embrace, and she continued even louder, "We're going out to celebrate with the others! Are you coming?"

"Sorry, girls, I can't tonight. I'm really not in the mood. Another time, okay?"

"Come on, you'll feel better with a beer in your hand," she said softly, understanding my state of mind. "Or do you want us to come back home with you? We could watch a movie."

"No, no need. I'll be fine," I reassured her, wanting them to enjoy themselves. After all, our gruesome training would start again on Monday. "I'm just going to go back home." As they were leaving, I suddenly remembered to not be an ass, plastered a fake smile on my face, and called, "Nat! Congrats on your fifth place!"

"Thanks." She laughed, throwing her rainbow hair behind her shoulder. I relaxed my face again, letting my disappointment at my own failure show as soon as they were out of sight.

In that instant, I just wanted to snuggle between Logan and Cody, and watch *The Office*.

Because if anyone talked about anything circus-related, I was going to cry.

Scratch that. I would hit said person. *That* would make me feel better.

Chapter 7

Fauve

Logan was—for once—at his parents', and like every Friday, Thibault was working, so instead of the flatmate sandwich I was originally planning for, I had to settle for snuggling on Cody's bed. The traitor had already watched half a season alone, and I swatted him playfully on his arm when I found out.

"Ouch," he complained while massaging his shoulder.

"You started without me!"

"I would have watched it again with you! I thought you were going to go out to celebrate. Thibault heard you passed and texted me. Congrats, by the way, that's awesome."

"Cody, honestly?" He raised a brow at me. "I don't want to talk about it. I was the last one to pass. The last! And as I was going out of NICAM, I kinda thought of hitting the first person who mentioned circus tonight, or bawling my eyes out. I already just hit you and I don't want to cry, so let's talk about it tomorrow, okay?"

"Okay, Fauvette, no problem. Come here, then."

He was watching the show on his computer in his lap, with his head propped up by some pillows, and extended an arm in my direction. I laid my head on his shoulder, and encouraged by the comfort I got from physical contact, intertwined our legs. Exhausted by the events of the last few weeks, I dozed off after a half-episode.

I woke up horny as hell. There was no other way to describe it. It was a common occurrence, and I usually took care of it on my own, but this time I woke up with my head still on Cody's chest, and his grey sweatpants-clad crotch right in my field of vision.

Keeping my breath even, taking advantage of the mass of red hair hiding my face, I decided to play a little, my left hand slowly venturing down south. I had no way of knowing if he was awake without revealing that I myself was, so I just started teasing, resting my hand on his lower stomach and caressing the skin between his t-shirt and pants with only my little finger. I was still obsessed by what he had said at the hospital. His latest ink was on his lower abs. Could I uncover it without him realising it?

"Fauvette, are you awake?" Cody murmured.

Busted. Well, I might as well make the most of it.

Saying nothing, I rose on my elbow, threw my hair over my shoulder, and leaned in to kiss him.

As I said, I was very, very horny, and didn't want to waste time. I rotated my hips so that I straddled him, grinding on his hardening dick while trying to pull his t-shirt up. Cody's body was pretty. There was no other way to say it. Contrary to Thibault and Loup, who worked out because they needed it to be good performers,

Cody took care of himself purely to be aesthetically pleasing. He wasn't as strong as them, but had defined shoulders and abs, and long, apparently tattooed legs that I wanted to free of clothes.

"Fauve, please stop for a minute. I need to check something," Cody said, pushing his glasses up his nose, all the intensity of his grey eyes fixed on me. "The Sunday after we made out, you were super uncomfortable while we were having tea. Was it because you wanted to ask me to go to the hospital with you?"

Wow, so not where I thought this was headed. I sat on my heels, still straddling him. He was hesitant, propped up on his elbows, looking up at me.

My skin already felt too sensitive, too hot. I needed his body to touch mine, his weight to ground me. His gaze was unflinching, though, and I knew I was going to have to come clean.

"No, our conversation wasn't why I felt awkward. Or not the only reason," I said, my voice still a bit sleepy. He raised an eyebrow at me, its unruly peak showing up above the frame of his glasses. I bit my lip, blushing a little. I would have to get better at these conversations, if these situations were going to keep happening. And since I very much wanted the sexy times to be happening, talking seemed imperative. "You remember that Loup called me the next day?" He nodded. "Well, I told him what happened, and umm...we got uhh..."

I was still looking for the appropriate words in between my hesitations when Cody cut me off, "Fauve, did you guys have phone sex over what happened between you, Thibault, and me?" he asked with a sly smile. I swatted his arm. Again. My flatmate was pushing my buttons tonight. "Ouch. So you masturbated and you're not particularly proud of it. Why aren't you proud of it, Fauve? Are you ashamed of us?" He pulled me down on him, nuzzling my neck, biting softly at my earlobe.

"I didn't say we did it." My denial came out way too breathy for him to take them seriously. He didn't.

"Really, Fauve." My name on his lips felt like a caress to my core. He said it with an emphasis on the 'f' sound, and it was legit one of the sexiest things I'd ever heard. "You're blushing even harder than when you were mumbling about it. If we weren't in this position, I would probably take you to a hospital. That colour does not look healthy." I hit him again on the shoulder, a little less playful this time. It was not a mature way to have this conversation, but his hot breath on my neck was way too distracting for me to do anything else. "Stop. Hitting. Me," he groaned.

To emphasise his words, he flipped us over, pulled my arms above my head, and held my wrists in his left hand. I could free myself, of course. Training every day as a circus artist meant I had enough upper body strength to match his. But his shift in position lowered his body onto me, and the pressure sent a shiver through my sensitive skin, making me moan. He didn't continue the way I wanted him to, though, reaching for something next to the bed and moving up to straddle my torso.

The new angle brought the still growing bulge in his dark sweatpants in my line of vision, distracting me from Cody tying me up to the bed frame.

"What are you doing?" I breathed.

"Making sure you're not going to hit me again. And I'm not strong enough to hold you down, so rope it is." I moaned, again, in frustration. For once, I would have really liked to be underestimated. Cody knelt between my spread legs, looking down on me. "You're so beautiful like this, Fauve, splayed out for me like an offering. I feel like driving you crazy, just like you made me feel when I thought you regretted what happened between us. You know I spent hours worrying about going too far with you?" He raised my t-shirt then, slowly exposing my ribs, then my naked breasts, and using it to trap my elbows and cover my eyes. The thin material crumpled around my upper arms, so my eyesight was effectively blocked. "Tell me to stop, and I will."

He started pulling down my jeans, taking off my panties and socks with them. I was naked from the neck down, and without being able to see his face, it felt oddly vulnerable. I felt the bed dip on each side of me, and he pushed up my t-shirt a little more, capturing my uncovered lips in a bruising kiss, undulating his hips to press the seams of his pants directly against my clit. I cried out in his mouth, the contact simultaneously too much, too rough, and not enough.

"What am I going to do to you now?" He rose again, and not knowing what he was doing, was slowly driving me insane. "I bet you're already wet for me. Do you like talking about your other lovers while you fuck? Such a dirty girl, we should have guessed from last time." He put both his hands on my upper thighs as he spoke, framing my throbbing core like a piece of art. He dragged his warm palms down on my splayed legs, pushing them apart as far as they would go—which was a lot, considering how flexible I was.

Taking advantage of the exposure, he blew on my clit, the cold air making me groan like a porn star. He hadn't even touched me where it mattered, and I was already really close to begging, feeling desperately empty.

"Please, Cody, I need you," I surrendered. "I woke up wanting you, and now—"

"Wait a minute, I'll grab a condom."

"Cody!" I moaned in protest.

"What? STIs aren't the only things they prevent. Are you sure you want to go bare?"

"Yes, and I have a contraceptive implant in my arm. Now forget about that and touch me!"

He spun me around suddenly, hands still on my thighs, so that I was belly down on his sheets. I felt even more exposed and vulnerable. He pushed my hips up, raising my ass in the air, setting a pillow under me to make me more comfortable.

I heard him move around in his room, then a popping sound, and then his steps brought him closer to the bed.

There was something deliciously taboo about my position, about the fact that he was still fully dressed, and I was stretched like a cat in heat, exposed and willing. I needed him to fill me, and I needed it now.

"You know, after last time, I bought us a present." 'Us'? As in Thibault and him? Or as in him and me? Or Thibault, me, and him? "Tell me you're okay with this Fauvette, I'm going to experiment a little. And if you don't like it, tell me, and I'll stop immediately, no questions asked." I moaned loudly. Whatever tests he had in mind, I wanted them. I wanted them all.

"Cody..." I said breathily.

I felt a cold substance run in between my ass cheeks. I was close to trembling, goosebumps all over my skin. "It's not too big, so it should start stretching you nicely. Do you want us to take you both at the same time someday?" My pussy clamped on air, and he slapped my ass cheek. "Answer me."

"Yes! Cody, yes...I want you both at the same time! I've thought about it, too." He chuckled, the sound masculine and self-confident.

A soft surface came in contact with my puckered hole, and I felt Cody slowly pushing in. "Relax, Gorgeous, it's small. It should feel really good," he said tenderly. I did what he said, and he pushed the lubed-up plug inside me. I moaned until the flared part came in contact with my ass cheeks. He started fucking me with it, and I couldn't take it anymore.

"Cody, please, I need you, please." My skin felt so tight it hurt, and I was pulling on my bindings, needing hands on me. If it had to be mine, then so be it.

But I was tied too tight and couldn't get free.

"Do you want me to leave it in, or...?"

"Leave it!"

"What do you need, Fauvette?"

"Fuck me! Get naked, and fuck me, Cody, or I swear I'll find a way to get free and finish myself off," I threatened. I heard a ruffling sound, and my threat must have worked because the next thing I knew, I was being stretched out deliciously. He roughly squeezed my hips as he buried himself inside me to the hilt, pressing his thumb on the sex toy in my ass. I was so wet from the anticipation that the stretch was pure pleasure. "Ah!" I yelled, feeling deliciously full. "*Yes*, Cody, fuck me."

And he started doing exactly that, slowly at first, and then hard and fast, making me cry out every time his pelvis met my ass. His palm slapped on my butt cheek and I yelped, feeling my orgasm close, but not quite there. I turned my head, repeating his name more or less intelligibly in the bedsheets.

"Do you guys need an extra pair of hands?" I suddenly heard Thibault say. In my sex-induced haze, I hadn't heard the door open. Too far gone to answer, I just moaned when I felt another presence between my legs.

Waiting for a hand on my clit, I whimpered when the contact that arrived was way too wet and warm to be a finger. Was Thibaut licking me? Nothing stopped that guy. Not even the perspective of getting up close and personal with his flatmate's balls. That was sexy as fuck.

"Cody, man, could you remove that pillow, please?" Cold air hit my clit when he spoke, proving it was indeed his mouth between my legs.

The pillow was removed from under my hips, and Cody, still standing with his knee against the bed, resumed his deep fucking, hitting that delicious spot inside me with every slow stroke. He took a step back and pulled my hips with him, so that his friend could sit between his legs and the bed, facing him. A long moan escaped my lips, when his tongue darted out to lick my dripping pussy, and Thibault then started sucking my clit in earnest.

It was too much. I was lost in the sensations, unable to focus on anything as my orgasm kept building like a tsunami. A hand—Thibault's?—started to caress my ribs, going up until it reached my breast, fondling it and tweaking its sensitive peak. A thumb—Cody's?—pushed harder on the anal plug then, sending my orgasm crashing through me, making me lose myself in the divine sexual pleasure and sensations. I cried out for what felt like hours. My muscles clamped around the plug and Cody's dick, and after a few strokes, he came too, leaning heavily on my lower back and groaning as he did.

He pulled out and I relaxed on the mattress, utterly spent. I felt someone untie me, and soon was faced with Thibault, a shit-eating grin plastered on his face. They were glistening with my juices, and he looked completely unbothered by it.

"Puss, that's definitely the hottest thing I've ever done. We should do that again, maybe just without Cody's balls slapping on my chin." I went to punch him in the shoulder, but Cody caught my arms from behind me.

"See why I tied her up?" he teased.

The trapezist winked. "I'm sure that's the only reason." He then leaned in and captured my lips in a bruising kiss, tasting like me.

After a handful of seconds, I broke it. "Cody, you need to stop playing with that toy, or I'm going to jump one of you."

"I don't see why that's an issue," he said without stopping his stroking.

Well, if he didn't see the issue, who was I to argue?

After at least five more orgasms for me and two each for the boys, we cuddled in a big pile of limbs to rest. I had finally explored every inch of Cody's skin, and traced every single one of his tattoos with either tongue or finger.

I was more or less in the middle of our cuddle puddle; my head propped up on Cody's biceps, and Thibault half lying on me with his legs between mine and his nose nuzzling my neck. It was a little weird, to have such a big, strong guy using me as a pillow, but I was warm and comfy as hell, so moving was not part of my plans.

The trapezist—I had caught myself calling him mine in my head several times and corrected my thoughts right away—was drawing abstract symbols on my belly, and the gesture would be arousing as fuck if I hadn't just been repeatedly, thoroughly fucked. Cody's hand was almost resting on Thibault's back, and suddenly remembering Loup's question from our conversation the other day, I asked, "Hey, sorry if this is an awkward thing to ask now, but are you guys bisexual? You have chemistry, and you kissed the other day, and now you're all comfy with each other..."

Both turned towards me, making me shift to see them at the same time, and I almost jumped their bones again. Really, with their sex hair and sleepy eyes, they were a mixture of cute and handsome that apparently turned me on even with a sore pussy. Down, girl.

Their gaze turned thoughtful, and a little bit embarrassed, too. It might have been better to broach the subject with each of them separately. But, well, they had been friends for a long time, and we were all naked in a big pile of limbs on Cody's bed. Surely, they could talk about this type of stuff together. Right?

Thibault opened his mouth to talk, but Cody cut him off, "You know, I've asked myself this question several times, but I've never really looked for the answer. You know how they say, 'Don't ask a question you don't want the answer to?' Well, I think this is one of those for me; every time it popped up in my head, I just shut it down. If I discovered that I am indeed bi, what would I do with that knowledge? Would I have to come out? It is scary as fuck, but would I be comfortable in the closet? I don't feel ready to even think about it." He lowered his voice to an almost whisper. "Although, the fact I don't have a clear answer to that question is probably answer enough."

"You know, Puss," Thibault chimed in, "I've read an article about a lot more people being bi than we think. It was on the Kinsey scale, I think. We place ourselves in those restricting categories, those boxes, which are super important, since they allow you to find people who are in the same boxes as you. But sometimes, they can also be prisons.

"For instance, if I'm attracted to women eighty per cent of the time, and men the twenty remaining per cent, I'm technically bi, but do people who feel like this, label themselves bi? I don't think so, they probably round it up and say they're heterosexual. At the same time, is it worth facing all the hate and prejudice if you're perfectly happy as a straight guy almost all the time?" Thibault and Cody shared an understanding look, their friendship and complicity palpable in the air. The trapezist then turned to me, two green lasers piercing my eyes. "Puss, can this conversation stay in this room, please? Neither of us feels comfortable about this."

I lifted my chin to softly kiss Cody, my neck bent at an odd angle since Thibault was still on top of me, then put my hand on the trapezist's jaw, raising his head to repeat the gesture.

"It'll be our secret," I whispered.

I went back to snuggle in Cody's embrace while caressing Thibault's hair. I understood what they were telling me more than most. Loup had already come out as bi when we met, but we still talked about it a lot. My boyfriend was particularly pissed at the fact that, since we had been dating for so long, most people thought that his coming out as bisexual was just the result of a rebellious teenage phase and he was now straight. Then, when he explained it wasn't a phase and he was just as bisexual now as he had been six years ago, we usually got awkward prejudiced questions like if I was worried he would cheat on me with a guy. Just to be clear, I wasn't. But my usual answer was to ask if my nosy interlocutor was worried their partner would cheat on them with someone better in bed. That usually took their misplaced curiosity down a notch.

I wasn't about to out Loup to Thibault and Cody though, so I silently laid there, soaking up their affection. I didn't believe you had to be close to someone to have sex with them, but good sex had a way to make people become intimate, not only physically but also emotionally and intellectually.

And at that moment, I really liked it.

•

Chapter 8

Fauve

With November, came the first snows and the endless lazy days inside, watching the outside world get covered in a white blanket.

Or that's what I dreamed of, actually. Instead, I had to brave the elements and get my ass to NICAM to attend classes, then practice, and then, when all that was over? Practice some more.

I wasn't complaining, though. Being selected last a couple of weeks ago had lit a fire under my ass, and I was more focused than ever.

Because of my almost complete business school degree, I dominated all the analytical subjects—like finance or marketing—having done one version or another of them before. Acrobatics was still my specialty, and I was one of the best in the class at all things balance, flexibility, and rhythm related. The aerials were outside my comfort zone, but everything considered, I was doing well. Balancing on objects was also under control, for the same reasons. Well, apart from unicycling. But after spending two entire days falling on my ass, I was certain their riders were supernatural beings that could levitate, so that didn't count.

The second bimester was also marked by my discovery that I really enjoyed learning magic tricks. Cardistry was surprisingly akin to juggling, all millimetric manipulation and resolute intent, except instead of being shown off, in cardistry, the manipulation had to be invisible. Levitations were also fun, calling to my soul as a flyer.

The look of astonishment on people's faces when a magic act was successful was deeply rewarding, satisfying the part of my brain that liked to always stay one step ahead of my audience. I was nowhere near sufficiently competent to create my own, but could memorize and reproduce existing acts well enough.

Thanks to Nathalie's tutoring, juggling classes were also under control.

There was one subject I really couldn't bear, though.

Clowning.

I loathed it with all my heart. It was legit one of the scariest things that I had ever done, and they made me wear ridiculous outfits to do it. Making people laugh was a lot harder than doing a handstand or—the money maker for acrobats—opening a split. Those guaranteed an applause. But to make an audience laugh, you had to bare your soul to them, and sometimes, depending on who they were and where they came from, it didn't even work, or worse, they could get offended. Most times, when I was the one telling the joke, no one laughed. My delivery was terrible, and I had no sense of timing, which sucked big, hairy balls.

I was going to have to work twice as hard on my second performance, because my grade in clowning was not looking good.

At home, Logan was noticeably absent. I knew he didn't actually live with us, so it wasn't preoccupying, but I missed his antics.

Whenever we could, Cody, Thibault, and I went out at night to have snowball fights. Even with the freezing cold, I loved it. Circus had always been my happy place where I went to let all the stress of the day go. The downside of trying to become a professional artist was that it had taken that refuge away from me, since almost all my worries were related to it.

Hence, snowball fights, where we rolled around on the ground like kids, and went back home panting and soaking wet.

On the weekends, I often studied at our living room table, next to Cody, who used that time to finish whatever task from his internship was the most urgent that week.

It was a comfortable routine, and I liked it.

"Wait a minute, *mon coeur*, I'm going to my room," I said, picking up my laptop from the table where I was studying when Loup called. I quickly crossed the corridor, and closed my bedroom door before sitting on my bed, my computer on my lap. I arranged the pillows to get more comfortable, knowing our calls usually lasted for a while. "I'm ready, Loup. How are you?" Then, taking in his scowl and tense shoulders, I added, "Did something happen? How was the party last night?" I knew he and his friends had organised an early Christmas party, since after that day some of them were travelling and there were no more available dates.

"It was good, I think there were about fifty people. We were at Matthieu's flat. He's my friend from work, do you remember him?"

"Yes, we met at that bar before I left, right?"

"Yeah, that's him. And it was cool, everyone brought lots of food, and drinks, too." He wrinkled his nose and ruffled his hair. "I'm actually pretty hungover right now, today isn't my greatest day so far." I smiled. Why did I find seeing people suffer from hangovers so amusing? "So, I got there, ate, and had a couple of drinks, and then we started talking with a friend of Matthieu's I'd never met before, Aurélie. Pretty cool. Attractive, too." I suddenly got a feeling I knew where this was going, and kept my face carefully neutral. "Anyway, next thing I know, we're making out in the bathroom, and she whips a condom out of her wallet." He was avoiding looking at the computer, and I felt the need to reassure him.

"Hey, that's okay. I'm not angry, we've talked about this, and it's cool. What happened next?" His back seemed to straighten a bit at that, and I breathed better. I didn't like him beating himself up over something when he hadn't done anything wrong.

"Well, we fucked, and made out for a bit after that. It was good, not mind-blowing, but we had had a bit to drink, so I guess that was expected.

"It was kind of nice, though, I missed being intimate with someone, you know?" I nodded. Being with Cody and Thibault was nice, so I couldn't really judge him for seeking physical comfort. "The tough part came after. A lot of people that were at the party know you, Plume. Or at least they know you exist, and that we've been together for a while.

"Nobody really talked to me about it—and a part of me is happy that they care so much about you—but the looks, Plume. The looks they threw me when we went out of that bathroom, it was obvious everyone knew what Aurélie and I had been doing—because of the noise, maybe? I don't know. Anyway, it was horrible. So judgemental and condemning, as if I was cheating on you and being a terrible boyfriend.

"Guilt has been gnawing at me ever since, and I couldn't really tell them what you're doing with your flatmates, because then I would have sounded like I just wanted to get back at you."

"Were you? Trying to even the score, I mean." As far as I knew, he hadn't hooked up with anyone since I left.

"No, I really wasn't. She was cool, and we got along fine, and I enjoyed fucking her." I probably was the weirdest person on earth because this conversation wasn't freaking me out. I wanted to be freaked out, as if to conform to what was expected of me in this specific situation, but I wasn't. In the end, now that he needed comforting, he was coming to me. I was the first person he wanted to tell his problem to, and in my mind, that was way more important than a drunk fuck in a bathroom.

"Then, that's fine, Loup, I'm really cool with it. As long as it wasn't to prove anything to me or get back at me. If you did it because it would make you feel good and you wanted it, then I'm not angry, or upset or anything..." And I meant it. I didn't want his hook-up to be out of spite, which was about as unhealthy as a behaviour could go, but if he wanted her for himself, then that was fine with me. "Do you want me to talk to your friends?" I offered. "Or we can change our relationship status on Facebook, if you want," I joked. "Make it known that I'm fully aware and on board with what you're doing."

"No, I'll talk to them. I'll explain the situation. I'm just annoyed it hasn't come up before. I hope they won't think I talked you into the open relationship thing. People are weird when it comes to accepting that women have sexual desires, too."

I really loved this guy, and told him so. He was amazing, and I couldn't wait to have him here. I still felt the need to change the subject.

"And how's therapy been going?" I asked. Since he was a kid, Loup had a very bad fear of heights. The first time I went to his house, he had a panic attack because he walked in on his mom standing on a stool to change a lightbulb. Over the years, it had slowly improved. He'd researched about his phobia, and explained it to people around him so they could help him avoid triggering situations.

When I had been accepted at NICAM, he decided to start seeing a therapist, knowing that aerial classes were part of the mandatory subjects. Ever the supporting boyfriend, Loup was pushing himself to be able to attend every single one of my performances. I felt a little guilty about it, if I were completely honest. I didn't want him to go through difficult situations, ever, and especially not because of me.

He winced at my question, though, and said, "Not great. It was going okay—the pictures of your aerial class helped, by the way, thanks for sending them—then *Docteur* Fabre asked me to stand on my chair and I spiralled again. He had to help me down." Loup ruffled his hair with his hand, giving me an uninterrupted view of his lean arm. "This is so fucking frustrating, Plume. I'm an acrobat who can't even stand on a *chair* without panicking."

My lips curled up in an apologetic grin. "Relax, *mon coeur*, these things take time. You have to be patient with yourself. I'm already so proud of you for doing this, and I'm sure your moms are, too."

"I know, I just thought it would go faster, I guess. Oh, and there is something else I have to tell you," he blurted, as if he had just remembered it. "Your mom is pissed that you're not answering her texts. She called me and told me to tell you to call her. Please do it, Plume, I know she's not going to say nice things, but I don't know what she'll do if you don't."

"Okay, fine, I will. I promise."

We started talking about lighter things then, while I was mustering up the courage to call mommy dearest.

He told me how he had already informed his boss about him resigning soon, how the visa paperwork was going nicely, and he hoped to arrive before my second NICAM presentation to help me with it. I chatted about my newfound routine, the unforgiving weather, and my friendship with Mary and Nathalie.

"*Mon coeur*, I need to hang up. I'm going to call my mom now before I chicken out."

"You do that, Plume. I love you, talk to you soon."

"Love you, too."

I hung up and clicked on the call button next to my mother's ID before even thinking of putting it off again. She loved me—in her way—of that I had no doubt. She had always been there for me when I needed her, but somehow, we could never have a nice, relaxing chat, and that's why our calls were rare and far apart.

She answered on my second try, and I tensed, prepared to be as accommodating as possible, to get it over with.

"Hello, *ma chérie*, how are you? I see you're too busy to call your mother, now?"

"Hey, Mom, sorry, classes have been really crazy lately, and they've changed the selection process this year, so now I have to create and rehearse acts on top of everything."

"Oh, yes, that's right, by now you must have had your first ranking. What was it?" I winced, reluctant to admit what I considered to be a failure.

"I ranked twenty-fifth, but I'm studying really hard now, and I'll do better next time."

"Twenty-fifth? See, I told you this program wasn't for you. You've never had much competitiveness, anyway. That's why you stopped gymnastics. At least, that was a real sport. Do you know your cousin had the best grade of the region at the Bac? I never expected that of you, but it's pretty impressive, don't you think?"

My mom loved to always compare me to anyone she deemed more successful, while never really congratulating me for my own victories. When I was accepted in my business school, she said it was only the third national best, so it wasn't really an accomplishment. When I received the letter from NICAM, well, it was only the one-year program, and not the true professional degree. The fact that she had made me apply to that specific program didn't seem to factor in the equation.

My cousin had graduated from high school in June—close to six months ago—and had achieved one of the best grades in History at the French national graduation exam, the Baccalauréat—or Bac, for short. My mother never missed an occasion to remind me that she was amazing, and I was me.

"Yes, Mom, she's very smart," I agreed. "I need to go now; I have to get back to studying."

"Studying, what could you possibly be studying in that clown school?" I ground my teeth. I wasn't about to take that bait and argue with her.

"Bye, Mom, I'll talk to you soon." Before she could answer, I hung up with a sigh. That was rude, but I didn't care that much.

Irritated, I took my computer back to the living room, where Cody was completely absorbed by a TV program I'd never seen him watch before. I put my computer down on the dining table to snuggle against his side on the couch.

"Hey, what are you watching?" He blushed, and I was growing more intrigued by the second, my irritation slowly replaced by curiosity.

"SpaceX might be testing the engines of its new rocket tonight. I'm watching preparation for the possible test," he explained. I raised an eyebrow. I knew from the posters in his room he had a bit of a space obsession, but had never seen him so absorbed in anything before.

"And what will happen in this test?"

"Oh, we don't know, that's why they test it. But they're not even sure they're ready yet, that's the third time they've announced it, and, the first two attempts, it got cancelled after four hours of preparation because there was a technical issue."

It turned out the filming of the preparation of the test was a fixed frame in low angle of the rocket engine, only interrupted sometimes by stalling journalists who visibly had no idea what was going on. It was the most boring thing I'd ever watched, but also oddly relaxing. After the day I'd had, being reminded there was an entire universe to be explored, and that my problems were in no way important in the grand scheme of things, felt—weirdly enough—good.

"Fauve, look, it's starting!" Cody leaned in, almost as if getting closer to the TV would help the engineers on screen. Huge flames erupted from the engines, burnt for a handful of seconds, and were then extinguished by water coming from everywhere. The whole action had maybe lasted a minute, and it was the most anticlimactic thing I'd ever witnessed. Cody didn't seem to think so, though. "Did you see that? Amazing!"

"So, the other two times when the test was cancelled, you stayed in front of the TV for four hours, waiting for this to happen?" I asked, biting hard on the inside of my cheek to keep in the roar of laughter that was threatening to come out.

"Of course! I didn't want to miss it!"

This time, I couldn't help it and started rolling on the sofa, holding my ribs, caught in an uncontrollable fit of giggles. Cody scowled at me in exasperation, but his lips were crooked up in a half-smile.

Chapter 9

Fauve

TWO WEEKS BEFORE THE Christmas break, Thibault threw a wrench in my comfy, reassuring, class-oriented routine.

"Puss, I need your help," he said, panicked. "Stephanie slipped on an ice sheet in the street today, and she sprained her wrist trying to cushion her fall. The owner of the cabaret where we work said I need to find a replacement, or he'll cancel our act altogether. It's only for two weeks, then the place will close for Christmas, and after the break, Stephanie will be good to perform again." I worried my lips all through his verbal vomit, taken aback.

"I don't know, Thibault," I deflected, "I have never seen your routine, never been on an aerial chandelier, and only started aerials a few weeks ago. Isn't there someone more qualified for this?"

Ever since Cody had told me about it, I had been dying to see Thibault's performance, but had somehow never found the time.

With the training and the exams, I had barely even gone out at all, aside from our late-night snowball fights.

"There isn't." He raised his hands in helplessness. "There are no aerialists in your class. In mine, the three aerialists are Stephanie, me, and another dude, and I need a woman partner for this. You have flexibility and your dancing is good, which is more important for a cabaret act than actually being an aerialist. Please, Puss, I'll owe you big time, and it's only for two weeks, then Steph will be back."

The reason why I wasn't jumping on this occasion to participate in my first professional performance was, of course, Loup. Even if he was far away, I had told him everything that was happening in my life, and it had helped us withstand the distance.

From our most recent conversation, it was obvious I couldn't tell him about performing on the aerial chandelier with Thibault. The photos I had sent him from the aerial class were nothing compared to what I would have to do in the next two weeks, if I agreed to help my flatmate. In those images, I was suspended upside down on the trapeze, my head hovering only twenty centimetres above the very fluffy mattress.

Thibault needed me to do daring poses, several metres above the ground—at least five of six times the height of the trapeze I was on in the pictures my boyfriend used for therapy. This meant I wouldn't be able to tell Loup right away, he would worry too much. I would have to lie. By omission, sure, but I considered it a lie, nonetheless. The thought didn't sit well with me.

Thibault directed puppy-dog eyes my way while taking my hand, pleading. My biggest problem was, I selfishly wanted to do it. From what Cody had told me, the aerial chandelier looked incredible, and I was excited to be paid to perform for the first time. I hated lying to Loup, but since it was only for those two Fridays, and he was in France, maybe I could tell him after the second presentation, so he'd know I was fine and unhurt.

"Okay, I'll do it. But only for two weeks," I amended. And I meant it. If Stephanie was still hurt after Christmas, Thibault could find himself another partner. "So, now, that gives us what, five days to transform me into a professional aerialist?"

And here we went again.

By Monday evening, I had discovered that Thibault had, in fact, three personalities. There was the joking flatmate with no sense of boundaries and personal space, who would do just about anything in the bedroom. Then, there was "Teacher Thibault", responsible, behaved, sure of himself, and hot as hell.

And then, there was "Artist Thibault", who I was quickly discovering to be a complete dictator.

"Point your toes," he yelled, slapping the bridge of my foot for good measure.

"Stop it, Thib," I pleaded, "I haven't even learned half the choreography yet, let me get it down first. We'll worry about the details later."

"If you don't learn it correctly from the start, you'll pick up bad habits, and then it'll take longer to fix them. So, point your toes, and start over," he retorted. I rolled my eyes, but obeyed anyway.

So far, we had only rehearsed at NICAM, on the available trapezes and aerial hoops, which added to my nervousness. I would see the venue for the first time on Thursday, and could only rehearse once on the actual chandelier. Thibault had tried to negotiate for more time, or to move the apparatus to NICAM for me to familiarise myself with it, but the owner of Cabaret Rouge wasn't having it. Ass.

I was doing a backbend on the trapeze bar, legs entwined in the ropes in a split, when Thibault started yelling again, "Fauve, that's not working. Your hips aren't aligned, and your shoulders are doing something weird. They should be above your hands. I already told you that. And you need to smile! Focus, it's not that difficult."

The urge was strong to get down, get the trapeze bar and hit him with it until he apologised, but I just tried to listen to his pointers, corrected my posture, and instead of smiling, rolled my eyes for approximately the nine hundredth time.

"That's better, keep going!" he shouted.

By the second day, I had the solo part of the sequence down, and after we'd finished training for the day, Thibault took his phone out of his pocket to show me videos of the duo.

My eyes went wide as I saw it. "Wow, this is hot." Thibault's smirk contained more smugness than I thought humanly possible. "And these are our costumes?" I asked.

I should have thought of it when he mentioned it was more of a cabaret number than a circus one, but well, the act that was being performed before my eyes was this close to sexual. High-end and sophisticated, but sexual in any case.

I suddenly understood why Thibault was adamant about me replacing Stephanie.

The music was "I Put a Spell on You" by Nina Simone. The sensual song required a great deal of exaggeratedly slow caresses and burning hot eye contact between the performers. The cabaret setting was likely responsible for Thibault's oiled bare chest and faux leather pants, and Stephanie's red corset with assorted panties and lace garter belt with fishnet stockings.

The performance was incredible, though, earning them standing ovations at the end. All the sparkling pendants on the apparatus added a mysterious lighting to the already dimly lit venue, and Thibault and Stephanie made challenging poses look fluid and sensual.

"Can we change the music?" I inquired, not completely comfortable with the idea of nearly having sex, with Thibault, on a chandelier, suspended several metres above the ground, in front of an audience while the sultry music played through the club.

"Not on such short notice. It's a live band, so they'd have to change their set list, and rehearse the new song. I'm sorry, Puss, but you're going to have to be all up close and personal with me over there." His predatory look confirmed that he was anything but apologetic.

Our dress rehearsal went badly, and for the umpteenth time this week, Thibault went all dictator on my ass.

I made all the mistakes he had told me to avoid, and I was pretty sure if you put Michael Scott up there with Thibault in my stead, the overall sexiness and fluidity would be about the same.

I tried to explain that it was what dress rehearsals were made for, identify everything that could go wrong to prevent it on the D-day, but he was too busy calling me an uncoordinated robot to actually pay attention to my sensible argument. I didn't know how Stephanie put up with this on a weekly basis. He and I were going to have a little conversation on Saturday because I wasn't going to accept two weeks of this.

Arriving at home, I curled up on Cody's bed to lick my wounds without even showering first, needing the affection, and maybe also a back rub. My body was *sore*.

"I take it you've met the Dragon, then, Fauvette?" Cody said when he saw my pitiful state.

"Is that what you call your dickhead of a friend when he starts being a dick for no reason at all? In this case, yes. Can you be my white knight and go slay it so we have our flatmate back?"

"He'll calm down, eventually. He always does. He's a bit of a perfectionist and an asshole, too, sometimes when he's like this, but I think that's part of what makes him so good at what he does."

I would rather plant a fork in my eye than admit it out loud, but his methods this week had been effective. Before the dress rehearsal where everything went wrong, our coordination was flawless, and I had truly started to think I knew what I was doing.

Apparently, I thought wrong.

Cody forced me to take a shower—what was it with these guys and giving orders, lately—and then went to great lengths to make me feel better, kissing and licking every inch of my body until I begged him to fuck me.

So, he did.

On Friday, Logan finally made an appearance at the flat.

"Hey, Thibault told me you have your first performance as a professional circus artist tonight, want me to do your makeup?"

"Um, what?" I asked, brows raised, dubious as fuck of his capabilities as a makeup artist.

"I've been doing Thib's makeup since we were kids, you know, because his hands are basically useless."

"Wait, what? Why are Thibault's hands useless? I saw him use them today."

"He trains so much that he can't really open them anymore, because of the calluses. And he can't really close them either. So, they're not exactly useless, but he's bad at all the precision stuff, like makeup or drawing. His handwriting is terrible, too. Since I was too young to be a tattoo artist, I figured that trying out drawing on people in a less permanent way could still be fun." He winked. "And I liked it, so now I'm Thibault's official MUA." I giggled.

"Okay then, what do you want me to do?"

Getting my makeup done by Logan was much more relaxing than I thought it would be. He did my skin first, making it look flawless and glowing, even with the stress of the last few days. Then, he focused on my mouth, painting it a deep red.

"Performance makeup has to be blunter than even a party one," he explained when he saw me glower at the bold colour, "otherwise the audience won't see your face, since they're far away and it's dark in the cabaret." He had a point, and his competent tone made me shut up and enjoy having him get me ready.

While he was doing my eyes—having commanded that I keep them closed so that the final design was a surprise—I finally asked the question that was on my mind.

"So, where were you these last few weeks?" I could hear him almost dropping whatever brush he was using, and then fumble in his makeup case.

"I wanted to tell you guys, I have a new boyfriend. I was at his place a lot, and then at my parents' a bit, too."

"You have a boyfriend?! Are you gay?"

"Yes, Fauve, I'm gay. I thought you knew. Believe it or not, but there are inhabitants of this flat that aren't head over heels for you."

"Well, technically...no, there aren't," I sassed. I could almost hear his eye roll.

"You three are cute together, though." He seemed to be thinking for a second, then lowered his voice and said, "Wait, did you meet the Dragon this week?"

"Yes, I did. I asked Cody to slay it for me, but he wouldn't. That's on my to-do list for tomorrow, though. I guess I'll have to be my own Prince Charming."

"Good luck, girl, you'll need it."

Chapter 10

Fauve

I arrived at Cabaret Rouge with my exaggeratedly long fake lashes full of snowflakes, wondering if the intricate pattern of eyeliner Logan had drawn over my eyelids was now running down my cheeks. I was blown away by his delicate and artistic work when he'd finally let me open my eyes. He had drawn three black eyeliner streaks—two of them were heavily winged, starting together at the outer corner of my eyes then branching out on my lid. The first one ended on top of my nose, just below my eyebrow, and was nestled in my lid crease. The second one was a more traditional design, following my upper lash line and ending at the inner corner of my eye. He had traced the third one below my lower lash line, ending it pointing almost downwards, to the tip of my nose. The space between the two upper black lines, basically my entire eyelid, had then been filled with multicolour glitter. I looked like a mix between an Egyptian princess and a cabaret dancer, my eyes dark and dramatic.

The most impressive quality of Logan's work wasn't its uniqueness or beauty, though. What had impressed me most was that both eyes were perfectly symmetric, and I had no idea how he had accomplished that.

I scanned the cabaret entrance—which was, for now, blissfully empty—hoping to find a back door, or even a kitchen one. There weren't any obvious signs, so I ventured through the main entry, passing in front of a smoking silhouette. I wasn't as stressed as I was for my evaluation performance, but I wasn't perfectly calm either, and only recognised her at the last second. "Hey, Stephanie!" I called out, "How are you? What are you doing here?"

"Hey, Fauve, I'm here to watch you and Thib," she spoke softly, but my stress level spiked anyway. What I was about to do was akin to performing a cover of a Beyoncé song in front of Beyoncé—no exaggeration here, I'm not that dramatic, remember?—"I also wanted to thank you for stepping up. I really like performing here, and we could have lost our jobs if we didn't find a substitute. So, thanks, Fauve. Really." She breathed out a mouthful of cigarette smoke. In the dim lighting of the street, I couldn't really make out her facial features—she was a brunette, with thick wavy hair and high cheekbones—but that was about it. It was freezing cold, and she was all wrapped up in her coat and scarf, her injured wrist hidden away by gloves. From observing her at NICAM, I knew she had that thin, flexible, strong body that seemed to be a given for all female aerialists. Her specialties were aerial hoop and silk, and all her clothing would probably be hiding the burns and bruises to match. Those two apparatuses were nasty.

"Honestly, I did it for you guys a little, but mostly for myself. Did you know that tonight's the first time I'm getting paid to perform? I was never a professional artist before, and I'm still deciding if I'm euphoric or terrified."

"I didn't know that. I've been trying to decide that same thing myself since Thibault and I put this act together. That feeling never really goes away, but that's part of the fun." In the depth of her hood, I could make out her mouth tilting up in a smirk. "If we wanted an activity that made us feel relaxed and calm, we would have picked meditation or yoga. Circus pumps you up so full of adrenaline you become an addict, and being in the spotlight is the only thing that can make you feel better."

"Amen to that, girl."

"Break a leg, Fauve, and tell Thibault, too, just in case I don't catch him before he goes on stage."

"Thanks, I will." I walked towards the front door, and went straight backstage to check my makeup, then started stretching. Logan's work had held on, even with the snow falling outside. I hoped he had a good makeup remover, because that shit was definitely waterproof and would be a bitch to get off otherwise.

"Good, there you are!" Thibault closed the distance between us in a series of big steps, coming back from the stage area. "I was just checking the rigging of our material and everything seems fine. I even cleaned the pendants of the chandelier; I think they were disgusting because I've never seen them sparkle like this. How are you feeling?" No trace of the Dragon so far. Perfect.

"Good, I think. I'm going to stretch and warm up; do you want to join me?" I offered.

"Sure. The rope is still up, we can start by going up and down a few times."

"Perfect, let me get changed, and I'll join you." I turned around to find a locker, but his hand on my upper arm stopped me.

"Logan really outdid himself, by the way. You look amazing. I can't wait to see you in costume," he teased. Only Thibault could make the people around us believe he wanted to see me dressed while telling me he really wanted the opposite.

I beamed at him. "I'll be right back."

I had my stage outfit under my clothes, the skimpy lingerie allowing me to easily get dressed above it, but I would wait to warm up to take them off. I ended up joining him in yoga pants and a tight t-shirt, while he threw me a disappointed look.

"Oh, stop it, you know very well I need to warm up before undressing," I scolded. "Otherwise, I could hurt myself or get sick."

He nodded, then came closer to whisper in my ear, "You should definitely wear a corset under your clothes more often, though. It makes your boobs look amazing."

He was right, the corset cinched my waist and pushed my small breasts up in a way that made them look indecent, and, even with a t-shirt on, they popped. The lingerie wasn't too tight—our routine included backbends, after all.

My yoga pants hid assorted red panties and the straps that hooked the black fishnet tights and linked them to my corset. I had spent a while ogling my own ass in the mirror at home before leaving, twisting and turning to see it from all angles. The two red bands of elastic that laid vertically across the milky skin of my barely-covered cheeks were sexy as fuck.

I swatted Thibault playfully in the side and headed for the rope dangling in the middle of the stage. I was glad he was his normal, flirty self, but hadn't forgotten his bad treatment during the week, so I didn't really feel like playing into his banter.

I went up and down the rope five times, my fingers screaming at me as they started to function, despite being cold. Then, I started stretching, Thibault imitating me. We moved backstage as soon as patrons settled at the tables, ordering food and drinks. The show would start soon, and my excitement was building exponentially.

I watched my flatmate from the corner of my eyes. Despite—or maybe because of—how strong he was, his flexibility was terrible. He could touch his feet with his legs extended in front of him, but just barely, and his right leg didn't even unfold properly. I made a mental note to ask him about it and to make him work on it, too.

I got to the part of my warm-up where I did splits with my front foot propped up on a chair, legs opened at an unnatural angle, when Thibault left for his rope number. Curious, I abandoned my exercises—I still had time before it was our turn as a duo, anyway—and approached to peep through the heavy curtains.

For this act, Thibault was wearing jeans, and he made a show of getting rid of a button-up shirt in a half striptease during the first few seconds, showing off the bare, muscled chest I knew very well. The fact that I was still annoyed with him didn't make my need to lick his abs any weaker.

As if purposely designed to have me drooling by the end of it, the routine was specifically thought out to showcase Thibault's strength. It was made of a succession of slow moves of contained power that had his skin rippling hypnotically. And he made it look easy, too. He rolled in the rope as sensually and lazily as if it was a bed, tying himself up and getting free to climb higher. He was giving me—and his audience too, probably—all sorts of mischievous ideas. After a controlled fall that made his back muscles pop out and his delicious abs flex while the spectators gasped, I decided I had seen enough and went back to my stretching. I needed to focus on our upcoming performance, and not on how gorgeous Thibault looked in his element.

Salivating over my flatmate's body had given me an idea, and I shot a quick text to Cody.

Fauve: Could you give us a minute before coming home after the show? I need to talk to Thibault alone, is that okay with you?

I didn't wait to see his answer. He would suspect what it was about, anyway, and I doubted he would have a problem with it.

A few minutes later, Thibault entered the backstage area beaming, breathing heavily, and once again, his pectorals caught my eye.

He erased the distance between us and, lifting my chin with one finger, met my gaze.

"What did you think?"

"You were amazing." His smile grew even wider. I wasn't petty enough to lie just to get back at him. My vengeance would come later and be much more...satisfying.

"I'm glad you liked it. Are you warmed up? We're on in about fifteen minutes. I'm going to go see if I can find Cody and Logan in the audience. I want the same eye makeup as yours; we need to match."

He disappeared between the tables I could barely make out in the darkness, only to come back a couple of minutes later with a visibly annoyed Logan.

"Couldn't you have thought of this before the show started?" he complained. "I was enjoying myself back there."

"I thought of it, actually. But I couldn't have the makeup on for the rope act, so get to work." He then added tentatively, "Please?"

Logan rolled his eyes in a way that had me snorting, and started looking for a black eyeliner in the mess of the backstage area.

He only drew two lines on Thibault's eyes, to match my makeup, but forewent the middle, traditional one. It made my partner's eyes less delicate and heavier, more...masculine, somehow.

"I'm not putting glitter or fake lashes on you, but you know mascara is indispensable, right?" Logan said in an authoritative tone.

"I know, and I can apply it myself if you want to go back out there," Thibault offered.

Logan pointed an authoritative finger in my direction. "You, check that he really does it," he ordered.

"Yes, sir!"

The tattoo artist stepped out, and Thibault started stripping out of his jeans while I checked him out unashamedly. I raised an eyebrow when he took off his underwear, too, and he answered my silent question.

"The leather pants are super tight; everyone will see the lines if I wear anything under them. But please stop looking at me like that, or they're going to get even tighter." His cock was indeed starting to stir under my gaze, and I averted my eyes, blushing slightly.

He shimmied inside the pants while I gathered all my self-control to not jump him then and there. I needed to focus. My lustful brain added that focusing on his perfect ass was still technically focus, but I shut down that unhelpful thought.

I undressed to my red lingerie and mentally went through our routine one last time. Thibault must have felt the shift in my thoughts because he said, "Remember, go slowly. Focus on the routine, but do not rush into it. Take your time, enjoy it." Then he added in a low voice, almost a whisper, "Thank you for doing this, Fauve." A quick glance towards the stage confirmed what I was thinking. "We're on."

We entered the stage hand in hand, wearing intensely seductive looks on our faces. The Dragon had made me rehearse all my facial expressions too; he was that anal retentive about his performances.

We placed ourselves on opposite sides of the chandelier that was hovering just above the ground, and the first notes of the song started playing, bewitching and enticing.

The act started with my solo, and I sensually walked between the pendants of the chandelier to the vertical bar in its middle. Thibault was watching me so intensely my skin burned from his gaze. Both the artist and the lover were present in his eyes, respectively analysing every aspect of my performance and capturing me in the intensity of those green depths.

His perusal reached my face when the singer declared I had put a spell on him. Our eye contact was torrid, and wouldn't be broken for the entirety of the routine—we had rehearsed that, too.

I stepped on one of the horizontal beams and used the middle section of the chandelier as a pole dance bar. My first pose was a front split against it, hands holding me while my legs were flat against the metal. In that instant, the chandelier rose in the air, Thibault dramatically reaching for me as if I was being torn away from him.

I went from the vertical middle bar to hanging on one of the horizontal bars, using it as a trapeze, holding my arms out while my legs were securing me, trying to get to him, but the distance was too great, the chandelier too high.

I started a slow dance between the metal beams then, never breaking our eye contact, moving sensually as if to enchant him.

The moment felt amazing. If it looked even half as good as it felt, I was killing it. The light refracted in the multiple glass pendants, casting rays on my skin. The singer had an incredible voice, deep and low, and while I felt awkward performing such sexy choreography on an aerial apparatus at rehearsal, I now felt powerful and confident.

As the music became more intense, the chandelier lowered, and Thibault started running towards it, grabbing it to make it spin. We rose up again, him holding onto one of the horizontal bars with only one arm. He did a series of effortless poses under the twirling apparatus, and then sat next to me. I crawled towards him, back arched, until I was in his lap.

We had rehearsed that crawl at least a million times. I never managed to get it perfectly, always scared I would miss the bars where I was supposed to put my feet, and fall to the ground. I executed it flawlessly this time, making it look as effortless as if I were on the ground, and not four metres above it.

I straddled him and caressed his torso and cheek. He flipped me over, so that my back was to his front, and leaned back against the vertical middle bar. The change in position allowed me to open my legs in a split above him, with his thighs grounding me and my feet on the horizontal bars. He made a show of touching me everywhere, as if truly bewitched.

Desire pooled in my belly. Was it wrong to be aroused by people watching Thibault touch me like this?

I joined my legs behind me, releasing the bars in my hands to grab both my feet and push them to my head. Thibault grabbed my hips as I did so, securing our position on the chandelier with his legs. The figure made both our pelvises come in contact, and he was definitely enjoying himself as much as I was.

The music ended abruptly with us holding that same pose, and we didn't move for a couple of seconds after, the sudden silence deafening.

Then the audience started clapping, and the chandelier was lowered again. We went down to salute.

I was panting, both from the physical activity I had just done, and the one I very much wanted to do. I didn't dare check if Thibault's pants were indeed as tight as he had claimed, preferring to hurry backstage instead, my partner hot on my heels.

He hugged me from behind, nipped at my ear, and whispered into my neck, "That was incredible. You're incredible, Fauve. Wanna get out of here?"

Yep. I definitely did.

Chapter 11

Fauve

THIBAULT AND I GRABBED our bags and made a beeline for the kitchen entrance I couldn't find on my way in, bumping into Stephanie on the way.

"You guys were amazing!" she exclaimed. "That was *so* hot. Like, literal fire. I think the guy sitting next to me got a boner. You need to help me train, Fauve, I'd love to be as flexible as you are!

"Really, guys, the chemistry between you two was... Wow, explosive! I didn't know you were an item, and I'm a little envious of the action we all know you're going to get tonight. If that was watching you work, imagine what watching you have sex must look like!"

Her verbal vomit was happening so fast I couldn't correct her on the status of our relationship, but not fast enough to prevent me from seriously blushing. Was she flirting with us? Fortunately, Thibault came to my rescue.

"Steph, thanks, but we were leaving. After the emotions of this week, we're pretty tired. I'll talk to you tomorrow, okay?"

"Oh. *Oh.* Yeah, sure, if you're tired, you should go home and rest." She winked at me. "Although, I'm suspecting you're going to tire yourselves some more."

We said our goodbyes and escaped, Thibault wrapping his huge arm across my shoulders in the street.

The subway trip home was pure torture. My trapezist flatmate never missed an occasion to touch me, caress me, or kiss me for the duration of the ride. I jumped on him as soon as we took off our coats. Literally.

He caught me effortlessly, princess style, as he had done all week.

"Shower time!" he exclaimed in a singsong voice while carrying me to the bathroom.

We each undressed ourselves, struggling with the already tight clothes that sweat and rosin had glued to our body. Since he just had his leather pants and t-shirt to remove, Thibault was done before me, and helped me with my corset and garter belt, before giving up and shredding my stockings to pieces in a move that would have made Superman jealous.

I won't lie, that was hot. Undoubtedly proud of himself, he nipped at my nipple.

He parted my thighs and carried me into the shower with his hands on my ass. He put me down to figure out the temperature of the jet, still keeping his left arm around me for warmth. Once satisfied with the temperature, he pulled me under the water, against his broad chest. I kissed it, nibbling his collarbone.

I then grabbed the soap and slowly washed him from top to bottom, wrapping my hands around his hard cock before moving on to his massive thighs. It was really a shame he had pants on for his rope act because they were magnificent, thick and muscled.

When I got to his feet, he pulled me up to return the favour, focusing on my hips, wrists, and ankle area, where he knew the sticky rosin was, since he had used it to hold me during our performance. I still hated the damn substance, but it was better than falling.

Once clean, he turned off the water, gathered me in his arms again, and proceeded to dry both of us before carrying me to his bedroom. He laid me down across his bed, feet dangling over the edge, and knelt between my legs.

"You're beautiful, Puss, and you've got an amazing body," he whispered, eyes fixed on my pussy. I chuckled.

I teased him, "Are you talking about my body in general or certain parts in particular?"

"There are definitely certain parts that I'm fonder of, but I was talking about you in general."

All the build-up from the performance, the subway, and our shower made me feel like my skin was on fire, my breasts sensitive and peaked. I tangled my hand in his hair to gently pull him where I wanted him.

Not unlike what Cody had done the night we ended up having a threesome, he pushed my legs as far apart as the bed allowed, and murmured, "This... this is amazing. Have you ever had sex while doing a split, Puss?"

I snorted. "Obviously." And, he growled.

Spreading his heavily calloused hands on my inner thighs, he started licking me, sucking on my clit and biting at my folds. I bucked my hips, making him tighten his grip to prevent me from moving.

I was dripping wet, and without warning, he pushed two fingers deep inside me, sucking harder on my clit. When he crooked them, I saw stars, and he went back and forth as my inner walls clamped around his knuckles.

As I came down from my high, I pulled him on top of me and flipped us over, straddling his hips. Having scratched that specific itch, I had him exactly where I wanted him, and it was time to put the plan I came up with earlier into action. An evil smile spread across my lips.

I kissed my way down his body, and when my eyes got to his crotch, I took him in my hand, caressing his shaft downwards until my fist closed around his balls.

Then I paused, kneeling on the ground next to the bed, waiting, lips parted in a predatory smile, and my fingers still squeezing slightly.

"Puss, what are you doing?" He propped himself up on his elbows, and our eyes met.

"Now that I have you by the balls—literally—you're going to listen to me. You are never, ever going to treat me the way you did this past week." I said it without aggression, but leaving no space for negotiation either. "I understand you have to be demanding, but this wasn't demanding, it was borderline abusive, and you know it.

"So next week, you're going to talk to me like I'm an actual human being when we rehearse. Hell, you could even talk to me like I'm your friend and we're on the same team, but I'll go easy on you and won't ask for too much, too soon." He opened his mouth to speak, but I cut him off by squeezing his balls a little harder, having no interest in hearing what he had to say. He closed his mouth, apparently understanding the message. "And, if you think I'm fucking you right now, well, you might have been misled. Oopsies, my bad. I hope having blue balls isn't too much of an inconvenience.

"Also, if you ever even think of treating me that way again, I'm going to rip these off and make you eat them." Well, that might have been a bit too much—drama queen and all, remember?

I punctuated the end of my sentence by dropping a feather-light kiss on his steel-hard cock, then got up and sashayed out of the room completely naked and smirking. Our clothes had stayed in the bathroom, so that's where I headed. Thank fuck, Cody and Logan were still wherever they went after the show.

I quickly took off my fake lashes, thoroughly removed the rest of my makeup and jumped into bed, loudly closing and locking my door to make sure Thibault got the message.

I was exhausted down to my very bones, and fell asleep almost immediately with a satisfied smile on my lips.

Dragon slaying, my ass. Grab them by the balls and make them your pet, that's much more efficient.

On Saturday night, having almost overdosed on testosterone during the week, I explicitly forbade my flatmates from putting even a toe in the living room, and invited Nathalie and Mary over for a girl's night. We ordered sushi, my two besties brought wine, and we put a makeover show on the TV. It was everything I didn't know I needed. Thibault had monopolised all my free time lately, to the point where I was too tired to even practice my juggling in the mornings.

I'd missed my girls.

"So," Nat started once we were all eating and already a bit tipsy, "how was last night? You know all the girls in our program are now jealous of you for training with our hot teacher, right?"

"And training with him is not all she does, right, Fauve?" Mary teased.

I blushed as they ganged up on me. "Well, Thibault doesn't grade us, so there's no conflict of interest since he's technically only a teacher's assistant. Plus, he was my friend before he was teaching our classes, I—"

"'Friend'?" Mary laughed, cutting me off. "Is that what we're calling it, now? Remind me how long you'd known him for when he first got you naked?" Sometimes, I hated my light, freckled skin. This moment was one of them, and I crossed my arms as I felt colour burning my cheeks.

Nathalie scowled at Mary and pulled my hand, forcing my arms to uncross and twining hers in my right one.

"Fauve, there's no judgment here, you know that, right?" Nathalie's words were soothing and comforting. "You sleep with whoever you want, whenever you want, we'll have your back if haters come for you. But"—a mischievous light lit up her eyes as she paused dramatically—"you can't be mad at us for wanting details, your sex life is much more interesting than ours."

Fun fact about me, I was apparently more comfortable in the middle of a hot threesome with my two flatmates than talking about said experience with my girlfriends.

So, I changed the subject. "About that, Nat, why did you choose to live with your seventeen-year-old sister? That probably doesn't help. And why don't you join your parents on tour? You're obviously as passionate as they are."

Her face fell, and I regretted my question instantly. "You don't have to answer if you don't want to," I added quickly.

"No, it's fine, it's good for me to talk about it, I guess." She shrugged. "My parents do want me to come with them, they've been wanting it for years, actually. But they never wanted my sister and I to grow up like they did, taking classes in the back of a car, living the circus life. They're adamant my sister has a stable education and graduates high school before she moves away from Montréal.

"They wanted the same for me, and they settled down for ten years until I was old enough for them to leave me with my aunt.

They're great parents, but not sedentary people. Ten years already had them stretched thin, you could feel their impatience and need for adventure when they left.

"So, when I was ten and my sister was four, we moved in with my mom's sister, and everything was fine until my aunt got together with her boyfriend." There wasn't a sound in the living room as Nathalie spoke. Until this point in her tale, her eyes had been fixed on the last lonely cucumber sushi left on her plate. She then looked around, meeting our gaze unflinchingly, almost challenging us to question her decision. "Let's just say that I can't let my baby sister live with him. Nothing happened to me, I got away in time, but I can't let her stay there." I nodded, my respect for her increasing tenfold. I didn't have siblings, but watching her care for her sister like this—sacrificing the best years of her life, some might say—was inspiring. I hugged her tight.

"I'm sure you're being a great big sister. Keira's lucky to have you," I said.

She snorted. "I know she doesn't think so most days, but she only dates assholes, so I get protective. I didn't do all this for her to get an idiot boyfriend." Mary and I chuckled. "The only reason I got a degree was to stay with her here!" Nat continued, "But it's going to be over soon. In June, she'll graduate and we'll join our parents on the road." Her excitement at the idea was palpable in the air. "The downside is that I have to make it to the top six at NICAM to be sure I stay until then."

We were quiet for a minute, the fact that, despite our friendship, we were in competition against each other, weighing heavily on the moment.

"Then, I propose a toast," Mary slurred drunkenly—she had been sipping steadily on her wine as Nat told us her story—"to you, badass big sis who ranked fifth in the first phase and will save Keira from a bad guy!"

MANUELA ROUGET

We laughed and applauded, Nat not as loudly as Mary and I, but it cheered us up, anyway. I went to look for my blanket in my room, and we all curled up under it to watch the end of the makeover show.

Chapter 12

Loup

"Love you Mava, tell Mapa I love her, too."

"*Bisous mon chéri*, say hi to Fauve for us!"

I made kissy noises at my phone's camera before hanging up, probably looking like an idiot to the travellers that surrounded me in the crowded airport. Adult men weren't supposed to be openly affectionate to their mom in public. Screw that, my moms deserved all the love I could send them, and then some.

Because they were perfect parents, of that I had no doubt. As with all human beings, they had their faults, of course, but when it came to raising me, they had done a damn good job.

When I was born, the plan was for me to call them Maman Va—short for Valérie—and Maman Pa—short for Patricia. Young me didn't like it and shortened it to Mava and Mapa. Really, what were they thinking? Those name ideas were way too long for a toddler who could barely speak. And in the end, my take on it was cute, so it stuck.

Mava was my biological mother. Even without the pregnancy pictures they had hanging in our living room, it would have been obvious. I had her blue eyes and blond hair, while Mapa had dark hair and almost black eyes, showcasing her Italian heritage. I had Mapa's complexion, which, obviously again, must have come from my father.

I didn't know who he was and never really felt like finding out. My mothers were incredible people, and more than enough, showering me with love and attention as I grew up. Hell, they had instantly adopted Fauve, too, when I first brought her home, and were more worried for her alone in Canada than her own parents.

Especially Mava. Then again, Mava was a bit paranoid when it came to, well, everything. The inadequacy of French laws on marriage and assisted reproduction for same-sex couples was to blame for that. Until 2013, she was my only legal parent. If something had happened to her, I would have been considered an orphan and put in the system, even if I still had someone I considered a parent. She relaxed a bit when they finally managed to get married, but over a decade of paranoia didn't disappear overnight, and even if I was legally an adult now, she still worried. A lot. About everything.

Mapa was a bit more relaxed, but fiercely protective of me. More than one school director not doing enough to stop the bullying I suffered for having lesbian moms ended up on the wrong side of her wrath. I almost felt bad for them. Almost.

I put my phone back in my pocket and headed towards the check-in area, pulling my massive suitcase behind me. It was mostly filled with food and wine, Mapa and Mava making sure that our Christmas dinner didn't lack the typical French delicacies. It wasn't exactly legal to import food in Canada this way, but I imagined that—if they found out—the customs authorities would just throw it away. I couldn't get arrested for smuggling in *foie gras* and *camembert* now, could I?

Fauve didn't know I was coming. I had started my visa procedure about a month before what I had told her, and it allowed me to travel now, just before Christmas, to surprise her. I knew doing this held a lot of potential drama—like arriving at her flat only to find her in bed with one of her flatmates—so I had let Cody in on the secret, and he had agreed to help me. He was friends with Fauve on Facebook, so it had been easy enough to get in touch.

Even if I wasn't of a jealous nature, my heart had done a happy dance in my chest when he had told me that she talked about me a lot, and she obviously missed me.

My surprise to Fauve also included a two-week stay in a romantic cabin in the Canadian wilderness—a Christmas present from my moms—for just the two of us. We would leave to go there on Saturday, and I couldn't wait. Her classes stopped for the holidays, so we would have fourteen full days to catch up, and I was eager to reacquaint myself with every centimetre of her gorgeous body. My cock twitched as that thought crossed my mind.

I missed my girlfriend *so* much.

Her getting into NICAM while I didn't had been bittersweet. A petty, malicious part of me would have preferred for neither of us to get in. I shut it down very quickly whenever it showed its ugly head. I was glad she was in. She was the one whose parents would prevent from pursuing a career as an artist if she didn't have a formal education to back her up. My moms would let me do more or less anything that made me happy, so explaining to them that I was following Fauve to Canada had been a no-brainer. They were wholeheartedly supportive of my endeavour. If the roles had been reversed between Fauve and I, I don't know what we would have done.

The objective was for us to get a gig in a small theatre while waiting for Fauve to finish the program, and hopefully get hired by the Cirque des Etoiles. She had told me yesterday that Donna Lowenberg authorised the students to get outside help—onstage and off—for their evaluation presentation.

This was another reason why I was happy to arrive earlier than planned. Her second presentation was at the end of January, and we needed to get to work as soon as possible. She had mentioned performing a more advanced version of the choreography that got her in, and I was here for it. Training with Fauve was almost as fun as fucking, and more often than not, one led to the other.

My daydreaming occupied me as I went through check-in, security, and customs. I took advantage of finally being seated, waiting for boarding to send a text to my girlfriend.

Loup: Hey, Plume! I'm not sure if I told you, but I'll be away with some friends for the weekend. Since tomorrow is the start of holiday, we decided to leave a day early to avoid traffic. It's away from the city so don't worry if I don't answer your texts, I might not get any signal. We'll talk on Monday, okay? Love you, Plume!

I stared at my phone fondly, remembering how she got that nickname. Fauve was reclusive as a teenager, extremely self-conscious of her body and on the verge of an eating disorder. Olympic gymnastics coaches had done a number on her, causing her to stop training, even if she was definitely good enough to continue to National Championship level, or maybe even European or World, who knew?

When we started training together, even if I towered over her, she was worried she was too heavy, and I wouldn't be strong enough to carry her. I picked her up effortlessly and answered that she was being silly because she was as light as a feather—"plume" in French. Once again, it stuck. I guess I'm just that good at naming stuff.

Needless to say, at that point, I was already smitten. The insecure redhead had captured my teenage heart, and the determination I discerned in her chocolate eyes had ensnared me with the efficiency of the strongest of nets. She had a boyfriend, so I let nothing show, ever the supporting, understanding friend.

The dickhead dug his own grave by getting jealous of me, showing off his homophobic personality. With a total lack of originality, he started picking on me for having two moms, and then he discovered it didn't faze me so moved on to practicing a sport where I had to do the splits and wear leotards. That was even more stupid. I was training in a discipline that made me confident, flexible, ripped, with mad control of my body, and gave me an excuse to parade in tight-ass clothes in front of a group of people. If that wasn't a sure recipe to get laid, I didn't know what was. Then again, he was a textbook example of toxic masculinity, so I didn't expect him to understand that.

The idiot was still calling me a faggot when I started sleeping with his then ex-girlfriend. Fauve had dumped his ass as soon as she discovered how badly he treated me. My Plume could get pretty intolerant—in the best of ways—when confronting bullies.

We had grown together and learned so much from each other. I looked forward to finding out what our future held. I liked to think that I helped her build the confidence she had now. She sure as hell taught me all there was to know about perseverance, and I was immensely grateful for that.

In twenty-four hours, we would be reunited.

I couldn't wait.

My entire body hurt when the plane finally landed. I needed to stretch, badly. Those tiny seats weren't made for someone my size. Scratch that, plane seats weren't made for any adult's size. Only kids might be comfortable in them.

I was thankful my fear of heights didn't make flying a problem, though. Since the plane floor was very solid and very close to me, my brain lacked the height perception that made me freak out. Small mercies. Seven hours of panic attacks wouldn't have been fun.

There was no way of knowing for sure, but we assumed my phobia was one of the reasons I didn't initially get into NICAM. I had been honest on my application, hoping that the admissions committee would be open-minded. Panic attacks weren't exactly easy to hide, and even with time and therapy, they weren't one hundred per cent gone. I guess the people studying my file weren't that accepting. Or I hadn't been good enough to get in, that was a possibility, too.

I grabbed my suitcase, which thankfully came out in the first round of baggage, and passed through customs without causing a diplomatic incident due to food trafficking. Right outside the duty-free area, as he had promised, Cody was waiting for me with a big sign that said, "Loup Dubois Rossi".

I slowly took him in. Plume's description was accurate. He was handsome, in a very put-together, polished way. Like most people, he was shorter than me. He looked fit, but I couldn't see if his clothes hid muscles.

His thick winter coat was open over a denim shirt tucked in black jeans. He had an orange beanie in his hand, and I suspected that was why his dark hair was tousled. The rest of his outfit was so carefully put together, he had probably combed it before going out, and the hat had messed it up.

He didn't see me at first, too busy cleaning his thick tortoiseshell glasses with a little cloth. Cody raised his head, put his glasses back on his nose, and aimed his storm grey gaze at me. He had intelligent eyes, observant and mischievous.

"Hey, you must be Loup!" he exclaimed. I was glad I still looked like myself after the endless flight because I certainly didn't feel like me.

"Hey Cody, have you been waiting for a long time?" I asked, not really interested in the answer.

We made small talk, and it was awkward. He seemed like a cool guy, but I was both jealous and grateful that he'd spent the past three months fucking my girlfriend, and the mixed feelings were throwing me off my game. I couldn't even decide which part was weirder: the jealousy or the thankfulness. From an outsider's point of view, the answer would be the former. But the latter actually bothered me more. Fauve and I had talked about this, and I was okay with it so far. Why was I getting jealous now? Because I was confronted with her sexy lover, and it made it all real? That was something my therapist would say.

Cody guided me towards the exit and to his car. By the time we reached it, I was shivering. It was much colder than Paris, with snow everywhere, and I would have to go shopping for an actual winter coat and boots. I hated shopping.

My new friend's eyes—that's what I decided to call Cody in my head, everything else was too weird—missed nothing though, and he said, very matter-of-factly, "I can lend you a coat for your trip, if you want. You won't have time to go shopping for one before you leave tomorrow."

He sounded sad, talking about our departure. Maybe he knew that, from now on, things would change between him and Fauve, since I was here. "It might be a bit short, but I think it should fit," he continued.

"That would be great, thanks, man." I was determined not to let the awkwardness I felt on the inside rear its head. Fake it until you make it, right?

"Where are we going, now, by the way?" I asked after a moment.

"Home. We'll be alone for now. Fauve and Thibault are in class, and then they're heading directly to the gig Thibault has on Friday night. His partner hurt her wrist slipping on an ice plate last week, and Fauve is replacing her. I thought we could head there after you rest for a bit. I was in the audience last week, and the act they put together is really cool. Then, you can surprise her when they're finished. What do you think?"

"That's perfect, thanks for helping," I said sincerely. I must have been very tired from the journey because even though I knew Thibault was a trapezist, I didn't even think of asking what the act was about.

I overslept.

Nestled in Plume's bed, surrounded by her scent, I slept like a baby and only awoke when Cody shook me, urging me to get ready since Thibault and Fauve were on in thirty minutes.

Fortunately, I had showered before going to bed, otherwise we wouldn't have made it.

We took the subway to the little cabaret where they performed. It was called Cabaret Rouge, and they had used that colour everywhere. The entrance had red neon that somehow managed to not look like a strip club. The walls were coated in carmine velvet. The tables had vermilion tablecloths and napkins. It was a bit overkill, if you asked me.

I didn't want to get blinded by the stage lights and trip on a chair leg or something, so I waited until Cody and I got seated to start watching the ongoing performance.

AERIAL

It turned out we had arrived just in time. On stage, a couple was suspended about four metres above the ground, dancing and posing in an amazing show of strength and flexibility. They were sexy as fuck, too, visibly knowing each other's body well, and taking advantage of a shared intimacy that showed in their every movement.

My sessions with *Docteur* Fabre had signalled what triggered my phobia and subsequent panic attacks the most was when I was caught unaware. So, when I recognised the redhead crawling on the man's lap on the aerial chandelier, time stopped. Fauve was up there.

She was up there, and if she fell, there was nothing I could do.

The thought started playing on repeat in my head.

My blood turned to ice in my veins, and I froze in my seat.

I sucked in air, as fast as I could, but was still suffocating.

I needed out.

"Loup, are you okay?" Cody asked, alerted by the noise I made. I shook my head. "Hey, calm down, what's happening?" He looked panicked.

In between heavy breaths, I managed to articulate, "Give me a minute. I'll be fine."

And I meant it. I didn't care that he was seeing me like this; I was fine freaking out in public, as paradoxical as that may sound. What I wasn't fine with was all the work I had put in during the past few months being for nothing. This got me angry, and my anger helped push my fear away.

I emptied my glass of wine, unceremoniously tossing it back as if it was a shot. Numbing my senses usually helped, too. Remembering my breathing exercises—thank you, *Docteur* Fabre—I put my hand on my stomach, and started focusing on the slow rhythm of the air coming in through my nose and out of my mouth, counting every cycle. My eyes closed of their own accord.

I managed to get my respirations under control, and, when the music stopped, I waited for a handful of seconds to give Fauve time to get back on the ground before opening my eyes.

A hopeful smile slowly grew on my lips.

All that work hadn't been for nothing, after all.

People around me started applauding, and I clapped my hands with them, finally taking in my gorgeous girlfriend on stage. She was wearing an exquisite red lingerie ensemble that I wanted to rip off of her.

"Do you want to go backstage?" Cody asked. I had forgotten he was here and snapped my eyes back in his direction. He looked at me as if I had grown three heads during his flatmates' performance.

"Yes," I answered, nodding eagerly.

Chapter 13

Fauve

I HAD MADE GOOD on my promise to myself and hadn't given in to Thibault's advances all week—he deserved to grovel for his behaviour—so I was ready to pounce on him the minute we were in private by the time we finished our performance. Fucking sexy routine, how did Stephanie do it? I was almost certain they had never slept together.

Cody barging in the backstage area with an eyebrow raised and a puzzled look on his face doused my libido with the efficiency of a freezing shower. He tipped his head to the back, as if to tell me to look behind him.

A tall, gorgeous man was following right behind him. He walked confidently, all lean, graceful muscles that I knew by heart. His light blond hair was a bit longer than when I had last seen him in person, just like his short, neatly trimmed beard. His skin was a bit paler as well.

He wore Cody's coat, and it was a little too short for him, the sleeves barely reaching his wrists. Our eyes met, and for a moment, time stopped as I lost myself in their turquoise depth.

Loup.

Loup was here.

A smug smirk twisted his lips at my astonishment, and he opened his arms.

So, I finally moved. Running towards him, I jumped, wrapping my arms around his neck and legs around his hips, nuzzling his neck as if trying to fuse our bodies together. He caught and held me up effortlessly, his arms tightening around me until my ribs started to protest. We must have made a pretty picture, him and I, holding on to each other like our lives depended on it, Loup in his street clothes while I hadn't taken off my stage costume.

"I did it, Plume," he whispered in my ear. It took me a moment to understand what he was talking about. I leaned back to look him in the eyes.

"You watched us?" If he had, it was massive, and I needed to get his therapist a nice Christmas present.

He shook his head, though. "No, I closed my eyes as soon as I saw who was on the chandelier, but I didn't lose it either." My eyes went wide, just as a pang of guilt hit my chest.

"*Mon coeur*, that's amazing! Are you okay?"

"A bit shaken, to be honest." He chuckled. I buried my face in his neck again, breathing him in.

"I missed you," I said on an exhale.

"I missed you, too." He angled his face towards mine, and following his lead, I let him catch my lips in a bruising kiss.

This kiss was everything. A love letter, a hot chocolate and a comfy blanket on a cold night, all at once. Our tongues tangled together, and my hips started rolling against his, my back arching sensually.

Someone cleared their throat, and I froze. As soon as I had seen Loup, the outside world had stopped existing, but Thibault and Cody were still there, watching us.

I wiggled to let Loup know I wanted him to put me back on the floor, and turned around to face my flatmates.

"Cody, Thibault," I started, "this is Loup, my boyfriend." I couldn't stop myself from beaming. He was really here. "Loup, these are Thibault and Cody, my—" I paused for a moment. How was I going to introduce to my boyfriend the ones who were essentially my lovers? "My friends," I finished lamely.

Completely unbothered by the history he knew we shared, Loup shook Thibault's hand, looking at him straight in the eyes.

He smiled his most genuine smile and said, "Thank you, guys, for taking care of her. I appreciate it."

Thibault had pursed his lips and straightened his back, as if to try to match Loup's height.

He looked dangerously like a rooster, proud and ready to start bickering over his female. Were we going to have a problem here?

I looked at Cody for support, and what I saw broke my heart. His lips were twisted in disappointment, and he frowned, his eyes twin pools of grey sadness.

The adrenaline that rode my body after the performance changed into a flash of anger. I had been honest with them, what did they expect? That Loup would arrive in Canada, and I would tell him it was over? It was never going to happen that way, and they knew it!

Loup's whisper against my neck interrupted my thoughts, "Let's go home, Plume, we'll sort it all out later."

He was right. Tonight, I would enjoy having him back, the mess with my flatmates could wait until tomorrow.

MANUELA ROUGET

In the silent car, I rested my head against the cold window, admiring the scenery to forget my discomfort.

I was feeling... weird. There were too many thoughts clashing in my head, and I was taking advantage of the drive to go through them.

Before taking off for our romantic getaway, leaving Cody and Thibault had been hard. Because of jet lag, Loup woke up at five in the morning and immediately got up to pick up the car he had rented for our trip. He then surprised me with breakfast in bed—decorating the tray with flowers and everything—and explained what his plans for the holidays were. I started packing as soon as he finished talking, excited to go on a trip with him.

We went down to our rental to put our bags in the trunk, and I jumped in the passenger seat—walking carefully on the icy sidewalk in between.

I let Loup focus on the robotic voice of the GPS, taking time to put some order in my thoughts and take in the fantastic views.

Leaving Cody and Thibault had been harder than I thought it would be. It felt final, somehow, as if things would never be the same again between us. And it couldn't be, now that my boyfriend was here, it had always been clear for us that, once he arrived in Montréal, we would be back together as a happy, exclusive couple.

But what if our relationship had changed, too? We had never been apart for so long before. Would it feel as if we had never been apart? Or had we changed enough for it to impact us?

Because I had changed. There was no way not to when you moved to another country, miles away from home. I just wasn't sure how, because nobody here knew the Fauve pre-NICAM.

Loup would be the first one to discover the new me. Would he like it? We had spoken a lot in those few months, but the thought still worried me.

There was also the subject of his phobia; he had seemed so happy to have survived our act while I performed high in the air, but I hated making him suffer like this. Would he be okay, seeing me go to my aerial's class every week? What if I hurt myself in it—that was always a possibility, after all—would it send him spiralling again? The last thing I wanted was to make his situation worse, even if I knew he wanted to work on it.

Another overwhelming feeling was that, despite feeling like I had just lost Cody and Thibault, I was deliriously happy Loup was here. His absence had made me feel like a part of me was missing, and I hadn't stopped touching him since he had arrived, always holding his hand, laying my head on his shoulder, or even plastering my body to his when we were alone. Our fingers were tangled tightly together on the armrest. I didn't want us to be separated again, and hoped everything would still be the way it was back in France.

"What are you thinking about?" Loup asked the moment we left the city, and the GPS quietened down a little.

Last week had been snowy, and everything was covered in a glistening, fluffy white blanket. I wished for us to take a break to jump in it. Almost.

The road was clear, though, and I was thankful for it, neither of us really used to driving on snow. Pines were bordering the road, and the forest landscape was sometimes interrupted by a lake, sparkling green or blue under the winter sun. Bridges took us above frozen creeks. It was beautiful.

"I'm preoccupied, I guess?" I answered truthfully. "Everything that's happened recently is clashing in my head. I want the cohabitation with Thibault and Cody to be nice while you look for a job so we can move out of the apartment. I'm worried that being closer to my classes at NICAM is going to make your phobia worse. And I'm happy you're here, but a part of me is worried things are going to be different between us because of the months we've spent apart." I laid it all on the table, leaving nothing out. It was why we had worked so well together, for so long, after all. We hid nothing from each other.

"Different isn't always bad," Loup simply said. He looked away from the road for an instant, so our eyes could meet. In the background behind him was an icy lake, and his eyes had taken the same light blue shade, stripped of its green undertones by the snowy décor. "People evolve, Plume, they grow and change, that's the whole point of life. Whatever happens now, we'll figure it out together." He turned back to focus on the road, but held my hand to his mouth and dropped a feather-light kiss on my knuckles. "I love you. Not the idea of you, or who I wish you'd be. I know who you are isn't fixed in stone, but that's my favourite part of it, actually. I loved you five years ago, I still did when you started college, and the half-second of your performance I actually watched yesterday made me fall in love with you all over again.

"We have two weeks alone just to take the time to be together, Plume, and I guarantee everything will be perfect."

He focused his attention back on the road, and I took a minute to shoot a quick text to the apartment's group chat, saying we were on the road and everything was okay.

"Is that them?" Loup asked, glancing briefly at my phone. I knew who he meant.

"Flatmate group chat," I answered.

"And how are you feeling? Have they said anything?"

"Not yet, they must still be sleeping." I sighed. "I'm not sure how I'm feeling, to be honest. Like it was fun while it lasted, I guess? We got along well, and I'm not sure how everything is gonna be now that you're here, and we're going to be living with them, then moving out... I feel weird."

"Would you have preferred it if I only arrived in January, like we'd planned?"

For a minute, I froze. How could he even ask that?

"No, *mon coeur*, of course not! I'm so happy you're here! I just wish I could have it all, you know? You're my priority, but your presence is going to impact my friendship with them—it's just a fact—and I wish it didn't."

He threw me a sideways glance and caressed my hand soothingly.

"I'm very happy to be here, too, Plume."

Appeased by his soothing words, I focused back on the road and the landscapes around us for the rest of the drive, never letting go of his hand, and when he needed it to park the car in front of the cabin his moms had rented for us, I just laid my palm on his knee.

We got the keys from the owner, who was waiting for us.

In the outskirts of Montréal, we had stopped to buy some groceries so we could enjoy our uninterrupted weeks of peace and quiet. Unloading the car took us a while because of it. As soon as we were done, we started making lunch and tidying up the place, putting our things away in the closet.

The cabin was charming, warm and cosy, with its high ceilings, big steel fireplace, and exposed wooden beams. It truly felt like a modern fairy-tale house. It had three rooms. The first one was the living room that was also a modern, open kitchen with an island in the middle. Then came a cute bedroom with wooden, soft grey walls and a massive king-size bed, almost hidden under a mountain of throw pillows. The last room was the bathroom, simple, but comfortable.

Loup was right, everything was absolutely perfect.

Once everything was where we wanted it to be, we had lunch, and then went for a walk around the neighbouring lake. Our living room had massive windows that let in the bright winter sun and gave us an uninterrupted view of the water body, now frozen and covered in snow.

"When I booked, they told me we might be able to ice-skate if it was cold enough, but I think it got a bit too cold," Loup remarked. I wasn't really disappointed. I had never ice skated before, and it would have been way too easy for me to break a wrist and be kicked out of the program I was working so hard for. Loup couldn't really ice skate either so he wouldn't be of much help.

"It's perfect," I told him, getting up on my pointed toes as much as my snow boots allowed, to kiss him. He met me halfway. "Thank you," I added when my heels were back on the ground.

We ate dinner, catching up on everything that had happened during the last few months. We already had talked about most of it, but hearing the stories through a video conference wasn't the same as in person. Living people didn't just pause in the middle of a grimace, and it did make a difference. We then went to bed, cuddling together in a big pile of limbs.

Chapter 14

Fauve

PROGRESSIVELY, I RELAXED, AND our holiday became truly enjoyable. We talked a lot, about everything, and it truly felt as if we had never been apart. The first full day we spent at the cabin started with us shedding our pajamas and making slow, sweet love while the sun rose on the horizon. We had breakfast, then Loup went to grab a bottle of wine that we started drinking in bed. Drunk, we forgot to make lunch and ended up heating a frozen pizza in the oven in the middle of the afternoon.

Loup had a bunch of tales of his disastrous adventures on Tinder that made me laugh out loud. He showed me the messages he got from people hitting on him, and he was right, the level of the pick-up phrases was low, from dick pics to pouting mouths. And boobs. Loads of boobs, all bigger than mine, and when that started to upset me, Loup tossed his phone on the armchair in the corner of the room, scooted down the bed so his eyes were level with my chest, and proceeded to show my small breasts how amazing they were, nipping at my nipple from time to time.

Idiot. Very lovable, but still, idiot.

I giggled for the entirety of his conversation with my boobs, kissing him after a while to make him stop.

That day, we kissed a lot, too. Quick, stolen pecks in passing as much as thorough explorations of each other's mouths, with tongues and teeth joining the dance. I had missed him so much.

We fell asleep early, after exploring each other's body as if we hadn't already done it a million times and taking a long, lazy shower to clean up.

Loup and I had almost spent the entirety of the day naked, and I found I didn't miss my clothes one bit.

I woke up with a tongue between my legs and an orgasm escaping my lips.

I never wanted to wake up any other way.

I pulled Loup up and crawled over him to return the favour. I was famished, in all senses of the word, so I went down on him enthusiastically, exactly the way I knew he liked and had spent five years perfecting. He came in my mouth with a groan, and I swallowed it all.

I had missed it, how easy, how right it felt to be together.

We ate a quick breakfast and went for another walk, during which I enjoyed the landscapes with all my heart. Even with our thick gloves on, we held hands for the duration of it, only letting go for the occasional snowball fight.

The wilderness was magnificent. I was used to the city and hadn't realised I missed being in such open spaces. Some deer and snow rabbits even came to greet us. We tried to feed them berries, but they apparently liked them better on the trees.

We went back to the cabin just before lunch and cooked together in companionable silence.

"How do you feel about starting to rehearse your second presentation this afternoon?" Loup asked while cutting vegetables.

"I'd love to! I didn't manage to find a decent Adagio partner at NICAM, can you believe that? It will be great to perform together again," I exclaimed.

We ate quickly, both eager to get started. We changed into our training outfits, and Loup put our favourite playlist on while we warmed up.

Obviously, the cabin wasn't planned to host a circus show rehearsal. There weren't any mattresses we could use to dampen our falls, and the ceilings weren't exactly high enough for some of our figures, but if we paid attention and chose carefully what we were going to do, I was confident we could make it work.

We had already put a first, easy version of an act together—planning to build up on it when we would be in a proper environment—when Loup started to throw playful glances my way.

"We've never trained naked, have we?" he asked, feigning innocence.

"I think I would remember it if we had," I teased.

"What do you say we give it a go? We can call it an experimental performance or whatever." So, we undressed in the name of art, my exposed nipples pebbling from more than the cold.

Lifting my eyes from the pile of clothes on the ground, I took my equally naked boyfriend in. He was all lean, dense muscles, and moved with graceful strength. Under my hungry eyes, his soft cock started to stir, attracting my attention to it and the valleys between his abs. He was magnificent.

MANUELA ROUGET

Loup was watching me as intently, then shook his head. "Come on, Plume, let's get started or I'll throw you on the bed and fuck you senseless. We need to practice."

Halfway through the routine, I understood what exactly my partner's goal was when he had wanted to get us naked. I sure suspected it but didn't know how exactly he would get us there. During a move where I twisted my body backward—a half twist and a backbend simultaneously—when he caught me and pushed me up, I found myself sitting on his shoulders with my crotch right in front of his face and my heels resting on his back.

His hands on my hips pushed my ass up to improve my balance, and his tongue darted out to lick me. It was an incredible sensation. I had no choice but to focus on every part of my body, otherwise the odds were that I would lose my balance and fall. It made me conscious of every centimetre of my skin touching his, and every way it did. I felt my clit as if it took root in my feet and finished in my fingers, making the smallest contact of the tip of his tongue a whole-body experience. I couldn't fully relax though, having to maintain my equilibrium, so my orgasm remained out of reach.

It was the sweetest form of torture.

Still in the same position, his tongue dancing between my legs, he started walking to the bedroom. He had to squat at some point for me not to bump my head on the doorframe—which was a bit ridiculous, but hey, what was the point of having a long-term partner if you couldn't do ridiculous sex stuff without killing the mood?

With me still on his shoulders, he sat on the edge of the bed, and using all the power in those perfect abs of his, laid back in a sexy as fuck move until he was flat on his back and my knees touched the bedspread. He kept me balanced over him as he did it, like the amazing base he was.

See? It was possible to sit graciously on someone's face, after all.

I needed to tell Nathalie that when we got back, she would find it hilarious.

Feeling playful, I extended my legs on each side of his head in an almost perfect split, tensing my thighs so that my pussy was hovering mere centimetres over his mouth.

"Come on, Plume, I know you can go lower than that, I've seen you in an oversplit before." He paused for a second, and I almost saw the metaphorical light bulb switch on above his head. "Wait, do you think it's possible for you to do a backbend now and suck my cock?"

"I can try," I flirted. If that worked, we would have to do it again some other day, because I wanted a picture. I was too far gone to stop to look for my phone now, though.

Lowering myself back on his mouth, legs still extended, I put my hand on his hips and arched my back as far as it would go, extending my hands to stop my fall. I completed the backbend, only to discover that the height difference between us was too big for me to reach his dick. I could see it, standing at attention, with a bead of pre-cum forming at its tip, but I needed to either use my legs or suddenly become quite taller to reach it.

Taking in the absurdity of my position, I giggled, then gasped when Loup pulled me down and started sucking on my clit. I straightened my back, back to my split position.

"Nope, not working, I'll have to suck you off the traditional way," I panted.

He licked me again, from my very exposed ass to my clit, taking some time to spear his tongue into my pussy. He pushed me up just a little to be able to talk.

"I think experiment time is over then. Bend your legs, Plume, I want to finish taking care of you." Echoing my thoughts from earlier, he added, "The acrobatic sex was hot as fuck, though. I kind of wish we had filmed it to watch again later."

I let out a decidedly girly scream when he flipped us over, his mouth still hovering over my pussy, but I needed more. I needed to be filled.

"There's already been too much foreplay today, don't you think?" I mused.

"I don't think there's such a thing as too much foreplay, Plume." As if to prove his point, he blew on my clit, and I whimpered.

"Let me rephrase, then. I need you inside me."

"You should have started with that. How?"

"Any comfortable position." I laughed. Splits and all were fun, but I needed the earth-shattering orgasm that I sensed coming, and didn't want to risk breaking my neck or pulling a muscle when it happened. Even acrobats had limits.

He put me on my side and spooned me from behind, his chest to my back. I shivered in anticipation. The height difference between the two of us made this position perfect.

"Is this comfortable enough for you, Plume?" he teased, nipping at my neck. I moaned, grinding my ass against his dick, making it obvious what I thought would feel even better.

He fisted his cock, using his hand to guide himself inside me. He moved agonisingly slowly as he entered me from behind, and I let him, my body putty from his ministrations.

When his hips finally came in contact with my ass, he tangled his left hand in my hair and used his hold on it to stretch my neck back to an almost painful angle. His other hand wrapped around my breast, and he rolled my nipple between his fingers.

Loup whispered against my neck, his voice suddenly low and possessive, "How beautiful you look, Plume, surrendering in my arms. I love it when you entrust me with your body, your pleasure, your heart, your pain, even. Will you come for me, if I slap your ass like it deserves? If I pull your hair and pinch your nipple?" I moaned, too far gone to speak.

While he spoke, Loup's hand had snaked down to my pussy. He dipped his finger where our bodies were joined and spread my wetness around. His fingers started sliding slowly back and forth on my clit, in time with the thrusts of his hips.

"And what if I do this?" he growled.

Then, he bit me on the neck, hard enough to leave an enormous mark. I came with a scream, my whole body tensing, trembling and clamping around him. My hand went up to his hair, to pull him down in encouragement or push him away, I wasn't sure. I was riding that fine line between pain and pleasure, and the sensations coursing through me were exquisite.

As I was coming down from my high, he pushed me down, so my front was to the bed, pulled my hips up in the air, and knelt behind me, his hand still in my hair. He pulled it harder than before and started fucking me in earnest, his balls slapping my clit every time his hips met my ass.

When I felt him close to finishing, I rubbed on my clit with two fingers and made myself come again. This time, he came with me.

We both collapsed on the bed, breathing heavily, and didn't move again for a very long time.

Chapter 15

Cody

SHE HADN'T CALLED. FAUVE hadn't called, had sent one miserable message and then nothing. If she were dead, I might have more news through her relatives. I hoped she wasn't, obviously.

From the minute she saw Loup, it was like Thibault and I ceased to exist.

I didn't even care that they were probably banging in every corner of the chalet he had rented, although I would very much like to be in his place. I wasn't jealous. I just thought she was my friend, and friends didn't disappear with barely a word.

But I was obviously wrong, otherwise she wouldn't have vanished without giving me a sign of life for four entire days.

I understood she had shit to deal with. Really, I did. Loup had been weird at Cabaret Rouge before they left. Add to it they hadn't seen each other for months while sleeping with other people, and you get a pretty messy situation.

But, come on. She had time to send more than a single text, didn't she? I didn't think he was the type to control her cell phone. Hell, had I just facilitated her going on a holiday in the Canadian wilderness with an abusive boyfriend? I needed to hear from her, and I needed it soon. My imagination of the worst case scenarios knew no boundaries.

I missed her, too. Loup was, for sure, a better person than I was—if he wasn't an abusive douche, that is—because I wouldn't have let her leave me to study abroad. It would have devastated me. It still might, actually, if she didn't win NICAM's program and had to go back to France.

Christmas afternoon, while I was pacing in my parents' living room like a caged lion, the text I had been waiting for finally came.

Fauvette: Merry Christmas, Cody! Sorry, I haven't texted earlier. I got caught up in everything and, well, I'm sorry. How has your holiday been so far?

I grinned like an idiot throughout the entire dinner.

Fauve

I felt slightly bad for texting my ex-lover while my boyfriend was busy in the kitchen, preparing me yet another surprise. Only slightly, because I knew Loup didn't expect me to stop talking to them. Even so, it felt awkward.

But I couldn't help it. Last night, a notification had appeared on my phone saying a SpaceX rocket had exploded a handful of seconds after landing successfully on earth, and I had felt Cody's absence as if one of my limbs was missing. I had to give it to him, he had managed to get me addicted to those stupid space exploration live streams.

I also had a whole season of *The Office* left to watch, and I wasn't sure I could do it without being curled up in his arms. I had become used to falling asleep that way after all this time.

Thinking of Cody brought back memories of Thibault, too, and I couldn't help but think we had unfinished business. I texted him the same message. Better late than never, right? And I couldn't not wish them a Merry Christmas.

What would it be like to live together, the three of us, along with Loup, when we came back from our trip? The plan included my boyfriend and I moving out after he found a day job, but I was going to miss my flatmates. Montréal was now intrinsically connected to them in my mind, and living in the city without being accompanied by my two favourite Canadians would take some getting used to. I was going to miss Logan, too, but since we hadn't slept together and he was gay, it would probably be less awkward to invite him for coffee when we got our new place. Thibault and Cody, well, I couldn't imagine being in the same space as them and not flirting, which would probably make Loup uncomfortable.

The fact that I felt this conflicted also made me weirdly happy. It revealed how amazing my experience with my flatmates had been, and I couldn't help but feel grateful about it. Some people spent their whole lives without feeling this intensely about anyone, after all.

I started getting ready for dinner. Even in my half-awake state, I had thought of packing a nice dress before leaving Montréal—just in case—and I planned on wearing it tonight.

I took a long shower, purposely making it last since Loup had decided to keep me out of the living room until he was ready. I had time, it was still early, so my skin was all wrinkled by the water when I opened the bathroom door, letting a cloud of billowing steam into the bedroom.

I shimmied into the skin-tight dress, one of my favourites, but that I couldn't wear often. It was a bit short and too tight to use during the day or a family dinner, and since I wasn't much of a party animal, I was limited on opportunities to wear it. But it would be perfect for tonight.

It was made of a sheer burgundy lace, with a lining underneath that was the same colour as my skin. The long sleeves reached my wrists, and the neckline dipped low, making it look like my cleavage was much more impressive than it actually was. The massive bruise Loup's bite had left on my neck was also shockingly apparent, the colour echoing the hue of the lace. If I had been going to a normal Christmas party, I would have had to be extremely careful not to flash my boobs or my ass to the room while sitting. Fortunately, this wasn't a problem I would have tonight. Since the cabin was well heated, I could go without pantyhose—I went without clothes most of these days, anyway—and just slipped on a pair of high-heeled pumps. If they seemed too uncomfortable, I could just ditch them under the table.

I blow-dried my hair, fluffing it up with my fingers until it looked like a fiery mane that fell down my back. My skin looked nice these days, so I moisturized it and left it natural, focusing on my eyes, instead. I was no Logan, but I wasn't bad at makeup either, plus NICAM's classes had helped boost my skills. This time, I went for a smoky look, confidently blending blacks and greys until my dark brown eyes looked deep and mysterious. Instead of lipstick, I preferred coloured lip balm, which would look less ridiculous if it ended up smeared all over my face for... reasons.

In the mirror of the bathroom, I did a last check-up, verifying I hadn't forgotten anything appearance-wise. I smirked. I looked good.

I belly-flopped back onto the bed to wait for my very own Paul Bocuse to be satisfied with his work.

I pretended not to hear him when he entered the room, knowing full well he had a very nice view of my ass from where he was standing, and feeling like teasing him. I was rewarded by a very loud slap on it.

"Ouch," I protested, "that hurt!"

"It was way too tempting." I turned my head around to look at him but hadn't really moved, so he pounced on me and bit the same ass cheek through my dress. Again, it wasn't exactly a playful bite.

"Stop it!" I wiggled out of his arms and made a move for the door, wobbling slightly on my high heels.

"No!" he shouted. "Stay here while I get ready, please? I smell like food, it's gross."

I nodded, sitting back on the bed. My butt still burnt slightly, courtesy of his hand and teeth.

Loup looked good in any outfit, really. He oozed self-confidence and strength, which would even make a penguin onesie look sexy. Maybe. But when he made an effort, I always had to pick my lower jaw up from the floor and remove the cartoon hearts from my eyes. He came out of the bathroom already dressed; his gaze pausing and heating when he took in the mark on my neck.

He was in a simple blue button-down shirt, leaving the top two buttons open and rolling the sleeves over his lean forearms. It was tucked into black slacks that hugged his perfect ass and long legs. It stopped just above his ankle, in a way that was trendy in France, but I didn't quite understand.

His short hair was artistically tousled, thanks to the hair wax I knew he liked. Our eyes met, and for a moment, I was lost in his.

He had bought a shirt that was the exact same shade of turquoise as his irises. It made the colour stand out, more intense, almost surreal. I was never letting him wear anything else.

"You look incredible, Plume. Come here." He extended a hand in my direction and helped me off the bed, pulling me close against his chest. In my heels, my nose was level with his clavicles, and I breathed in his scent, recognising the fancy cologne I had given him years ago.

"So do you," I said. I pushed the collar of his shirt aside to lay a feather-light kiss where his shoulder met his neck, and he shivered in response.

"Let's do this," he announced. He turned me around, putting his hands over my eyes, entirely blocking my vision. He pressed his body against my back, telling me without words to walk towards the door.

"Open the door, Plume." I blindly reached for the doorknob and turned it. "On three," he breathed in my ear after guiding me inside the living room. "One, two, and three." Loup removed his hands.

My lips formed an "O", but no sound came out of them. I was rendered speechless, wide-eyed at the amazing work he had done.

He had covered every available surface in little glass vases with candles floating in them, while the lights were off. He had pushed the sofa against the window, leaving more space around the dining table that he had decorated, too.

"Did you go out this afternoon?" I asked.

"I had to; I wanted to cut down a Christmas tree, like in movies, but never found one small enough, so I picked up branches instead."

"It's perfect."

He had artistically arranged branches in the middle of the table, around three big red candles that would provide the light we'd need to eat. It was romantic and festive, and I loved it all.

"Sit, I'll get the food," Loup ordered. Who would say no to this?

He pushed my chair under me like the gentleman he was and went to the fridge to get everything he had prepared. It turned out to be a feast.

The starters included *foie gras*, smoked salmon, and toasts from what he told me was homemade bread. *Homemade* bread.

"Aren't you supposed to let it rest at a certain temperature for several days for it to turn out good?" I asked.

"I did, actually. The dough's been in the oven for some time now, I've been distracting enough for you not to find it." The idiot winked.

He popped open a bottle of champagne I assumed came in his suitcases, and we toasted, our glasses clinking together while we looked in each other's eyes, exaggeratedly opening them as French people always did. The saying was that you had to suffer through seven years of bad luck in bed if you didn't make eye contact while toasting. Nobody was ever willing to risk it.

We waited for the capon—he had managed to find a fucking capon, *the* traditional French Christmas turkey—to finish roasting while sipping on our drinks. The typical food from my homeland was making me wistful. Until now, I had spent all my Christmases with my family, close and extended, at someone's place—either my parents', one of my aunts' or my grandparents'. This year, even with all the amazing things Loup had done for me today, I felt homesick.

I hadn't truly missed my family since I arrived, too busy with classes and presentations and flatmate drama. But I missed them now. Christmas did not feel like a true Christmas without noise, laughter, and, paradoxically, my mom's annoying remarks.

"It's okay to miss them, you know?" Loup said, his azure eyes missing nothing.

"I know, it's just weird. It's hitting me now, and I almost feel... bad about it. Like I should have missed them earlier or something."

"I know. You shouldn't, though. Feel bad, I mean. You had other things to think about," he reassured me. His phone pinged, catching his attention. "I think the capon's ready now, it smelled really good before, but was a bit raw. I stuffed it with chestnut and *foie gras*. I don't want to sound like I'm gloating, but the stuffing was amazing."

I giggled. He definitely had earned some bragging rights on this one.

I ate until I was so full it felt like I was going to have to roll to the bedroom, the skin of my belly pushing through my dress in a decidedly unladylike way. He laughed when he saw me relax against the backrest of my chair like I was pregnant.

"I brought cheese from France, too, do you want some? Or should we have dessert instead?"

"Yes!" I blurted. I hadn't eaten decent cheese in months, and I was sure my stomach could handle more food.

He fetched a cheese platter from the fridge, removed its cover, and opened a bottle of red wine to go with it. It smelled amazing. Like old, dirty gym clothes and vinegar. The cheese, not the wine.

I was already full, so I only ate a little as there would be leftovers for tomorrow.

For dessert, Loup had made a dark chocolate mousse. He joked he felt it would have been overambitious to venture into patisserie. He was probably right, and I loved the dessert he had picked anyway. He had even used his mom's recipe for it, in which she removed one egg, and added solid chocolate chips, to make sure it was concentrated to the point of slightly bitter. It was incredible.

I was going to burst, but I ate some anyway.

"Where do you put all this?" Loup teased.

"I'm training a lot; I need the calories. Plus, the food was great, and I think our bodies are smart enough to automatically create more stomach space when what's coming down is tasty."

He smiled sweetly at my antics. I wasn't so relaxed about my eating habits when we first met. I knew he considered getting me excited about food and not controlling every calorie I ate a victory. Honestly, so did I. I was never truly an anorexic, but it was a close call.

"Do you want to open your present?" he asked. "And before you feel bad, I know you didn't get me anything; you didn't know I would be here, so relax. It's a present for both of us, really." My body had indeed started to tense, and it immediately relaxed at his words.

He got up, disappeared in the bedroom for a moment, and put a box the size of a dictionary in my hands, wrapped in a pretty pink gift paper with a silver bow. It was lighter, though.

I opened just a corner of it and recognised the brand. I knew it... intimately.

"Do you like it?" he asked.

"I'm curious, but on this subject, you have my complete trust. What does this one do that's better than the other one?" I managed to say the complete sentence without blushing, like an adult woman confident about her sexuality.

"Oh, this one is shaped like a U, so one side is a clit stimulator, and the other a vaginal one. And this side allows for a partner to penetrate you at the same time, since it's flatter. Obviously, it's remote controlled, too."

I couldn't hold it in anymore and giggled while blushing bright red. My boyfriend had a theory that sex should be treated as any hobby, and therefore have time and/or money invested in getting better at it. Bringing it up during such a familial holiday was a first, though.

In my hands, freed from the pink gift wrap, I held a sleek black box, containing another high-tech sex toy.

And I loved it.

I woke up warm, comfy, and happy.

After dinner, we had both gone to bed and passed out from a food coma. The night had been perfect, my present was perfect, and my boyfriend was perfect. These were the thoughts that accompanied me to the land of dreams. Not bad.

I felt Loup move against my back from where he spooned me, and I realised he was awake. I wiggled to turn around and face him, and softly kissed his lips.

"I wanted to talk to you about something," I started.

"Sure, Plume, what is it?" I worried my lip.

"About your fear... I don't want you to push yourself too much, okay? You're making progress, and I'm scared if you're not careful, it will end up making it all worse, like an overdose of sorts."

"I promise I won't take it too far, Plume. I am starting to know myself, and I'll still have my virtual weekly sessions with *Docteur* Fabre to talk about it. You don't have to feel responsible for this, I'm an adult, and capable of making my own decisions."

"I just can't help but wonder if there's anything more I can do to help."

He scratched his head, thoughtful for an instant. "I think it would help if you told me every time you performed or trained up high. I know it's annoying, and I totally understand if you forget sometimes, or even don't want to talk about it, but it truly helps when I have time to mentally prepare for these situations."

"Deal," I immediately said. "I like telling you everything."

Chapter 16

Fauve

Coming back to Montréal was as awkward as I thought it would be. The apartment was quiet and empty, everyone making themselves scarce. We still talked occasionally on our group chat, but it just wasn't the same as before.

Loup was looking for both a job and a new place for us while I studied. Then, we rehearsed my second evaluation presentation during all our "free" time. Often, I had absolutely no idea what Cody, Thibault, and Logan were doing. Then again, I had decided figuring out my love life could wait until after my exams. Not ranking last again was the priority in my life. I couldn't mess up this opportunity, and definitely not for boys. To quote Lady Gaga, "Your career will never wake up and tell you that it doesn't love you anymore."

Yeah, I was in denial too.

MANUELA ROUGET

In the dead of night, when sleep escaped me—you know those nights, everybody does—I admitted to myself I missed the easy relationship I had with Cody and Thibault at the beginning of the school year. Having Loup here was incredible, but a long-term relationship came with more pressure than a newfound one, and that made things less exciting sometimes. Screwing up my relationship with my boyfriend wasn't an option, it was too important. Since it was all so new, the consequences of messing up with Cody and Thibault were less dramatic, which made me experiment more.

I missed that carelessness.

To top it all off, my mom had suddenly decided she wanted to know what I was up to, and with the amount of stress I was already under, I had no other solution but to ignore her calls. She had lectured me enough right after my last result, I didn't want to expose myself to another judgemental discourse, disguised as a pep talk. At some point, she would get irritated and call Loup, then I'd call her back. I wasn't talking to her any more than I absolutely had to.

I focused on my classes, and that was what mattered. Under Nathalie's tutoring, my juggling skills had improved a lot. It wasn't my comfort zone yet, but my religious, daily training was paying off. I was compensating for my lack of talent with sheer, constant, unwavering stubbornness.

Back in September, I thought it would take me years to figure it out, but again, I was determined. It turned out that in almost three months, I was a decent juggler. Well, decent in my book, not compared to the ones at NICAM. I could juggle with three balls, without making one fall, for about a hundred throws or so, and even managed to start finding it relaxing. Indeed, it was a very physical manifestation of how focused I was. If I started thinking about anything else, the balls fell, it was that simple.

AERIAL

The clowning exam was another problem altogether. After several trials and failures, I had given up on telling jokes. It didn't work. But this grade would be important for my total average, so I couldn't give up on the subject.

To my horror, the exam consisted of a quick presentation. Since we were only twenty-five students in this phase of the program, it was possible to organise in almost every class. I didn't like it, but it made sense, too. As a performer, what good could it do to have passed written clowning tests?

So I had three minutes to fill with things that my audience would hopefully find funny, and it quickly turned out to be a nightmare. To compensate for my lack of ideas, I was studying a lot. I watched videos of every single comical performance I could find. I researched the great clowns in history. I even went through theatre plays, and dissected the forms of comedy in the Comedia Dell'Arte movement.

I loved learning these new things, and hated that it wasn't helpful at all.

Until juggling brought the solution I was looking for. I was learning my first trick, and all the balls had just fallen on the floor. I went to pick up one, but stepped on another while doing so, and almost fell on my face, sending both Mary and Nathalie rolling to the floor in laughter.

Clowning didn't have to be verbal, did it?

So, on the day of my performance, I dressed as a gigantic baby, and with my head held high, I strolled down past the tables to the front of the classroom. My act was simple, really. I was a baby learning to walk, and falling on my ass most of the time. It was also relatable, since most people had been an infant, and sometimes even seen one, too.

The really funny part was that I was using my acrobat training to fall in completely over-the-top manners, like some kind of Hollywood stuntman, except dressed as an enormous baby, with padding, pacifier, wails and all. I was completely unable to fake-cry convincingly, so I had used sounds found on the internet to create a soundtrack, including a disapproving mother.

I had timed it all perfectly, and the other students were all caught in fits of giggles. The grand finale was me getting up, taking two uneasy steps, wobbling from one side to the other, falling backwards, catching myself up by doing a backflip, landing on my feet, raising my arms to the air in victory, and face-planting three forward steps later.

Everyone laughed, some students were holding their ribs, others were even crying.

It was a triumph.

I beamed, immensely proud.

All my exams had gone well, and I was better prepared for my second evaluation presentation than for the first, so I was confidently waiting backstage when Loup arrived. We hadn't warmed up yet, since we wouldn't perform for another hour or so. He had come early so that I wouldn't have to wait alone, or go back home in the freezing cold after my classes.

"Plume, can I talk to you for a second?"

"Yes, of course," I answered, preoccupied. Loup was scowling and looked oddly serious. Not focused, but... nervous, which was unlike him.

We went to a corner of the dressing room, trying to find some semblance of privacy in the busy backstage area.

"Ever since we've been back from our trip, you've been unhappy," he started, cutting right to the chase. I opened my mouth to speak, but he didn't let me. Apparently, he knew more about my inner turmoil than I thought. "Please, let me say what I have to say. I promise it won't impact our performance in a bad way. If anything, I think it will help." My heart stopped pounding in my chest, and I started breathing more normally. "You haven't been yourself, and I don't like it. Even when we video chatted, you seemed more lively than now that I'm here. You don't look unhappy all the time, of course, but I never see you laugh out loud, or get excited by things either. I miss it, and it made me think about what's changed since I last saw you happy." He held my chin between his thumb and index finger and tilted my head backwards until our eyes met.

"It's me, Plume. I arrived, and your life changed. And I hate it. You can't be like that because of me, that's just not what I want to be for you. That's actually the exact opposite." He wasn't wrong, not exactly. I felt like I was cut in two halves, and very purposefully ignoring one. My professional side was overjoyed at the success it felt was near. My personal life, on the other hand, was gloomy. I had avoided Thibault and Cody, losing Logan and a part of me in the process. I didn't want to go back home at night, knowing it would be empty and sad, and it had made it that much easier to throw myself into my studies.

We hadn't had sex since the cabin either. The walls of our apartment were too thin, it felt rude. Also, I was too exhausted at night to think about it.

In that instant, I realised that my relationship with Loup had become strained this past month.

"So I thought about it, and if you want to be with the three of us, I want to try to make it work. If they want to be with us, of course.

"I trust you, and I trust your heart, so let's have a go at it and see what happens. Plus, they're nice to look at." I was dumbstruck, so he nipped at my nose, causing me to squeal. We both chuckled. I didn't expect Loup to have picked up on those feelings, since I wasn't acknowledging them myself. But, of course, he had.

"What if you end up unhappy, then? I don't want to make you feel bad either," I said.

"Then we'll find another solution. You're the love of my life, my partner in crime, and my best friend. I have no doubt we'll find a way if this doesn't work. And I promise to tell you if it doesn't." Loup raised his other hand, cupping my cheeks, once more ensnaring me in the turquoise depth of his eyes. "Between you and any other person in the world, I'll always pick you, Plume. But between you and me, I'll always pick me. I'm not going to sacrifice my happiness for yours. All I'm saying is that I'm willing to try and be happy with them, too." A weight was lifted off my shoulders. He was offering me everything.

"And what about the future? Our relationship would not exactly be common."

"Well, in the future, if it all works out, then we'll have a big, loud, messy, unconventional, happy family. I grew up with two moms, and you know that I was happier in my family than a lot of people with heterosexual parents. I am sure kids can grow up fine with three dads and a mom. They'll be more loved, more cared for, and I don't see how that can be a problem.

"But that's jumping pretty far ahead, don't you think? For all we know, they're going to screw up all on their own like the grown men they are, and I'll have you all to myself again in a couple of months." He smiled, so I knew he meant it as a joke.

"Plume, the important thing is, this isn't a big deal. You aren't doing anything wrong. If anything, I'm ecstatic and a bit scared that you were willing to go to such great lengths to make me happy.

"It stops now, and I'm returning the favour. Do what you can to be with the men you love, Plume. All of them."

"I'm not in love with t—"

"Uh-uh, you can lie to yourself all you want, but not to me. You're in love with them, and it's fine. We live in such a messed up, hateful world. There are many people doing terrible things without feeling any shame. You shouldn't, either, when all you're doing is daring to fight for the people you love."

I jumped into his arms then, wrapping my legs around him. He held me effortlessly, using the wall against my back to support me. I put my forehead against his and closed my eyes. Maybe Thibault and Cody wouldn't want me anymore, after I had stayed away from them for weeks. Maybe they would resent me, and we would indeed have to move out. But in that instant, it didn't matter. I felt hopeful and confident that it would all work out.

"I love you, and have I told you how much I've missed you?"

"I love you, too. Now, let's show your teachers what the Duo Animal is capable of."

Thibault

I shouldn't be here. As a TA, I was allowed to, but still, I shouldn't.

The second selection presentation was just starting, and even if Fauve—*my* Puss—had been ghosting me for weeks, I wanted to be here, to support her—or at least that's what I told myself. A masochistic part of my brain also wanted me to witness what I'd lost with my own eyes, and maybe, finally, find a way to move on. After all, it had been weeks since our presentation in December, and she now had a perfect life, with her perfect boyfriend.

A perfect life that didn't include me. Cody. *Us*.

Loup and Fauve stepped on stage, announced as the Duo Animal. Their parents obviously had the same weird naming tastes. Wolf and Big Cat, in French. Their stage name fit them like a glove.

Like the sun and the sky, they looked incredible together, too. She was all fiery and flamboyant, in a very sexy set of white lingerie I had never seen on her. He was more subdued, in the background, shirtless and in loose thin black sweatpants. Casual, allowing her to shine, but looking gorgeous, nonetheless.

I had never seen them perform together. Their act was all I wanted for my performance with Fauve on the aerial chandelier to be, without quite getting there. We lacked training and experience. Fauve had never been as comfortable with me as she was with Loup. A pang of jealousy speared my chest. I shouldn't be watching this. It only added to my misery.

Their routine was sexy, sensual, sexual, almost. They exchanged unapologetically heated looks, intense and at the same time, incredibly happy. She was radiant tonight. I couldn't remember if she looked this joyful these last few weeks.

Daring poses and extreme figures followed themselves one after the other, and I was gradually coming to a decision that I was going to leave the room and pretend I had never been here in the first place. Pretend that tonight and all the perfect months before Loup's arrival had never happened.

Then, I saw it, and understood it all.

For a fraction of a second, as she was elegantly, flawlessly flying in the air where he had thrown her, her whole body relaxed completely. Like a seabird, she was gliding, as if an imaginary draft carried her. Unbothered by gravity, unconcerned by the laws of physics, she flew.

As a circus artist, I understood how dangerous that was. Your body wasn't ever supposed to be relaxed. You had to always be careful because that fraction of a second could always be the last one. When flying, you were supposed to protect yourself, be attentive to anything that might happen, and this state of mind is what made a presentation that only lasted a handful of minutes as tiring as an hour-long workout.

She was suspended in the air, three metres high, upside down, and she was as relaxed as if she was lounging on a bed.

In this position, if he didn't catch her, she was dead. Or quadriplegic, at least.

For a gutting, heart-wrenching fraction of a second, she even closed her eyes.

She flew, gracious as a bird, relaxed as a cat.

She trusted him.

He caught her.

And I could breathe again.

Their presentation continued, but I wasn't paying attention anymore.

This split second told me everything I needed to know about them.

Have you ever realised how certain expressions lose their meaning when too many people start using them? They wear out, like old clothes only hanging by a thread. "Trust one with one's life" is one of those, for me. Hollywood's used the shit out of it, and it doesn't make sense anymore. It's diluted, bland.

Seeing Fauve and Loup together changed that. She trusted him with her life, completely, to the point where she didn't even pay attention when she was falling headfirst towards the ground, because the possibility of him missing her didn't exist in her mind.

This was love, pure and simple.

I felt threatened when he arrived, as if I had to defend my place with Fauve. It was foolish, but true. I shouldn't have, that spot by her side was never even mine. It had been lent, and she had told me several times her boyfriend would take it back. To Loup, I wasn't even threatening. At all.

I understood now why it was obvious that opening their relationship would work. This was not the kind of love that considered a few months of sex with other partners a threat, and I was stupid to put myself in this category, hoping that she would pick me in the end.

She was honest from the get-go, and I didn't listen.

What happened between us on stage was undeniable chemistry and desire. But what they had was years and years of training, falling and learning together. It was love and trust, the kind that moved mountains and was felt across continents. This was the real deal, the one that stories were made of.

I couldn't compete with it.

I shouldn't want to compete with it.

And I didn't want to, not really. I just wanted in.

My dilemma had only one solution. I was going to woo them both.

Chapter 17

Fauve

Like for the first presentation, we all assembled in the main hall on Friday—twenty-four hours after our performance. I was calmer this time around, less agitated. Pumped by our conversation, Loup and I had performed exceptionally well, and I was almost certain I would pass on to the next phase, even if it got more competitive. My business school background helped, too, since I didn't need to spend as much time studying all of the analytical subjects, while they were challenging for others.

Donna Loewenberg had prepared an introductory speech, but my mind was elsewhere. It was starting to all sound the same, anyway. Give me the damn results now!

"Without further ado," she continued, "our best student for this phase is... Fauve Laurent!"

I gasped, spacing out for a moment. People applauded. I was expecting to pass, but didn't anticipate being called out first. Donna kept going, but I was dumbstruck, until Mary elbowed me in the ribs.

"You did it, girl! Congratulations!" Her voice was strained, and I started paying attention again. Neither she nor Nathalie had been called yet. My anxiety rose. NICAM wouldn't be the same without them.

"In fourth place, Mary Sue Shevchenko!" Two out of three. Donna just had to call Nathalie now, and I could relax.

"In eighth place, Nathalie Roy," Donna announced after what felt like hours.

I let out a long sigh and shook my shoulders, trying to relax my tense muscles.

Out of respect, we waited for the five remaining students to be called, never taking our eyes off the podium. It turned out two of them were the almost identical sister that had made fun of me and Nathalie, when we'd fallen during that first acrobatics class.

As soon as the last student had been called, Mary and I hugged each other, jumping around in celebration. We were on for another term, along with eleven other hard-working students. We weren't lucky. Luck had nothing to do with it.

"Fauve, call that boyfriend of yours. This time, you're coming with us to celebrate," Mary ordered. "I won't take no for an answer, not from you, and not today. You deserve a fun night, filled with alcohol and junk food."

"Yes!" I was still bouncing around on my toes, not fully believing what happened recently, but definitely up for some partying. I texted Loup, telling him the good news and to meet us at the bar where everyone was headed. "Are we going right now? Or can I go home to change first?" Unlike last time a verdict was announced, our aerials class had been maintained today.

"Nope, we're going right now. I'm not letting your sweaty ass miss happy hour."

I laughed, the enormity of what had just happened finally sinking in. I was the best student. I truly was a performer, and not simply a circus artist wannabe, too arrogant for her own good.

"I have to check up on my sister first," Nathalie said, "but I'll meet you there." I mentally scolded myself for forgetting about her situation. Eighth wasn't a good ranking for her. It meant that she would have to work twice as hard to be sure to make it until June, since, next time, when we would be ranked, they'd only keep six students.

"Are you okay, Nat?" I asked. "It'll all be fine, you'll see. You have three months now to gain only two places."

"I know," she grumbled. "I'll see you soon, behave while I'm gone!" she said, already walking away from us.

"Always!" Mary shouted.

We arrived at the bar, and I drank my first beer, Loup joining us right when I was ordering my second one. He quickly stole it from me, claiming he had to catch up.

He had met Mary before, but it was the first time they truly had the opportunity to get to know each other, and he didn't miss a beat before starting a conversation. I watched them silently for a moment, happy that she and my boyfriend were getting along so well. At the same time, knowing how important she was to me, Loup had launched a befriending operation, doing everything he could to make her like him. Seeing in his behaviour the proof of how much my happiness meant to him gave me a warm, fuzzy feeling inside.

Or maybe it was my third beer... that was a possibility too.

By my fourth beer, Nathalie still hadn't arrived, so, starting to worry, I stepped out of the bar to call her. Mary and Loup came with me, dancing from one foot to the other in the chilly atmosphere.

"Hey, Nat!" I started when she picked up, "Are you okay? Are you still coming, or did you decide to stay at home? We were getting worried!" The alcohol I had in my system was making my words harder to articulate.

"Well, about that..." she hesitated, which made my heart skip a bit. "I don't think I'll be hanging out with you and Mary anymore." I scowled, and Loup and Mary immediately crowded me, trying to eavesdrop the conversation on the phone.

"What?" I protested. "What are you talking about, Nat? It's fine if you stay at home today. I understand, I didn't feel like going out last time either."

"No, you don't understand. Since they announced the verdict, I've been thinking." Uh-oh. Her voice was strong and resolute. "I've been taking care of my sister since I was eighteen, and now I only need to pass into the next phase, to hold on for six more months, and Keira and I will be free. This is more important than anything else, Fauve. I can't afford to be distracted right now. And you guys are worse than distractions, you're my competitors!"

"But, Nat, we've always known we were competing against each other, why is it an issue now?" I didn't understand. This was so... sudden.

"Because I never thought you guys would make it to this phase! You were twentieth and twenty-fifth last term, and now you're first and fourth! What were the chances of this happening? Now, there are only six spots for the next step. Six! Do you know how unlikely that is for the three of us to pass together? I'm sorry, but I'm going to have to start treating you like the threats you are, especially since you're in front of me, for now.

"Also, you guys will have to do without me for the juggling. Goodbye, Fauve, I'll see you on Monday."

Without explaining herself further, she hung up. I quickly filled Mary and Loup in with the content of the other side of the conversation. She tried calling Nat back several times, and so did I, but our friend never picked up.

"Fuck," Mary raged, "this is so stupid. The three of us can totally make it together to the top six. I know we can, she doesn't have to do this." She dialled on her phone again, but I laid my hand on the screen.

"Let's talk to her on Monday. She seemed pretty determined just now, and my feet are freezing. Let's go back inside."

The worst part of it all was I understood Nat's reasoning for her relationship with me and Mary. If our grade in juggling didn't keep improving while she trained hard at everything else, it might impact our average enough to fall in the ranking. And she only needed to climb two ranks to be in the top six and watch over her sister until she graduated.

I didn't agree with it, but I understood, and it broke my heart.

I was also getting pissed at her comments on how she thought I would be going home by now. Had she befriended and helped us only because she didn't feel threatened by Mary and me?

So, I did what anyone who had just won a sports competition and possibly lost a friend would do.

I went straight to the bar—Loup and Mary hot on my heels—and ordered us three tequilas.

Thibault

As far as post-recovery performances went, this one was okay. I could tell Stephanie was hesitant to really use her hand, but we made it work, anyway. Still, I wasn't fully satisfied—then again, was I ever?—and we scheduled a rehearsal for the middle of the upcoming week.

I was distracted, too. Stephanie had heard from a friend that Puss had ranked first in the intensive program today, and they were celebrating in a trendy bar nearby. I couldn't believe work had made me miss the first part of the night, and I hurried out of Cabaret Rouge to meet them, hoping they hadn't gone home yet.

I texted Cody, filling him in about my plans. He passed, claiming he had work to do. Work, really, at eleven on a Friday night? He was one of my best friends, but he really took me for an idiot on that one.

My interpretation of the situation was: he was pissed at Fauve. I had tried explaining to him my epiphany of the day before, but he had called it "a truckload of bullshit," and me a "pussy-whipped chucklehead." Fuck him. I had to do things the right way. First, I had to win Loup over. Then, I would make Cody see reason. What we had right here was too good to miss out on.

I entered the bar and was immediately assaulted by a very drunk mass of red hair jumping to my neck.

"Thibault, you came!" she shrieked. How drunk was she? Considering her sway, I guessed it was very. Loup didn't look much better, either. "I'm so happy. I missed you, we haven't seen each other in *so* long." Puss pouted. She was adorable, still climbing me like a baby koala.

"Hey, Puss, I'm happy to see you, too. I heard you came in first. Congratulations!"

"I want a winner's kiss," she ordered, an equally inebriated Mary rolling her eyes behind her. I leaned back a bit, trying to extricate myself from Fauve's embrace to see her expression. She was serious. I looked back and forth between Puss and Loup, trying to understand this change in situation. When our eyes met, Loup winked. He goddamned winked, and I took it for the authorisation it was. Not that she needed his permission for anything, but I didn't want to start a fight in the middle of a bar. Men in relationships could be stupid, and I wanted my approach to be subtle. But if I read the situation correctly, I wouldn't need to tread so carefully after all. It was a damn relief.

Our lips met, and I suddenly remembered why I was so put out the night she had left me hanging. Kissing her felt like fireworks. It was both amazing and arousing, and I never ever wanted to stop doing it, even if she tasted like cheap beer and greasy french fries. She smelled like sweat, too.

Theoretically, it was the worst kiss ever. In practice, I never wanted it to stop.

I deepened it, cupping her nape with my right hand and making her open her mouth for me. We devoured each other as her boyfriend watched, and she didn't seem to be the least bit uncomfortable, moaning in my arms.

I wasn't sure she wouldn't have second thoughts in the morning, though, so I regretfully broke the kiss. After this short interaction, I was hopeful it wouldn't be our last one.

"You know I helped her win, right? Do I get a kiss, too?" Loup teased.

"Of course, you get a kiss, dummy!" Puss mumbled. Almost without touching the ground, she jumped from my arms to his. She was an exceptionally agile drunk, for sure. She kissed the shit out of him, just as she had done with me mere seconds ago. His eyes never left mine, though, and I suddenly wasn't sure of what I had heard him say. Did Loup want me to kiss him? Or had he really talked to his girlfriend, like she had understood?

"Let's have some more tequila!" Puss interrupted my thoughts by climbing down her boyfriend and almost running to the bar. This late, it was emptier, and they had left their things at a booth when they got up to meet me.

Apart from agile, Puss was also a very enthusiastic drunk, and by the time I got to her, she had ordered and paid for six tequila shots.

"Puss, you're not drinking two more shots," I asserted softly yet in a stern manner. Sometimes, antagonizing a drunk person was the worst thing to do, as they wouldn't listen to anything you said anymore and weren't in the right mind to make decisions for themselves.

"Oh, I know." She giggled. "I'm already tipsy." She was way more than tipsy in my book, but I could accept that term. "There's one for me, one for Loup, and four for you! It's my party, and I say we're getting drunk together."

I hadn't seen that one coming, but the lady had spoken, so I obliged. I also needed a break. I looked around and saw that Mary had probably taken a page out of our book and was shoving her tongue deep into a dark stranger's throat. She seemed totally happy there, so I focused back on my tequilas.

With Mary busy, I went on a mission to prevent Fauve from drinking more. A part of her seemed to agree with me because all I received, when I stole her drinks for myself, were playful nips on my ears, or slaps on my butt. Needless to say, I wasn't dissuaded at all. If anything, it encouraged me, and I soaked up her attention. She was sandwiched between Loup and me, and looked so excited. I never wanted that look gone from her face.

The bar started to close, and I was as drunk as the others when we got back home.

It would probably have been a ten-minute walk on a normal day, but we ended up spending what I estimated to be close to forty-five minutes staggering in the winter cold. It wasn't on our way at all, but we made sure Mary got back home okay.

It would be a miracle if we weren't sick in the morning.

At our apartment, Fauve and Loup went to their room as I went to mine when I suddenly heard a big falling noise, followed by giggles. In my drunken state, I thought it was a good idea to go into the room, only to find them entangled on the floor, Puss probably having jumped on Loup for the umpteenth time tonight. Except, this time, he was too drunk and tired to properly catch her. They were both laughing loudly, heads thrown back, though, so I guessed no one was hurt.

"Do you guys need help?" I asked them.

Loup threw me an apologetic look that was answer enough. I lifted his girlfriend from him so he could stand.

"Could you help me undress her? She refuses to stand still."

In other circumstances, I might have jumped on the occasion to escalate the situation. But she was way too inebriated, and I didn't want her to regret anything about tonight in the morning—except, maybe the quantity of booze she had drunk, which she would and should most definitely regret.

I held her up in a steady position while Loup took off her pants, then her t-shirt, before pulling one of his own over her head. He took his own clothes off, and I did my best not to ogle either of the two while they were getting into bed. I might have caught glimpses, though. At the same time, they were both almost naked and gorgeous. Sue me.

I turned around to go back to my room when I felt a small hand grab my t-shirt.

"You're not leaving," Puss announced, the certainty in her voice unwavering.

I glanced at Loup questioningly. It was his bed, too. He shrugged and scooted to the side, pulling her with him to make space for me.

"Okay, just let me switch off the light first."

I could have found the switch and only then undressed. Really, I could have. I was balanced enough to take my clothes off in the dark.

Did I, though? Of course not.

Two pairs of hungry eyes followed my every move as I took off my t-shirt and then peeled my jeans down my legs. I might have slightly exaggerated the slowness of my motions, too. The expression on their faces when I looked back up made my strip show totally worth it.

I turned off the light and laid down next to Fauve. She curled up at my side, Loup spooning her from behind.

I kissed her on the forehead, and then, emboldened by the alcohol still buzzing in my veins, did the same for him.

"Good night, Puss. Good night, Wolfie. Sleep tight," I whispered.

Day one of my seduction attempts, and I was already sleeping in their bed. Maybe this would work way more easily than I had planned. Then, it would just be a matter of convincing Cody.

A guy could hope, right?

I woke up to the gross sound of someone puking their guts out in the bathroom. It wasn't a nice sound to wake up to. A quick inventory of who was still in the bed told me who was paying now for last night's sins.

"She's been throwing up for about thirty minutes," Loup informed me.

"What time is it?"

"Seven in the morning, I think. It's still early, go back to sleep if you want."

"Is she okay?"

"I think so. It's just a really bad hangover, and it was expected, considering all she drank last night. I tried to help her, hold her hair or some shit, but she threw me out of the bathroom." I chuckled and turned on my side to face him. There must have been only thirty centimetres between us, and I caught myself staring at his full lips.

"You know, I never really apologised." It was something I'd been meaning to tell him for a long time now, but was too angry to do it. Everything had changed in the last forty-eight hours, though.

"Apologise for what?"

"For convincing Fauve to do the gig with me, on the aerial chandelier. She wasn't sure about it at first, but I insisted. I didn't know about your phobia. So, I wanted to tell you that I'm sorry. And if you want to keep me from her so it doesn't happen again, I understand." I would fight him, though. But I would understand his point.

"Fauve and I talked about it, and it's fine. I would appreciate it if you told me about it first, though. I know that makes me sound like a controlling asshole, but it's a phobia, and I am still learning how to deal with it." His expression was open, vulnerable almost, his arms wrapped around his body as if to protect himself. "I'm talking to a therapist, too. I don't want to make her feel like she has to avoid doing things because of me." I wanted to hug the guy. Really, I did. He was trying incredibly hard to overcome his fear so he wouldn't limit his girlfriend; it was awe-inspiring.

I didn't know how he would react to the contact, though, so I just patted his shoulder and reassured him awkwardly, "It's fine, Loup. I'm sure she understands."

Fauve entered the room as I finished my sentence. She looked horrible. Like death warmed over, and her pale skin was decidedly greenish. I couldn't stop the smirk gracing my lips.

She took us both in and how close we were on the bed, then made a gagging sound, covered her mouth with her hand, and ran back to the bathroom while holding her stomach.

"Well, if that's how she reacts to seeing us both in bed, I might tell her I changed my mind about us all being together," he teased.

MANUELA ROUGET

We chuckled, before what Loup had said really registered. Tell her what now?

Chapter 18

Fauve

THE THIRTEEN SURVIVORS OF the second elimination round of NICAM's intensive program were, for the first time, all gathered together in the same room.

It was Monday morning, and after the worst forty-eight hours of my life, I finally felt like myself again. I was done drinking alcohol. Never again. It was not for me.

I had stopped throwing up around three on Saturday, and managed to drink the Coca-Cola Thibault had bought me—after shaking it to remove the carbonation—around six. Then, late in the evening, my stomach finally accepted food again. Yesterday morning, I had devoured my breakfast like I hadn't eaten in months and started feeling a lot better. Now, it was like nothing had ever happened, which would probably make it difficult to uphold my "no drinking rule." Fuck it, I wouldn't be the first one to break one of those.

MANUELA ROUGET

I was glad to feel better because today, we were starting one of the most exciting subjects of the entire year. Considering how enthusiastic I was about the program, that was saying a lot.

Donna Loewenberg entered the room, and silence immediately followed her.

"Hello, everyone! Congratulations to you all on passing the second selection round on Friday, and welcome to your first aerial silk class."

At her words, we all looked around to truly take in our competition. Besides Mary, Nathalie and I, ten more people had stayed, and I had talked to them all, at least once now.

I was happy that Stacy and Clarissa—the quick-changing Barbies—had passed. I found their act immensely entertaining, and they had a witty sense of humour that made any situation lighter. I couldn't figure out how they did it, though, even after seeing them rehearse and fight over a mistake one of the two had made.

Jennifer, standing next to them, was both a contortionist and an antipodist—juggling with her four limbs while folding her body in gross positions—and even if I liked her as a person, I wasn't a fan of her act. I knew some of the things I did were pretty close, but contortion was really something I didn't like to watch.

Carlos, to my right, had come from Mexico with his little trained dog, Bruno. He did an acrobatics routine, and had trained the pup to climb and pose on him while he did. They both always executed their acts flawlessly, and it was honestly pretty creative and impressive. I had never managed to make an animal like me—let alone obey me—so I was always dumbstruck when Bruno stood on his hind legs on Carlos's moving body. Who wouldn't be?

Silvana and Luis, both from Cuba, had a roller-skating number they performed together since they were kids. Silvana made me uneasy. Because of the centrifugal force when he held her feet while they turned, her eyes were always injected with blood from burst capillaries, and it was creepy as fuck.

Nathan—the winner of the first phase—was unremarkable in his daily life. He changed completely when he was on stage, though, going from timid to exuberant as soon as the projectors were on him. He was a unicyclist, and his signature act consisted of an obstacle course that he overcame without falling. Last time, he jumped over a table. Without touching its upper surface.

Jonathan, a.k.a. Alisja Adore, was a knife-throwing drag queen, and both he and his drag persona scared me in more ways than one. First off, they were knife-throwers, so duh. You would have to be stupid not to fear that. Then, they were absurdly creative, and completely unpredictable performers, which made them entertaining as hell. You never knew what costume they would pick, what the setting or makeup would be... It was a complete surprise every single time they got on stage. To top it all off, they were super technical artists, having great balance on heels and off, flexibility, sense of rhythm, style, and makeup skills... They were definitely a threat.

Last but not the least came Ana and Eva, the Adagio sisters. They scared me, too. I had no idea if the fact that they were both in the program while Loup was not would help or hinder them. Their whole act was based on elegance and flexibility, while we were all about sensuality and chemistry. We had beat them this time, but we would have to step up our game to keep ahead of them, and I had no idea what that would entail.

Nathalie was as far from Mary and me as possible while staying in the circle, royally ignoring us, and that hurt more than everything she had said on the phone.

I distracted myself by finally looking back at our teacher of the day, fangirling *hard*. She had foregone her usual pantsuits in favour of skin-tight shorts and a tank top, her grey hair pulled back in a long braid. She looked just as regal as she did in her business attire, authority oozing through the pink lycra.

Behind her, stood Thibault, Stephanie, and Daniel, the three aerialists in their year, who had all tutored us during our basic aerials training.

"Now, you all know that I like to teach aerial silk," she announced, "so I can make sure you don't start off with bad habits." Thibault winked at me, as if to say, "I told you so." Idiot. He knew our dean was my idol.

"But I can't do that if there are twenty-five students in the class. It's just dangerous, and I don't have the time to teach all three groups, unfortunately," she continued. "Even though I just had to send home twelve incredible performers, a part of me rejoices that it now allows me to teach this class, so we'll get started right away. Any questions?"

"I just have one," Mary started. I glowered at her. We did not upset the Queen. "Could we have a demonstration?" I maintained my scowl, but inside, I was thrilled. I was about to witness an aerial silk presentation from *the* Donna Loewenberg. Maybe.

"I'm sorry, I haven't learned all of your names yet. Could you remind me of yours...?"

"Mary," she replied.

"Mary. Good. You're the blunt one, I see." Our teacher looked thoughtful for a moment. "Of course. I haven't trained in a while, but I guess I could put together something real quick." I couldn't tell if she was joking. I relished the moment anyway, eyes wide and expectant.

It turned out, she was joking. Maybe not about the "not having trained in a while" part, but definitely on improvising her performance. Or maybe she was improvising, which made it even more impressive.

Donna Loewenberg climbed up the aerial silk with the agility of a feline, and as soon as she was about seven metres high, it looked like she was dancing in water. If humans could breathe underwater, that is, because she didn't look like she was suffocating *at all*. Obviously.

She made it look easy, going up, twirling, and suddenly falling almost to the floor, stopping mere centimetres away from the mattress, and earning a gasp from her audience. It was official, I wanted to be her when I grew up.

"Now, I am going to show you some exercises, and since those three"—our teacher gestured towards her assistants—"must have taught you well and you're all in good shape, we'll build up to learning small falls pretty quickly. When we do, just remember to always have an error margin, and for this, you need to climb relatively high. The height shouldn't be what scares you. It gives you time to react and control your fall. You should always be afraid of the ground because it will hurt you." A grave silence followed her words, as we were all trying to commit them to memory, and then we got to work.

The beginning of the class was simple enough. Then, as planned, we got to the falls, during which we had to tangle our bodies in the silk in a very precise way, to control our rapid descent towards the ground.

I soon started feeling like I had been put in a washing machine, rolling from side to side and upside down, only to be stopped brutally.

"Your muscles need to remain contracted even when you're falling, Fauve. Otherwise, you'll look like a dead fish, still flopping on the floor," our teacher screamed from the other side of the room. "And smile! You need to make it look easy, it's part of the magic." Nothing got past her.

Obviously, I had paired up with Mary, and we alternated our tries on the multi-coloured silk. There were seven of them, suspended all around the room, all colours of the rainbow. Except the one we had picked—the prettiest—which was striped with all the other shades.

When it was my turn again, I went for another one of the figures Donna demonstrated in the beginning of the class, and she got closer.

"Remember, immediately after you let go, put your hands on your hips, to block your fall once the rotation is complete—don't start the trick now, go a little higher... Perfect!"

I felt like I was way higher than necessary, but I wasn't going to discuss it while dangling in the air. I did a foot lock around each of my feet, using my other foot to complete the first one, and my left hand to complete the second one while my right hand held me up. Once secured, I crossed the two strands of the silk behind my back, pushed my shoulders back and inverted my body in what our teacher had called aerial silk's catcher position. I wasn't going to carry anyone, but it was good to know. Then I caught the silk on the side of my butt and pulled myself up again.

In that position, with the silk behind my back and my arms holding it above my head, the floor really seemed far away, and the fall a lot more impressive than it had when Donna demonstrated it.

"Aleee, hup!" she yelled.

It was stronger than me. A pure reflex. Every circus artist knew this was the signal to start whatever figure you were about to do.

I let go.

I fell forward, the silk catching me so it looked like I did a front flip while rolling in the stretchy fabric.

Except, someone let out an alarmed yell as I spun and, because of the adrenaline that rushed through my veins, I completely forgot to catch the silk around my hips. I did a second half-turn, the floor rushing closer at an impressive speed. The foot locks finally caught me, and I ended up dangling by my feet from the ceiling like a smoked ham. I was breathing hard, and a smirking Thibault appeared in my field of view to help me, or possibly mock me from up close. He didn't say a word, though. I had been lucky Donna had seen me and told me to climb some more—or maybe that was why there were four teachers in this class; it was dangerous. If I had started the trick where I wanted to, my head would have hit the floor. Hard.

"And that is why you have to start your falls from high up, everyone," Donna Loewenberg taunted me. "Now do it again, Fauve. Right away, otherwise you'll get scared of this figure, and it'll be a lot harder to reproduce.

Those words might have sounded harsh, but it was circus culture. When you fell, if you weren't badly injured, you got up and tried again. Immediately. Even in the middle of a presentation. It was one of the most basic rules.

"And you," Donna continued, facing away from me, "what's your name?" Still hanging upside down, I couldn't see who she was talking to.

"Nathalie," my apparently former friend responded.

"Why did you scream? She could have really hurt herself!"

"Oh, I thought one of her feet wasn't locked properly, I just wanted to warn her." Our teacher didn't seem convinced. I didn't know what to think. Had Nathalie decided to not only stop helping us, but also get rid of the competition? I looked back at where she was practicing her own locks and falls, having paired up with Eva and Ana since we were now an odd number. The three of them were whispering together and smiling.

Steel blue eyes zeroed in on me again. "Fauve, what are you waiting for? Up you go!"

So, I untangled my feet, got down on the floor, took two deep breaths, and started climbing.

MANUELA ROUGET

It was Saturday, and I had invited Mary for coffee right after lunch so we would have the entire afternoon to just gossip. I had once again banned the guys from the living room. Cody was making his presence scarce, pretending he had a lot of work to do. Then again, it was the end of the semester, and he really might have exams. I wouldn't know, we hadn't spoken in so long. Thibault had told me Logan was giving us space to figure out our shit—Logan's words, not his. And then Thibault and Loup were doing whatever they did when I left them alone together. I wasn't sure I wanted to know.

They had bonded during the past week; mostly over how impressive my hangover was. They had teamed up to make fun of me, and if I had been told a month ago this could solve the situation this easily, I would have got hammered way sooner. I suspected there was more going on, though.

"Hey girl, how are you doing? Did you already find another apartment?" Donna Loewenberg had been right when she'd called Mary "the blunt one". She never beat around the bush.

We had also made a deal this last week to not talk about the situation with Nathalie today. She had ignored us all week, with the exception of little events like my fall on Monday, when she did random things to make us lose focus and generally fail at whatever we were doing.

Mary and I had talked about it enough, and we were both disappointed and sad. There was no point of having the same conversation all over again.

"Actually, I forgot to tell you what happened, but Loup and I stopped looking for another flat this week," I said, looking everywhere but at her.

"Really? But I thought the guys didn't get along and it was weird?" she questioned. I had told her as much, but everything had changed last weekend, and she hadn't got the update yet.

"Well, Cody's still weird. I think I know what's going on with him, but I need to catch him so we can talk about it.

"Thibault and Loup, well, that's a different story. Something happened last weekend, I'm not sure what—I was super drunk, then hung-over—but the three of us slept together in the same bed and they have a sort of a bromance going on now."

"You have a magic bed, that must be it. Can I borrow it?" she joked.

As if on cue, Loup's voice came from the hallway, loud but teasing.

"T-Bone, what did you do with my underwear that was drying in the bathroom? I think you took it along with yours yesterday; give it back!"

"T-Bone?" Mary questioned, eyebrows raised.

"I have no idea where that came from," I answered, shaking my head for good measure.

She giggled.

"And what about the Cody situation, then? You guys are going to all live together, with an ex-lover of yours that's acting like he's been spurned?"

"Well, for now, he's just working and studying a lot. Next week, his exams end, so we'll have more time to hopefully talk about what's been going on with him."

"And do you know what you want? Are you really going to have three boyfriends?"

"Loup keeps telling me it's possible to make it work, but yeah, sometimes I feel like a greedy bitch. I genuinely miss Cody, though."

"Hey, no judgement here, girl. I just want to know where you found Loup and if they make more like him."

That sentence sent us rolling to the ground, caught in a fit of laughter.

Afternoon coffees with friends were the best.

Chapter 19

Cody

I WENT TO THE back of my massive finite elements book to check if the result of the exercise I was doing was correct. Just like during my first four trials, my answer was wrong, and I had no idea why. What was the point of computing n-dimensional matrices anyway? I would forget it all as soon as the exam was over, and never use it during my career.

Or at least, I hoped.

Since Thibault had left me alone in my resentment of Loup and Fauve, I had trouble focusing. Scratch that. I could at least admit to myself that since Loup had arrived, I couldn't focus, at all. I would fail all my tests if I continued like this. I wanted to give in, ask them for help, but it would be like opening a Pandora's box. Would I be able to let them help me relax for my exams, and not give in to the four-way relationship they wanted me to join? Did they even want me to join in? How would that even work?

MANUELA ROUGET

I wasn't stupid, I knew what my reaction to Fauve's text on Christmas morning meant. My feelings for her were very real; difficult not to catch some when you slept with someone you also lived with and considered a friend. The boyfriend thing hadn't stopped that.

I was genuinely trying to help when I had arranged for him to see her performance at Cabaret Rouge. Thibault and Fauve looked incredible together, and since I knew Loup was aware of everything that had happened between them, I just thought he would like it. I had no idea his fear of heights even existed; he was an acrobat, for fuck's sake.

Thibault had told me all about his epiphany during Fauve's evaluation presentation. All bullshit, honestly. All of us together, in a foursome. That would never work. I didn't, couldn't even allow myself to consider it. Neither of us lived in Wonderland, and in our society, this kind of arrangement was just impossible. At some point, someone had to be pragmatic.

Plus, Loup and Fauve weren't even Canadians, so they couldn't live legally in Montréal without having to go through a fuck-ton of bureaucratic procedures. I was dizzy from reading the governmental websites alone. In a moment of weakness, I had searched for more information on visas.

A part of me wanted to give in. I had loved Thibault forever, and I had always assumed that what I felt for him was what best friends felt for each other, without really questioning it further. Fauve's interrogation in the beginning of the year had made me think more about it, but without really reaching any sort of conclusion.

Now that he had sided with the French couple, it felt like my heart had been ripped out of my chest. Twice over, to be precise. And all of them were still physically here.

What would it feel like if Loup and Fauve went back to France at the end of the school year, and we never saw them again? I wasn't sure I could survive it.

It was better not to give in, less risky.
I had to protect myself.

Loup

Fauve had described to me what NICAM looked like, and how it was laid out inside, so I felt like I already knew the place, even having been there only once.

Why Thibault had asked me to meet him here at seven in the evening, though, I had no idea. I joined him in the flying trapeze gymnasium. Those three words already gave me chills. I would be more comfortable hearing "torture chamber" than I was hearing them. Was static trapeze not scary enough? They had to invent a flying one?

The trapezist was sitting on a mattress, scrolling on his phone, when I entered the room. We had grown close scarily fast, but it was also something that could have been expected. After all, two of our main centres of interest were the same—circus and Fauve—so we had things to bond over, and it wasn't difficult to find conversational subjects.

"T-Bone!" I exclaimed, forcing joy into my voice. He immediately raised his head.

"Wolfie!" The cutesy nicknames had appeared while we were drunk, and since Fauve had been drunker than the two of us combined, she didn't remember it at all. Her puzzled face whenever she heard them was too good to pass up, so we had decided to keep them. I was embarrassed to have used it in this context, though. Nerves. "Man, I needed you to meet me here because I have an idea for Fauve's next presentation, but I need your help."

Without further preamble, Thibault launched into his explanation of the act he had in mind, and the longer it went on, the wider my eyes got. It was crazy ambitious, and difficult, but genius at the same time. I had never seen anything like it.

"Are you confident you can pull off your part?" I asked, without judgement or prejudice. I had seen him perform for a grand total of half a second.

"Yup," he answered, without an ounce of doubt. It was impressive in itself. "I already tried, actually. It's difficult to really know the result without having two other performers with me, but my part is doable. I know Fauve can do hers, too." I understood where he was going with this.

"But what if I can't pull off mine?" I asked, suddenly feeling insecure, which wasn't like me at all. But Thibault had very high expectations of what I was capable of.

"That's why I asked you to come, actually. I want to start training just the two of us, and if we can make it, then we tell Fauve."

"What if she finds out? And can you participate in her presentation? You're her teacher, right? Wouldn't that be unethical?"

"Then we tell her the truth, it's not even that big of a secret anyway. I just don't want to get her hopes up if we can't pull this off in the end." He shrugged. "And for the teacher part, I asked Donna. Since she took over the aerial class, I will have less influence on Fauve's grade—not that I had much to start with—so the dean said it's fine."

"I'm okay with that. Where do we start?" I asked.

"Come here." Thibault gestured towards the corner of the room where a rope was dangling above a pit, filled with foam cubes. "I've fallen into this countless times, and in all the positions you can imagine, so I can promise you, nothing will happen to you if you do." He pulled one of the thinner mattresses, and put it above the foam.

"Doesn't doing that defeat the purpose of the pit?" I questioned.

"I just told you that nothing will happen if you fall. Now, I put the mattress here so I can stand next to the rope and make sure you will not fall. Are you comfortable with trying to climb? Have you ever tried?"

His sharp green eyes were open and free of judgement, caring even. He genuinely wanted me to succeed. All traces of his teasing personality were gone. He was being a pro, and to my surprise, arousal started mixing in with the fear and confusion I was already feeling. It was a welcome sentiment.

I shook my head. "My therapist makes me stand on stuff sometimes, but that never went well, so far. I'll try climbing, maybe it'll be different."

I walked towards the pit, trying to keep my breathing even as my hands started to sweat.

"Good," he said once I managed to join him and stand on the thin mattress. Those foam cubes were hell to walk through, and I had no idea how he had made it look easy. "Put your back to me. I will have to touch you to help explain certain things, is that okay?"

"We've shared a bed all of last weekend, I think that makes it okay for you to touch me," I joked, all conscious thoughts lost in my nervousness.

"No, it doesn't." He smiled. "I promise that what you just said will stay between us. Imagine what your girlfriend would say if she knew you thought sharing a bed once gives you permission to touch someone."

I glared at him, then smiled.

Though I felt panic start to rise, I was grateful for what he was doing. He was giving me a safe space to try and conquer my fear.

My therapist couldn't give me that, not exactly. We talked about things, of course, but I didn't feel as safe with him as I felt with Thibault. The aging man would never catch me if I fell, and his body didn't exude the same raw strength. Fauve couldn't truly help me, either, even if she wanted to. She was way too small to efficiently hold me up or prevent me from falling. Thibault, on the other hand, was huge. I felt almost delicate next to him. He was slightly shorter, but a lot bulkier, and I had no doubt he could do what he had promised, and not let me fall. It gave me a certain physical sort of reassurance that was lacking during my therapy sessions.

And he was gorgeous, which was a welcome distraction, too.

He taught me how to wind my legs around the rope, and step with my left foot on my right to stay up. The moment I was suspended in the air, I started feeling uneasy. It was ridiculous, really. I was hovering ten centimetres above the ground, and I was scared.

"Get back on the mattress now, Loup. You did great, I didn't know if you would be able to climb."

He put his hands on my waist to stabilise me and helped me step down.

"How do you feel? he asked.

"Okay, I think."

"Let's take it real slow, okay? I would really like for you to be rid of the fear, but I think it's not going to happen this soon. Getting you up on the static trapeze looks like an attainable goal, especially if it's low enough, so I don't want to trigger you by going too fast. I want you to associate here with a pleasant experience, always, so you're more comfortable to confront your fear. What do you think?"

His monologue had been at the same time delivered in a completely professional way, and oddly sensual, since we were standing so close to each other, and the subject was intimate.

"It sounds good. As I told you last week, I don't want my fear to limit Fauve."

"Very well. Then, up you go again."

My record for the day was forty centimetres. When I tried going just a little higher, my body started shaking, and Thibault announced I was done. He then made me kneel on the floor, loosely holding my ankles with my hands and putting my forehead on the mattress.

Knowing his jokester personality, I was still waiting for him to pull a prank on me, and started doubting him as soon as he described the vulnerable position he wanted me in. I glowered, and he said, with hands held flat in front of him, "Trust me. Safe space, remember? I'm not going to make fun of you, I swear."

So, I followed his instructions, and had to repress an embarrassingly loud moan of delight when he started massaging the sides of my spine. I was tense, more from the nerves than the exercise. The position he had put me in stretched my back deliciously, and he had massive, strong hands that knew exactly what they were doing. My eyes closed, and I allowed my muscles to unwind.

After a moment that ended with me almost drooling on the gym mattress under me, Thibault stopped, and I almost growled in protest.

"How are you feeling?" he asked. Despite the unpleasant reason for our encounter, I felt deliciously relaxed, and he had asked me a version of this question almost fifty times already.

"Okay, I guess. You're very good at giving massages."

"Do you think we could do this every day, then?" Thibault was still in his very professional persona, a behaviour I was still deciding if I liked. It was unsettling, to see him so serious. Kinda hot, too. Any other day, Thibault would have joked or made a sexual comment about me complimenting his massaging skills.

"Maybe? Let's take it one day at a time, okay?" I paused, trying to think it through. The part where I had to climb on the rope wasn't nice, not even close, and I would be the happiest man on earth to decide it wasn't for me and never do it again. But Thibault's idea for Fauve's third presentation was genius and depended on my participation. Surely, I could be brave for that for one day and then go back to being afraid, couldn't I? Also, was it shallow and selfish to admit I wanted more massages? I shivered, my back cold without his touch.

Thibault smirked, probably guessing where my mind had been. I was sure the bastard had premeditated it. Flies, honey, and all that jazz.

"How about you? How do you feel?" I asked.

"About what?"

I did an arm gesture that was both ominous and noncommittal, to encompass the whole situation. He smiled his usual insolent, flirty smile.

"Will you think I'm insane if I say I feel really good? I like you, and well, it's difficult to imagine a life without Fauve, now."

"Not really, I feel that way, too," I answered, even if his question had been a rhetorical one. "Relationships are a social construct. Five hundred years ago, my moms probably would have burnt at the stake for being together. Now their relationship is tolerated." I winced, that word was a horror, but there just wasn't a better one. Saying it was accepted would have been a lie. "Fewer and fewer couples are forming purely for the sake of reproduction. Maybe, at some point, people will realise the whole idea of pairing a person that has a body made for multiple orgasms with one that can only come once, is stupid. When you think about it, if the objective is desire and pleasure, homosexuality makes a lot more sense than heterosexuality. Or for women to have multiple partners, that's logical, too. It's just a question of finding out what the goal of love is. Simple, really."

Thibault was looking at me as if I had three heads.

Feigning innocence, I asked, "What?"

He stood up, turned towards me, and extended his hand. When I raised my arm, he grabbed my wrist—forcing me to hold onto his in a weird trapeze handshake—to help me up. Once on my feet, he didn't let go immediately, goosebumps appearing on my skin at how close our bodies were.

"You're weird, Wolfie."

"I'll take that as a compliment, T-Bone."

He let my arm slide in his calloused hand, our fingers brushing for a moment before letting go. Shoulder to shoulder, we started walking towards the exit.

"What about Cody, though?" I asked.

"Cody got in his head about this. He says he's being pragmatic by keeping his distance. I think he wants in, but he's afraid it won't work, and fearful of feeling left out. It doesn't help that we're all circus artists. I have an idea that might contribute to changing his mind, though. Do you know if Fauve knows how to ice skate?"

"No, it wasn't common where we grew up. Let's hope your idea will work, then."

"Eager to share Fauve with another dude?" he teased.

"Eager to see her happy," I answered.

After the conversation, we walked the chilly streets home in companionable silence.

Chapter 20

Cody

"Come on, it's already organised, so now you have to come," Thibault admonished.

"I don't want to celebrate today, I still need to study," I said.

"You're coming. A break will do you good. Get ready."

"You didn't even tell me what we were doing," I yelled while he disappeared in the corridor.

Fauve

"I am not going to ice skate," I protested.

"Oh yes, you are," Thibault's voice chimed in from behind me.

Loup had brought me to a frozen river, where families were having fun gliding, racing, and playing catch with each other. There was a little cabin on the side where people were renting their skates, and the surrounding trees were covered in snow. It was incredibly cute, and cold as... well, not hell.

"If I break a wrist and have to give up the program, I'll murder you all," I threatened.

"Seems like a reasonable threat," Thibault mused, "but Cody will make sure nothing happens to you." Cody glowered at him, apparently pissed at Thibault for volunteering him as my ice-skating teacher. "Come on, man," he continued, "it's your birthday, you need a break, and you love ice skating. I thought it would be perfect for Fauve to keep you company."

"What?" I blurted, staring at Cody. "You were born on Valentine's Day?"

"Yep, ruined my parents' romantic evenings with birthday celebrations for almost two decades," Cody said, without real humour in his words.

"Why can't you go skate with him?" I asked, looking pointedly at the trapezist.

"I hurt my leg when I was a kid and now can't even walk properly when it's cold. Have you never noticed I have a limp?"

The truth was, whenever Thibault was around, I wasn't looking at the way he walked. Too many distracting elements got in the way. Sue me.

"And I'll keep Thibault company." Of course, Loup would say that. Traitor.

I stared accusingly at Thibault for making me do this. He waited for Cody to take three steps towards the ice, then grabbed my upper arm and whispered in my ear, "Fix this."

AERIAL

Our eyes met, and he appeared dead serious. He then cocked his head in Cody's direction as if to say, "Move along."

Reluctantly, I made my way in the snow towards the cabin, reflecting on the trapezist's words. He was right, I had been incredibly lucky that he and Loup had figured their shit out on their own. Relationship conversations freaked me out, but it seemed that if I wanted things to work out with Cody, I would have to have a long, serious one. Maybe it didn't have to be today though, did it? Maybe today could just be a warm-up? It was his birthday, after all, not a day for difficult talks.

Following Cody, I noticed he had a big bag on his shoulder, resembling the ones I used to put rollerblades in when I was a kid. I didn't need to be a genius to understand that those were his skates. The fact that he owned some already clued me in on why Thibault thought he could protect me on the ice.

He sat on a bench next to the skating rink and started taking off his shoes, to replace them with the skates. They looked... aggressive. Covering his ankle, they had a robust plastic support to hold the blade, and no brake thingy on the front like the ones I had seen at Christmas markets.

"You need to go to the cabin if you want to rent some," he informed me. At that moment, I felt the effect of culture shock, and oddly vulnerable. Spending most of my time cooped up studying or training at NICAM, I hadn't really taken the time to truly experience Canada and what it had to offer.

"I don't know how," I said. He sighed. Asshole.

"Just go there and ask for your size."

"I don't know my size. French shoe sizes are different."

"You've been here for six months and haven't bought a single pair of shoes?" he asked incredulously.

"Not everyone is as fashionable as you are," I mocked. Unlike Thibault, Loup, and I who mostly wore sports clothes, Cody was always well dressed. His shoes were polished, his shirts were ironed, his hair was combed, and all the colours of his outfits matched while somehow showcasing his personality. I loved that about him, but would absolutely never, ever admit it.

He looked irritated, but stood up in his skates, anyway. I noticed they had plastic protections on, allowing him to walk on the rubber grill carpet that prevented people from slipping without dulling the blades. Clever.

"Sit here, and give me your shoe," he ordered.

I did, and he went away with it to rent the skates for me. I took off my other shoe as he came back with a navy-blue pair dangling from his fist.

"Do you know how to put them on?"

"Like shoes?" I snarked.

He rolled his eyes and left me to it, preferring to walk towards the ice. I took a while to figure out the laces that got tangled while the skates were in his hands. When ready, I finally raised my eyes. He had already stepped onto the ice and was making lazy circles at an impressive speed.

Mesmerised, I watched him for a moment. He was going faster than everyone else but still effortlessly avoided the families, with their clumsy kids that threw themselves in his way. His movements were slow and assured, and even from afar, I saw his shoulders and jaw relax. He was in his element.

I stood, and he must have been watching me from the corner of his eye because he instantly turned to move towards me. He accelerated until I was sure he wouldn't be able to stop in time, and a fraction of a second before hitting the fence, he turned both skates to the side and braked with a loud scratching noise. My eyes went wide, arm halfway around my body to protect me from the impact I thought was unavoidable.

"Let me guess, you thought Logan and Thibault were the two athletes and I was the intellectual one."

I was dumbstruck, but managed to mumble, "Mmh, something like that."

"Well, I played ice hockey for eleven years. Careful, you're drooling."

I did something I am not proud of. I stuck out my tongue at him.

He was right, though. I undoubtedly had a thing for athletes, and even if Cody's mind had attracted me first, seeing him control his body like this did something to me.

It was nice to hear him joke again, too.

"Shut up. Let's do this." I stood up on wobbly legs, and he stabilised me by holding my arm. He guided me gently on the ice. As soon as I put a foot on it, I almost fell. I knew it was ice, and I knew the skates wouldn't find much purchase, but I still didn't expect it to be this slippery. I yelped.

"Have you never ice skated before?" Cody asked.

"Nope," I answered, popping the *'p'* for effect. "Complete ice-skating virgin here."

I would deny doing it if anyone asked me about it later, but I then completely assumed the role of the damsel in distress. I shrieked, and wobbled, and almost fell a hundred times, letting Cody act as my white knight while surreptitiously getting closer to him. I figured, since he hadn't helped me slay the Dragon, he owed me that.

I wasn't in any way sure of myself. But with the sense of balance I had, I would have done much better if falling didn't mean I was rescued by Cody's arms.

"Wow, you're really bad at this, aren't you? Here, let me help."

Extricating himself from my arms, he went to stand in front of me and put his hands on my hips.

"Extend your arms on the sides," he ordered, "and slowly push your right foot outwards. Yes, like that, exactly. Now, left foot. No, bring your right foot back, *yes*, very good.

"Now, we're going to stop. Point your foot, and use the serrated part to break your momentum."

I pretended to follow his instructions. "Pretended" being the key word here. I failed to brake completely and crashed into his chest. He was steady on his feet, though, and caught me in a hug to prevent us from falling.

I couldn't help it, I threw my head back and laughed. A happy, careless laugh. Soon, he joined me, all traces of his bad mood from earlier gone.

"Do you like it?" Cody asked.

"I'm not sure it's my thing, but we should do this again sometime, it was fun." I very purposefully angled my head towards his, raising my chin and exposing my mouth, just to see what he would do.

With his cheeks reddened by the cold, glasses periodically fogging up to the rhythm of his breathing, and hair tousled by the winter air, he looked younger, more carefree. I liked this version of Cody a lot.

He didn't disappoint, and leaned down to kiss me. A sweet, feather-light kiss, barely a peck on the lips, only lasting long enough for me to feel the freezing tip of his nose against my cheek.

"I miss you," I whispered after he had broken the kiss. I had said this a lot in recent times. It didn't make the sentence any less true.

"You seemed to be having fun. Are Thibault and Loup not taking care of you?"

"They're not you."

"Fauve, you have two godlike men warming your bed every night, and you still waste time wanting me?"

"Wanting you is not a waste of time."

He nuzzled my nose, the tenderness of his gesture contrasting with the harshness of his words.

"You don't need me, Fauve. Go back to your trapezist and your acrobat, who look like top models, to live happily ever after, while I grow old in the company of my beer belly."

Was Cody... insecure? It seemed insensitive to ask.

"Cody, stop it, you're totally silver-fox material. With your sense of fashion and those eyes of yours, you'll have my granny panties wet in no time—"

"*If* you guys stay at the end of the school year," he cut me off, voice full of anticipated regret, "and we all know how likely that is. I do believe in you. You're super talented, and a hard worker if I ever saw one. But all the other students in your program are, too, and I just can't take that risk."

He stepped back from our hug, guided me to the fence, and hurried off the ice without waiting for me.

My chest hurt, and I couldn't decide if today had been progress or not.

Thibault

"You're an evil genius, T-bone," Loup said while we watched Cody and Fauve kiss.

"She totally overdid it, though, didn't she?"

"Yep. Even wasted, she wasn't that unbalanced," he confirmed.

"And he fell right for it," I added. We high-fived, then did one of those weird side bro hugs that brought his very full, very kissable lips way too close to my eyes for me not to stare at them. For an instant, he looked at my lips too, and time stopped with our faces angled towards each other.

Then, his eyes flicked back to the ice ring, and he growled, eyes darkening with rage. "Oh, no. Oh, I'm going to murder him."

I turned back, taking in the ice ring; Fauve, looking shaken, holding the fence like a lifeline, and Cody storming off in the snow.

Loup's body tensed, and I tightened my hug, trying to prevent him from doing something stupid I wasn't sure he even wanted to do.

Fuck.

Chapter 21

Fauve

THIBAULT, LOUP, AND I went back home. On the metro ride back, I explained what had happened.

"Did he say he didn't want to be with you? Us?" Loup asked for what felt like the hundredth time.

"No, Loup. He just gave some bullshit excuses about why it wouldn't work."

He was practically fuming; his protectiveness kicked into high gear. He didn't like seeing me hurt and had threatened Cody in every way I could have thought of, and then some.

I wasn't feeling great, but I wanted to handle it myself.

Sounds of TV filtered through our door. Someone was in the living room. With my heart in my throat, I turned the key in the lock, took off my coat, gloves, and shoes, and immediately went to find Cody and Logan watching *The Office* on our couch. Without me.

"Cody, can I talk to you for a second?" I asked.

"I'd like to watch the end of the episode, please. Then, I need to get back to studying."

The reason I hated relationship conversations so much is because they stressed me out. I imagined everything that had and still could go wrong, and every little thing I could have done better for days on end. Then, I rehearsed speeches in my head without ever being able to deliver them fully. It was horrible. There was no way I was letting myself stew like that this time. We were ripping off the Band-Aid right here and right now.

With my mind made, I settled next to him.

"Cody, I need to know why you don't want to be with me. Give me half a good reason, and this conversation is over. But I need to understand."

"You need a good reason? Let me give you several.

"I'm the only one that's always left out. You spend your days together and come back home with your private jokes and references that I don't have, all in your own world. I don't know if I can even exist in a relationship like that.

"Then, there's the ridiculousness of being in a relationship with three people. Three people, Fauve, how insane does that sound? How do you plan on telling this to your family? 'Oh, by the way, Mom, we've figured out a schedule for us. Cody sleeps with me on Mondays and Thursdays, Loup on Tuesdays and Fridays, Thibault on Sundays and Wednesdays, and Saturday is orgy night?'

"And what happens when your visa expires? If you're not the top one per cent of your class, in the most competitive circus school in the world, then you're going back to France in June, and we're going to stay here, lonely as fuck with our thumbs up our asses. I'm not taking that chance."

He stormed off after his monologue, leaving an awkward silence in his place.

"He's not wrong, you know?" Logan supplied.

"What?" Loup retorted. "Of course, he is wrong, it's all a bunch of bullshit! There's no way it's like that!" He threw his hands in the air.

"I didn't say he was a saint and you guys were assholes, Loup. Relax, I know there are two sides to every story. Fauve did get more distant this past month, and now that you guys are doing this he should be on board just like that?"

"But he wants to!" my acrobat protested. That was classic Loup, thinking that people should do what they wanted when they wanted it, without fear or worry. My boyfriend dove headfirst into whatever new experience appealed to him, without being scared by the consequences. This was why Cody and him would either never work, or be absolutely amazing together. They were polar opposites.

"I know," Logan soothed, "but he's sad, scared, and hopeful, all at the same time. Cut him some slack."

"I'm gonna talk to him," I announced absent-mindedly. Logan was right. Still, I was fixing this today.

Full of newfound resolve, I walked towards Cody's room. This time, I wasn't letting him escape.

I was growing increasingly irritated with his behaviour. Granted, I had been distant. But he hadn't exactly been forthcoming either. It took two people to screw up a relationship, and both of us had stopped trying, not just me.

I went to his room and knocked on the door, then barged in when he didn't answer. "Cody?" I called.

"What do you want?" he grunted. He was laying on his side, back to the door, on his bed, and was scrolling aimlessly on his phone. Shutting me out.

That wasn't going to fly.

Without even taking my shoes off, I kneeled on the bed and straddled him, reaching for his phone to throw it into a pile of clothes discarded on the floor. Tangling my fingers in his, I pinned him down on his bed, arms spread out. I got as close to his face as I dared, forcing him to look at me and stop hiding away. The intensity of the eye contact made me repress a shiver.

"Cody, the reasons you've explained are not good enough for me. I've never heard that you don't want us or that sharing me is not enough for you. I would understand that. I've only heard a baby babbling about how walking is scary because you risk falling. Guess what? Falling is part of the fun," I whispered, centimetres away from his face.

"First of all, you're not left out. You're pushing us away. Thibault, Loup, and I are part of the same world; that is true. But you're the one that reminds me the universe exists. I'm sorry I caused you to feel like this wasn't true, but I need you as much as I need them, and if it is reassurance you need, I can give that to you." I was practically begging at that point. "You want time alone, then nothing would make me happier than to watch your stupid rocket tests right now. You've opened my mind to so many incredible things, and I want to know what you'll teach me next. Don't you?

"And I know I can't predict what will happen at the end of the year. It's a difficult situation, really. But I'd rather enjoy what I have now to the fullest than worry about the future. If we decide we want to do this, right now, we still have four months together, and maybe an entire life after that, if we decide to keep fighting. Wouldn't it be worth the risk? I have made my decision and I will be brave, even if I end up with a broken heart. Will you?"

"I can't, Fauve. I'm sorry. Not like this. I need time, I need—" His voice broke, moisture glimmering in his eyes.

Despite his words, his steel-like resolve was cracking. I was tearing down his walls; I could feel it. He just needed another little push in the right direction, and he'd join us for months—months, for fuck's sake—of happiness and pleasure.

"Cody, I'm sorry for this past month, and I promise it will never, *ever* happen again. Let me make it up to you. Let me prove how serious I am. Please, give us a chance." Our noses were touching, and restraining from kissing him was probably the hardest thing I'd ever done. He had to take the first step, though. Otherwise, it would never work.

Loup

I was trying to control myself to hold the rage I was reeling with inside. Even if she wanted to handle it on her own, Cody was hurting Fauve, and I couldn't live with it.

It was funny how, in our weird four-way relationship, all of them brought forward a different side of me—and, yes, I considered Cody a part of it. Fauve wanted him, and it was enough.

I wanted to take care of Fauve. Protect her while at the same time propel her to new heights, and she somehow ended up bringing me with her. She accepted me, loved me, and knew me—inside and out.

Thibault pushed me to be better, bolder, braver. He would never let me be happy in my comfort zone, and made me feel safe while I took the necessary risks to venture out of it.

Cody, now, brought out of me the beast that was my namesake. In that instant, I wanted to shove my dick down his throat and fuck his mouth until all the bullshit stopped coming out of it. I wanted to tear apart his neatly pressed clothes and mess up his perfect hair. I wanted to see him unravel and lose control before me.

Yeah, that seemed appropriate.

I brought my mind back to the present situation; Thibault and Logan's bickering about what we could do to stay in Canada if Fauve didn't win NICAM's program.

"Even if they did find a job as performers, most companies would want them to be able to work legally in Canada, so they don't have to go through all the visa paperwork," Thibault argued.

"You guys could always get married. I'm almost certain that would help," Logan chimed in.

"Logan, Fauve can't marry three guys, not legally at least." He rolled his eyes.

"No, but Fauve can marry Cody, and you marry Loup and poof, problem solved. Canadian visa sponsorship for everyone!"

A dangerous spark lit up in Thibault's eyes. He liked that idea, and I knew I probably wouldn't fancy whatever was about to come out of his mouth.

"That would be perfect, actually. That way, Loup can be Fauve's boyfriend, Cody, her fiancé, and I would be her... partner? It's either that or her boyfriend's fiancé. Anyway, it would be so cool. Imagine all the surreal conversations she could have with innocent bystanders? Like: 'Oh, my life at home is so complicated. My boyfriend will only eat french fries, but my partner hates them, and my fiancé is allergic to potatoes.'" The trapezist's eyes widened in excitement. "The look on people's faces would be hilarious."

It wasn't, per se, a bad idea.

"Don't we have to prove we're a couple for the visa sponsorship to be valid?" I asked.

"Aren't you?" Logan retorted. "You live together under the same roof, you spend all your days together—and trust me, no one who looks at you when you train is going to believe that your relationship is purely platonic—and you even sleep in the same bed most nights! Okay, you've never actually had sex, but is it really something that's needed to validate a relationship in the eyes of the law? It's not as if you were going to tell the immigration agent, 'By the way, Officer, we're married and have been sleeping together for months, but my dick has never actually been in his ass,' right?"

Idiot. He wasn't wrong, but still. Idiot.

"I can't take it anymore," I stated, standing up before anyone could stop me. "They've been talking for hours. I'm going in."

"Yeah, more like ten minutes, dude, but whatever," Logan mocked.

I walked down the hallway towards Cody's bedroom, from where arguing voices were coming. I had never been in it, but it didn't matter. I barged in, barely knocking first, to find Cody lying down on his bed—probably frustrated he had nowhere to escape to—while Fauve was straddling him, looking fierce. When he saw me, he carefully pushed on her hip so she'd free him, and stood straight, chin raised defiantly.

Even angry, arguing with my girlfriend, Cody was hot as hell. He had thrown the bag containing his skates in the corner of the room and was still wearing the pants he had on, on the ice.

Since I had met them, my relationships with Thibault and Cody were difficult to separate from the tales of their sexploits with Fauve. I had been jealous of it, at first, even if I'd hidden it well, but since I had decided to share her, the memories were only arousing, making me feel as if I knew them more intimately than I did.

My arousal mixed with my anger, twirling in my head and heart until I detonated. I wanted the situation resolved, and I wanted that now.

Taking two big steps, I closed the distance between Cody and me, crowding his space.

"I know we hurt you, and for that I'm sorry. I also know you're scared, but I'm fucking done seeing her get hurt by you. I don't care if it was voluntary or not; she's sad, and it's at least partially your fault. It stops now." I got even closer, grabbed him by the neck with my right hand, my thumb brushing the bottom of his ear lobe.

"We need an answer, Cody. Are you with us, yes or no?" His mouth opened and stayed that way, agape, as if he was too dumbstruck to think properly.

"Do you know what I think?" I continued. "I think you're terrified of losing control, and you want someone to decide for you. Well, as much as I'd like to bury myself inside you while you fuck Fauve, and show you what you're missing, that's not going to happen. I'm not risking you breaking her heart tomorrow, if you end up running away from us like a coward."

Challenging him like this had my dick hard as steel in my pants. I wanted to crash against him and find out where the night would take us, but I meant what I had said. It needed to be a conscious decision on his part. Didn't mean I couldn't give him a little nudge in the right direction, though.

I threw a glance at Plume, wanting to check her reaction to my ultimatum. The expression on her face was of pure lust; her pupils so dilated her dark brown eyes seemed black. Good. My girlfriend and I were going to put on a show, and it would either make the four of us into what we were supposed to be, or break us.

I took off my t-shirt, still close enough to feel his breath on my skin, and strolled towards Fauve. Our eyes met, and I was surprised sparks didn't appear between us. Our connection was just that tangible.

"Are you okay, Plume?"

She nodded. "That was hot." She squirmed on the bed, pressing her legs together.

"Now, Cody, if you don't mind, I'd like to fuck my girlfriend. Either participate or get out." I didn't look to check if he obeyed, only hearing sounds of his heavy breathing.

"But it's my bedr—" he stuttered, protesting the fact that I was throwing him out of his space.

"I can't see how that's my problem. Move." I said, cutting him off.

Fauve was observing our interaction with interest, letting me take the lead.

"Take off your clothes," I growled to both of them as I started peeling my jeans off my legs, my underwear with them.

My girlfriend happily obliged, ending up completely naked in the blink of an eye. I loved how sure of herself she had become in the past years. She wouldn't even let me see her in a swimsuit when we first got together. Now, she was completely bare in front of two men, devouring her with their eyes, and looked regal while we did it.

I wanted to roll her and the comforter into a giant burrito, take her to our room, make at least three litres of hot chocolate with marshmallows, and spoon-feed her until I was sure she was okay, and the bullshit coming out of Cody's mouth hadn't really hurt her.

However, that would probably ruin the moment and the sexy alpha-hole persona my anger had brought forward. Sensing my hesitation, Fauve threw me an encouraging glance, and the pure lust I saw in her eyes convinced me she was fine. More like horny as fuck, actually.

I grabbed the back of her bent knees and pulled her towards me down the bed, helping her up while wrapping her right thigh around my waist. My other hand went to her nape, ironically not unlike how I'd held Cody just moments ago. I pulled on her hair, and she moaned, arching her back while her lips parted for me. I captured her mouth in a cinema-worthy, bruising kiss. Our tongues danced together, and I could feel wetness gathering where her core was in contact with my cock.

I lifted her off the ground to line us up, but resisted the urge to bury myself in her, preferring instead to grab her ankle wrapped around my butt and put it on my shoulder. I blocked her other foot with my shin, in a way her legs were opened in a split in front of me. Plume wrapped her small hand around my cock and pushed it inside her.

"*Fuck.*" I heard Cody say behind me.

I didn't resist the urge to taunt him. "Oh, so you're still here."

"Man, there's no way I'm leaving the room now, and you know it."

I started moving my hips in slow, lazy pumps, nipping at Plume's lips and swallowing the breathy moans that escaped from them.

"Can you give me a hand, then?" I asked. "Mine are a bit full at the moment."

I heard the tell-tale ruffling of clothes as Cody undressed. I turned us around so Fauve's back was to him, and he hurriedly came closer to the two of us. She leaned back on him, looking for his lips. They exchanged a heated kiss, his hand snaking around her to find her clit, tangling in my pubes in the process. Accelerating my rhythm, I sucked one of Fauve's nipples in my mouth, nipping at it and licking the underside of her breast.

Shortly after, I felt her clamp around me, her legs shaking and her back arching at an unnatural angle as she climaxed. I wasn't done with her, not even close, and I lowered the leg that was still on my shoulder, until her foot touched the floor. She turned to Cody.

"If you act like an asshole tomorrow, we're moving out. I really want this to work, but you have to want it, too. If we all decide we're in this together, I'm sure we can figure the details out later. Together. Not lashing out at each other, or avoiding each other. Do you agree, Loup?" I nodded slowly. "So, what do you want, Cody?"

I wanted to ravage her. My Plume was standing there, completely naked, graceful and fierce as a wildcat, confronting her lover, and all I wanted was to bury myself inside her warm, wet pussy. She was amazing.

"I want you," he said, looking her right in the eyes. Then, turning towards me, he added, "and you. And I miss Thibault like crazy."

"Is there anything you don't want to do now?" Fauve inquired.

"No. Show me that I belong." His order sounded like a plea to me.

I surrendered to what I had wanted to do since I had stepped into the room.

Cupping his face in my hands, I kissed the shit out of him, groaning when he started kissing me back.

Plume got down on her knees between us, her hand wrapping around my still-hard cock, then starting to stroke me. Because of the whimpering noises that came from his mouth, I assumed she was doing the same to Cody. Then, she started licking me and him, pulling us closer together. Soon, her saliva made it all so wet I had no idea if it was her tongue or his dick touching my own shaft.

He motioned to pull away and break the kiss, but my hand tangled in his hair, preventing him from escaping me. I had tousled it to my heart's desire and was positive he would look even more handsome that way. When he pushed harder on my hold of his nape, I let him break the kiss.

"Wait, wait, Fauvette, I'm going to come if you keep going like this." I opened my eyes to be faced with a pair of askew glasses, and the soft grey gaze they showcased.

"Then come," I whispered against his lips. I nipped at his neck, and his hand went up to pull me closer. I got used to Thibault's touch during the moments he helped me overcome my fear, and it was eerie how different Cody's was. His palms and fingers were soft, free of calluses, his nails longer when they grazed my shoulder. I liked it a lot.

My hand went to cup his balls while Fauve swallowed him down in frenzy, her other hand still massaging me.

My cock started twitching, and Cody's balls tightened in my hand. She pulled him out of her mouth, and we came all over each other's abs.

The three of us collapsed on the bed in a big pile of sticky limbs.

"Happy fucking birthday to me," Cody said, breathless.

Plume laughed.

Chapter 22

Fauve

OUR WALK OF SHAME took us back to the living room. I had gathered my red curls into a high ponytail, without really managing to tame down the sex hair vibes coming from them, and Cody's glasses were still smudged from Loup's cheeks, but we didn't care. Only Logan and Thibault would see us, after all.

"Are you done hate-fucking? Or love-fucking? I don't know, whatever the fuck you were doing? I want to eat cake now," Logan scolded.

"I am so jealous Cody got laid before me now that we're all a thing again," Thibault whined, "I have been playing nice for days."

"We didn't have sex," Cody protested. I immediately frowned, looking at him with a question in my eyes. "What? Nobody penetrated anybody."

"Penetrative sex is so overrated." Loup rolled his eyes. "But, if we're being honest, I did have my dick inside Fauve at some point."

Cody sat on the couch and threw his hands in the air. "Yeah, for probably the nine-thousandth time, so it doesn't matter."

"Let's agree to disagree on that one," I objected. Coming with my boyfriend's dick inside me was definitely something that mattered to me.

"Okay, forget about the cock-in-hole part for two seconds. Did everyone involved orgasm?" Thibault inquired.

"Yes," Cody, Loup, and I said in unison.

"Good, so you had sex. I call dibs on the penetrative sex, though."

I laughed, then crossed my arms. "Shouldn't I be the judge of that?"

"I don't know. Did I say you'd be the one getting lucky?" Smartass.

I swatted the back of his head, then sat in Cody's lap since all the spots on the couch were taken.

"Cody!" Thibault shrieked. "Where's the rope? She's getting violent again!"

"Well, this conversation is very entertaining," Logan interrupted, "and a little bit arousing, but I really want cake now. Ready to blow out your candles, Birthday Boy? And just to be clear, I mean the ones we're going to put on the cake."

Cody rolled his eyes while Thibault stood to get the cake we had bought for him. I went with the trapezist to the kitchen to help him light the twenty-four candles on the cake, and we sang as we slowly walked back to the living room.

I was trying to play it cool and not grin like an idiot, but it was difficult. I couldn't remember the last time I had been this happy. Loup threw me a knowing look and a nod as if to say, "Mission accomplished." I pressed a quick peck on his lips before sitting down and devouring my cake.

Gaining a new boyfriend had made me ravenous.

Life became somewhat simpler after Cody's birthday.

My flatmates and I resumed the same lazy rhythm we had before Loup arrived, and my boyfriend slipped into it effortlessly. He mostly spent his days looking for a job or walking around the city. We sometimes also slipped him into NICAM so we could practice our Adagio routine.

He was watching *a lot* of TV shows, too, but had given up on *The Office* after three episodes, joining Thibault in the *this-show-is-bullshit* team.

Loup claimed he was bored to death, but I envied him, sometimes.

The sleeping arrangements between the guys were an issue at first, but we had quickly realised that the only problem was none of us liked sleeping alone, and we didn't own a bed big enough to fit the four of us. Or a room big enough to fit said bed.

The first days, we had organised a rotation of who would sleep with me, clearly frustrating the guys.

Then, Cody's turn had arrived. It was one of those nights when Thibault and Loup came back home late, wearing conspiratorial smiles. I'd eventually make them reveal what their secret activity was, but for now, I was so happy to see them bonding over something that I didn't want to intrude. Cody and I hadn't waited for them to go to bed.

In the morning, when I had barged into Thibault's room to wake him up so we wouldn't be late to class, I had found Loup sleeping like a baby, curled up in the trapezist's big arms. I had swooned a little. How cute was that?

The next night, Thibault slept with me, and I found Cody cuddled in Loup's arms in the morning. Seeing them like that made me want to jump in bed and wake them up in the best of ways. Why did I have to get to class again?

To my surprise, it had taken more time for Cody and Thibault to share a bed together than with Loup. I guessed, threatening decades of friendship was a pretty big deterrent. I felt like they wanted to, though, noticing they usually woke up grumpier when they had slept alone in their own beds. So, one night, I offered to tuck them in, pretending not to have noticed they hadn't shared a bed yet. One thing led to another, and they ended up both sleeping in Thibault's room, relaxed after a couple of orgasms each. In the morning, I found Cody caressing Thibault's hair while he slept, head propped up on the engineer's bicep. When he saw my head coming through the barely open door, he made a shushing gesture in my direction and promptly went back to his stroking.

Yeah, my men were cuddlers through and through.

I hadn't started to work on my third evaluation presentation yet, and that worried me. Thibault kept telling me creativity couldn't be forced, a good idea would come to me when I was looking for it the least, and to believe in myself, but it was easier said than done. Even if they had been intense, only three weeks had passed since my second performance, so I had time until the third one. Still, I was stressed.

I didn't want to ask for my boyfriends' help, feeling like I needed to do this alone. It felt silly, but it was important to me.

So, I looked for good ideas, realising in the process what fickle little things they were. Just like bars of soap, the more you tried to catch them, the more they slipped through your fingers. It was unnerving.

"Don't worry," Thibault told me one day after I confided in him, "it will be fine." He then deftly changed the subject. "You know, Puss, I wanted to ask you something." He seemed embarrassed, so I wrapped him in a hug.

"Anything, T-Bone." Loup's ridiculous name for him had grown on me.

"Will you go on a date with me? I don't think we've spent a whole evening and night, just the two of us, before. I know it sucks that I work on Fridays, but maybe we can go next Saturday?"

"Or," I countered, "maybe, I can come see you at Cabaret Rouge? I've never actually seen you perform from the audience. If you'd like that, of course. Then we could go for a late dinner?"

He beamed. "I'd like that very much." He seemed thoughtful for an instant. "Aren't people supposed to spend their time together when they go on dates, though? Is it okay for you to be alone in the audience?"

"And have the opportunity to drool all over you while holding a sign saying, 'This man is mine'? Trust me, I'll be fine. Maybe I'll just forget the sign. But I remember your rope performance from before Christmas. It was pretty amazing to watch, and really frustrating that I couldn't openly express how proud I was, since I was alone backstage. I'd love to see it again."

My answer convinced him and he kissed me softly before going to class.

Thibault

"We have to tell Plume our idea soon," Loup declared.

We were finishing one of our sessions, and he had been amazing. He could now climb until his feet were about a metre and a half from the ground. It seemed the first metre had been the hardest, and he was now making progress at an impressive speed.

I didn't have any phobias, so I couldn't exactly understand what he was going through, but was amazed anyway.

It helped that I was really good at reading him. Whenever I saw he was getting uncomfortable, I declared it was massage time, and he now associated reaching his limit with a pleasant experience. Being able to help him like this made me genuinely happy, and I couldn't wait to show Fauve what we had accomplished together.

However, there was one milestone left to reach. I was unsure if I could help him on that front, and even more insecure to ask. The time had come, though.

"I agree," I answered. "She's getting super stressed over not having ideas for her presentation, and it doesn't seem right to hide ours from her like that.

"There's just one thing that we need to do before we tell her. You are also triggered when people you care about are high up, right? Like when you were feeling bad, watching Fauve and I at Cabaret Rouge?" He nodded. I took a deep breath before asking, "Do I fit into that category?" He looked at me incredulously, then grabbed my arm and caught me in a hug.

"Of course, you do, you idiot. Were you scared to ask?"

"A little." My gaze was resolutely glued to the ground until he used a single finger to push my chin up and made me dive into the depth of his turquoise blue eyes. He was smirking, head tilted to the side.

"I know we haven't known each other for very long, but I do like you, Thibault. I like you very much. It means a lot that you're helping me do this."

I felt a smile creep on my face.

"You know you're going to have to watch Fauve do some pretty dangerous shit, though. Are you okay with that?"

"I think I can ignore it until my cue, look somewhere else, then if I'm the one catching her, I realise I'm not that scared. At least I have some semblance of control over the situation, and it helps keep my phobia under wraps. It doesn't make a lot of sense, but fear isn't logical in the first place, so..." I nodded.

"Do you think you'd be up for watching me train for a bit? Just to be sure you won't get triggered?"

"Yeah, what's on your mind?"

"Since you've been doing so well, I was thinking of just doing some swings on the flying trapeze. I know it's much higher than what we've done so far, but I think you can do it."

"I don't know, man. Maybe just climb on the ladder, and I'll tell you when it feels like you're too high."

Was it wrong to be happy that he could get scared for me even before I reached the platform? It was as if I had this tangible proof of how important I was to him. For a very selfish second, I rejoiced at the idea.

I started going up the ladder, and as I was about six metres up—almost at the platform—when I heard his strangled voice saying, "Get down."

I hurried back down, more a controlled fall than a descent, really, and found him sitting on the floor breathing heavily, legs bent in front of him, and head in his hands. I wrapped myself around him.

"Hey, hey, hey, I'm here, Wolfie. I'm here, I'm fine. Just breathe," I soothed.

I deliberately slowed down my breathing to show him what to do.

"I can't do it, Thib, I can't. We cannot tell her yet; she'll be feeling guilty as hell if she sees me like this."

"I know, I know, don't worry, we won't tell Fauve yet. Today was just the first time we tried it, and you watched me climb so high, I was almost at the platform! We'll take it one step at a time, just like we did with climbing. You made so much progress already. I'm proud of you, and I'm sure you'll do well." I was turning into a mushy shit, but I didn't care. It was all true, and he deserved to feel good about what he had accomplished.

Long minutes passed, and he finally raised his head. He had been crying. Fuuuuck. What do I do with a crying dude in my arms? At a loss, I did the first thing I could think of to make him feel better. The fact I had wanted to do it for weeks didn't factor into the equation, or so I told myself.

I kissed him, long and deep, tasting salt from both his tears and sweat. He opened his mouth for me, grabbing my hair in his hand. I had noticed he did that to Fauve a lot, and now I understood why. It felt fucking nice. I laid down on the floor, pulling him on top of me. My hand couldn't get enough of him, exploring his body, from his broad shoulders, to his perfect abs, narrow waist, and tight butt. I ground my hips against him, tangling our legs together.

"You know, if you two wanted to be together, you didn't have to do it behind my back."

Her voice resonated in the deserted gymnasium.

Fauve. Double fuck.

Chapter 23

Cody

"WHAT HAVE YOU TWO dickheads done?" I yelled as soon as they stepped foot in the apartment. Whether they looked guilty because I shouted at them or if they looked that way before, I couldn't remember. I had started yelling too fast.

I had just received a text from Fauve telling me not to worry about her and that she would be back at the flat tomorrow. Oddly enough, telling me not to worry had had the exact opposite effect. If she told me not to, it meant I could have been worried, and since I was utterly relaxed beforehand, it made me wonder what I should have been worried about. Hence, worry.

The two idiots were staring pointedly at the floor. They had done something, then. Not good. I had been in this for a few days only, and deliriously happy. Mostly, I felt like I was floating in the sky, airborne; gliding, free-falling; and making love instead of fucking.

I had been in love before, but this over-the-top, strange relationship was making me feel so much more. They were my friends, my lovers, my partners. Thibault and Loup weren't screwing this up. Not if I could prevent it.

"Start talking now," I ordered, tapping my foot on the floor.

They told me the unabridged version. How Thibault wanted to help Loup with his fear of heights. Why they didn't want to tell Fauve yet. How great Loup was doing, until he wasn't. How she walked in on them making out on the floor.

Yeah, that didn't sound good.

"You know, it looks like you were hiding your relationship from her, right? Did you talk to her, at some point, about being together?"

"Not really, no..."

"Are you going to leave us?" I asked, scared of the response and maybe a bit hurt, too? I was jealous of Thibault and Loup's easy camaraderie, to be honest. I doubted myself all the time, especially when it came to my best friend.

They looked at each other, then at me, eyes wide and lips parted. Thibault opened his mouth to speak, then seemed to change his mind and closed it. I guessed I'd take that as a no.

"You know with the information she has, Fauve will think it's the most straightforward explanation to your behaviour, right?" I pushed. "That you're gay, and you want it to be just the two of you?"

"No!" Loup started, "I mean, yes, but no!"

Thibault looked like a goldfish, dumb and unresponsive.

"Well, now, go to bed," I demanded. "She wants space, we'll give her space. She's probably at Mary's, anyway. But you two had better prepare a great speech, explaining what you did and why, because I'm not letting you ruin what we have. It took us long enough to build it."

I could have sworn I heard one of the two say, "Yes, Daddy." Not funny, kids, not funny.

I texted Fauve back.

Cody: The two idiots and I are at home; just come back whenever you're ready. Please talk to them before you decide anything. We'll miss you <3

I wanted it short, simple, encouraging, and relatively neutral. I guess, common sense dictated I stayed out of it. I wouldn't, though. I would act as a middleman, until everyone was as happy as I was two hours ago.

Fauve

I had fled from NICAM as if the devil himself was following me and ran to Mary's flat, texting her on the way. When I stepped through the door, she took one look at my face and ushered me into the shower, grumbling about how I couldn't sit on her sofa smelling like this. She was right; I had been coming back from the gym when passing the gymnasium. I had heard muffled moans coming out of it, and that was when my curiosity had backfired—big time.

The shower helped me calm down, wrapping me in a comforting cloud of my bestie's smell. I smiled when I saw she used peach kids' shampoo, but an expensive body wash—full of contradictions, this one. There were baggy sweatpants, a loose tank top, and a hoodie waiting for me on the toilet lid when I got out.

"I am not lending you underwear, girl. There are limits to any friendship. But I swear those pants are so soft inside, your fanny will never want to be in contact with anything else ever again," Mary yelled from the living room as soon as she heard the shower stop running. My favourite thing about her was precisely this. You always knew where you stood. She told you exactly what she thought, and laid it out accordingly. There was no second-guessing her, or her behaviour.

Her apartment was small because she had decided to live alone and couldn't afford a much bigger one. If I had to guess, the reasons for her choosing this over a shared flat, was—to put it simply—men. It was her first time living without her parents, and she wanted to enjoy herself. Naughty girl.

The kitchen had a little bar area from where you could see the living room, which was also her bedroom, thanks to a Murphy bed. Cody was openly jealous of it and only waiting for the right occasion to pull it apart and find out how it worked. Engineers, go figure.

We sat on each side of the bar.

"I'm making pasta," she announced. "There aren't a lot of situations in life that pasta cannot make better. I'm assuming you're not at home because you've got boy trouble. Therefore, the present one does not fall into that category.

"And I only have tomato sauce, so it will have to do. On the plus side, we can hide it under a mountain of grated parmesan. I bought like three bags the last time I went grocery shopping."

I started eating, and to no one's surprise, I felt better, too.

"Now, spill." Mary leaned back on the sofa where we were eating.

I took a deep breath, then blurted it out in one go, "I walked in on Thibault and Loup making out on the floor at NICAM."

"Hot." I scowled at her. "What?"

"Why were they hiding? They know I'm not against them having a relationship. I told them, I love how they have bonded so fast. They've been sneaking around for some time now; I just didn't think they were, you know, *together* when they did."

"I don't know." She shrugged. "Maybe they were just doing something else, and it happened? Maybe they trained together for some reason? You should talk to them before jumping to conclusions."

"And what if they've discovered they're gay and in love, and they want to leave me? Since he got his visa later, Loup will be able to stay longer than me if I don't get selected at the end of the school year."

"Girl, you will only get these questions answered if you talk to them. They've always been open and honest with you; why would they hide that stuff from you now?"

I continued on with my ranting. "But what if they got tired of me and don't want to say it yet?"

"How do I have to say it? Talk to them!" she sing-songed.

"I have to talk to them tomorrow, don't I?"

"Finally, *yes*, that's an excellent idea. I don't know who's the genius that suggested it in the first place, but it must truly be an amazing person."

I poked her in the ribs with my index finger.

"Ouch. Cody is right; you *are* violent."

I chuckled. After what I had witnessed, I badly needed some headspace to think things through, and the talk with Mary had provided me with it. Thibault, Loup, and I needed to have a conversation in the morning. Including Cody would probably be a good idea, too. I frowned. I hated heartfelt conversations that were supposed to discuss relationships, but almost messing up badly with Cody had taught me they were necessary.

Mary had been puzzled by another aspect of our talk, though, and true to herself, said what was on her mind.

"Are you sure you wouldn't be able to stay if you don't get the job?"

The topic had gone a bit too serious for my liking.

"Are you going to let me win if I say yes?" I joked. Her long face didn't let up. I backtracked. "It's not that I wouldn't be able to; it's that it would be stupid to do so. Without a stable job or a degree, it would be a lot harder to get a visa, and I'd probably end up doing something that I don't want to do. I am lucky enough to have parents that can pay for my degree, and a business school that agreed to wait for me. Going back and finishing may not be what I want to do, but it's the smart choice here.

"Maybe in two years, I can come back and audition for the Cirque de la Lune again. If I don't get picked in June, that is." I winked, finishing the last part.

"Sometimes, you're too responsible for your own good, you know?"

I could only smile. "I know. Girl, what about you, though? I feel like we haven't properly talked in a while, and then it was always about me, the boys, or Nathalie. What's up with you? How's your family?"

When we were in class, she often talked about her parents' technique to teach kids specific movements at their gym, back in England. I would have loved to have had such understanding and caring coaches.

"Yeah, well, you had a lot on your plate." Blunt, funny, and kind. She was the best friend anyone could dream of. She continued, "My family's good. I talked to my parents last weekend. The gym's team is doing well at championships this year, so they're pumped. They're even buying new equipment and everything."

"That's great! Are they hiring new staff, too?"

"They're considering it. Why? You applying?" she teased.

"I might."

She blushed, and I became very curious about what she was about to say. Despite her light skin, Mary was so sure of herself, her cheeks rarely coloured.

"I also wanted to tell you, I've met someone."

"What?! Who, where?! Is it serious?!" I exclaimed. "Wait, I'm going to need all the little details, and we're going to need wine for this. Do you have any?"

She went to the fridge, grabbed a bottle of red wine, and fumbled through her cupboard to find glasses.

"What was red wine doing in the fridge?"

"Chilling." She winked. "Well, do you want to hear the story or not?"

Mary then proceeded to tell me about her new beau. After the break, she had found an advanced Cyr Wheel Act Creation class in one of the independent studios, surrounding NICAM, and had met Liam there.

I listened attentively, forgetting my troubles for a moment.

"Do you have pictures?" I asked.

She pulled out her phone and showed me some shots from his Instagram. He was the epitome of tall, dark, and handsome, with a sharp, strong jawline, bronze skin, and hazel eyes. He was shirtless in the picture, his torso and arms covered in tattoos.

"Wow, he's hot," I admired. She blushed beet red. "Is he taking the class, too?" I pat her arm with the back of my hand. "And wait, is he the one from the bar?"

"He's the teacher, actually. And yes, I invited him."

I waggled my eyebrows. "Dating our teachers now, are we?"

"Well, you're one to talk."

"Thibault was my flatmate before he was my teacher!" I protested.

"I'm not sure that makes it better." We got caught in a fit of laughter at her words. When we were able to catch our breath again, I resumed the conversation.

"How old is he, anyway?"

She looked resolutely at the floor. "Twenty-seven."

"Oh, and we're dating older men now, too. What a naughty girl you are, Mary Sue Shevchenko!"

She rolled her eyes. "Yeah, well, it's fun, okay? And we're putting a Cyr wheel act together. It looks pretty good so far."

I could totally believe it. They probably looked good just standing next to each other.

The next day at NICAM was uneventful. I thankfully didn't run into the two idiots I didn't want to see, allowing me to plan our conversation of the evening properly. I had texted them I was indeed coming back and we needed to talk.

Coming into our apartment, I barely got the time to remove my coat before Thibault nearly tackled me, wrapping his arms around me in a suffocating bear hug.

"I'm sorry, I'm sorry, I'm sorry," he whispered without interruption.

I kissed his nose. "Thibault, are Loup and Cody here? The three of us need to have a conversation, and I was hoping to get it out of the way."

"Cody, Loup, bring your asses in here," he immediately yelled.

We all sat in the living room, and taking a page out of Mary's book, I asked without preamble, "Loup, Thibault, what are you hiding from me?"

They cringed.

The trapezist looked at the acrobat. "So, who's starting?"

"I am."

My boyfriend looked at the coffee table, then at his knee, finally meeting my eyes again. He rubbed the side of his throat, tilted his head, then he started, "Thibault has been helping me work on controlling my fear." I was taken aback; I hadn't seen that one coming. "We've had an idea for your third final presentation." Thibault growled and scowled at Loup, and I raised an eyebrow. "Actually, Thibault had an idea. It's genius, but it involves me getting off the ground, and we didn't want to tell you until we were sure I could do it."

I was slowly getting upset for an entirely different catalogue of reasons. First, it didn't explain how they had ended up kissing. Second, they were making decisions for me and micromanaging my life. Third, they had hidden things from me. And fourth, they made me get anxious over a problem—my evaluation presentation ideas, or lack thereof—they had a solution to.

I crossed my arms and glared at both of them.

"And how did you end up making out on the floor like teenagers? Why?"

"It was my fault," Thibault started. "I pushed too hard, too fast, and almost started one of his panic attacks. I needed to calm him, so I did what I could, and that's when you walked in on us."

"It wasn't your fault," Loup protested, frowning at Thibault. Then, he turned towards me. "I wanted to tell you what we were doing, but we had to make sure I could do it first. This made Thibault push me, and that started it all."

I felt both like hugging and punching them. Not necessarily in that order. I turned to Cody, who had stayed eerily silent since the beginning of the conversation.

"What do you think?"

"They're dickheads, but they meant well. And just to be clear, I refuse to be on anybody's side. I am on *our* side. As in, I don't think I've ever been happier than during this past week. You guys have been, too. It's visible. I am not letting anyone ruin that."

I stopped for a minute to think. This conversation was necessary, and I very much wanted it to be the last one we had on this subject. For at least a month. It didn't seem realistic to be in a relationship with three people and ban relationship conversations, as much as I hated them.

"Thibault, you can't make those decisions for me behind my back. I would accept and value your help if you offered it, but you cannot decide I need help and start planning stuff for me without me. I would have asked for your help eventually if I felt like I needed it. Or you could have come to me and explained what you were thinking."

"Fauve, this last part is my fault," Loup interrupted, "I didn't want you to see me struggling."

I threw my arms in the air. "I've seen you struggle plenty of times."

"Exactly, and it always worries you. How would you have felt if you knew for a fact that I was pushing myself for you?"

I paused for a moment. He had a point.

"You should have told me anyway. I would have given you space to figure out whatever needs figuring out."

"Would you, really?"

Again, I thought about my answer before speaking.

"Maybe not," I conceded.

"See? That doesn't excuse hiding things from you, but I needed Thibault's help. I was dubious at first, but it does help a lot more than my sessions with *Docteur* Fabre. And we were planning on telling you soon—as soon as possible, really."

I was still upset over the whole situation, but I understood their side, too.

"Are you ready, now, to tell me about this mysterious idea?"

Loup cringed. "Not really, no. I'm okay with climbing, but seeing people I care about high up still makes me freak out."

"Exactly," Thibault chimed in, "and that's why my tongue was in his mouth when you saw us."

I rolled my eyes, Cody sighed, and Loup glowered at him.

"I take it you're not leaving us, then?" I finally asked.

"No!" they shouted in unison.

"Cody, you're still in whatever this is, too?"

"Yes, Fauvette. It took me a moment to pull my head out of my ass, but it's fully out now, and not going back in."

"Ew, gross." I narrowed my eyes at the images his comment had evoked in my mind. "Okay, so we're all officially in a relationship, then?"

Loup grabbed my hand, Cody securing the other one. Thibault went to kneel between my legs, where he barely fit.

"I think we are," my boyfriend said—the French one.

"Wait, so I have three boyfriends now?"

"No," Thibault protested. I looked at him incredulously. "We've decided that Cody has to propose to you and I to Loup, so Cody is your fiancé, Loup is your boyfriend, and I am your partner. Or your boyfriend's fiancé, it's your choice."

I blinked. Several times.

"What?!"

"Oh, and it would make it much easier for you guys to get a visa, too. If we got married and not just engaged, that is."

"That's insane, Thib. Not happening."

"So, you're going to call us what, Boyfriend 1, Boyfriend 2, and Boyfriend 3? I'm number 1, if that's the case."

I sighed. This had just started and was already exhausting. Fortunately, being in a four-way relationship meant that I had backup to deal with Thibault's antics.

Cody smacked him behind the head while telling him to shut up, and pulled me against him.

"Is there anything else, Fauvette?"

"Actually, yes. I know now that it wasn't what you were doing, but if you guys ever want to be together, I'm all for it. I like to see you getting close."

"I think that was obvious, Puss," Thibault said, "and I would be careful if I were you; Loup liked Canadian kisses."

"Thibault!" Loup scolded.

"Too soon?"

"Yes," I confirmed, "too soon."

"Oops." The trapezist didn't look the least bit apologetic. "And what can I do to make you forgive me?"

I rolled my eyes. "You idiot." I quickly relented, though. "I want a kiss. A good one."

He obliged.

Mary was right about communicating, after all.

Chapter 24

Fauve

The rest of the week was a lot calmer, anticlimactic, almost, after the way it had started. I studied and often trained on my own, sometimes with Mary, but gave space to Loup and Thibault to figure out Loup's phobia, as I had told them I would.

Waiting another week to start training for the evaluation presentation was making me nervous as hell. I tried to hide it as best as possible, and hoped Loup wouldn't pick up on it. Obviously, out of the three, he was best at reading me.

Friday came, and with it, the moment to get ready for my date with Thibault. I noticed last time that the audience at Cabaret Rouge was relatively well dressed, not full suits and ball gowns, but chic anyway, so I decided to blend in.

I gathered my hair in a high bun, kept in place by a myriad of pins, only letting a couple of crimson strands escape, the curls falling in front of my eyes. I applied a golden eyeshadow on my lids, light and subdued, only for the sparkle, and painted my lips with a deep carmine lipstick I absolutely adored. Three layers of mascara complemented my look, my lashes looking impossibly long.

My French business school had invited a tailor to make us custom suits, and I got two. Two years ago, imagining a future as a circus artist was a complete impossibility, so I thought I would need a formal businesswoman attire. And I still might. I took one out of my closet and quickly donned it. It was entirely white, which I loved since, in the winter, people tended to wear darker colours. Even in the audience, I would stand out. Would Thibault see me?

The pants were straight, reaching my ankles, and the blazer was tailored close to my body, with only one button to close it. The twist to make my business school outfit date appropriate? I wouldn't wear anything under the blazer. The neckline dropped nearly to my belly button, and if I bent forward too much, Thibault was sure to catch a glimpse of my breasts. Oops.

I put on the black pumps I wore for Christmas and twirled in front of my mirror. They exposed the top of my feet, letting yet another burn mark—from aerial silk this time—show, but I wasn't hiding them. I would wear the shoes I wanted to wear, even if it showed off the angry red slashes.

After observing myself for a minute, I added a long gold necklace with a little circus tent as a pendant—a belated Christmas present from Cody. The ornament rested exactly in the middle of my chest, and it was sure to attract my trapezist's attention where I wanted it.

On my heart, of course.

Satisfied with my slutty-chic look, I took off my pumps, put them in my bag, and grabbed my snow boots and coat to put them on. There was no way I was losing a toe to frostbite because of style.

I headed out, and the bouncer immediately spotted me when I arrived at Cabaret Rouge. I knew Roger from the times I had performed there. He gestured for me to cut the line and come right to the front.

"Hey Fauve, how have you been lately?" the mountain of muscles asked. Seriously, he was even bigger than Thibault and Loup, combined.

"I'm good. How's everyone here?"

"Good as well. I was told you're part of the audience tonight. Thibault reserved the table closest to the stage for you. Do you know how to get there?"

"Of course."

"Good, enjoy the view, then. I heard he was on fire tonight." He winked. I'd never seen a winking mountain before.

I made my way inside the cabaret, leaving my coat and snow boots at the coat check. I sat at my table and waited as the seats started to fill. Nobody came to sit with me, but it didn't bother me in the least. I was actually glad Thibault had made sure I had breathing space. He also arranged for me to have the best table. I was so close to the stage it would be possible to see every movement and muscle as he performed in the air. A shiver of anticipation ran through my body.

A few minutes before the light went out, I saw the heavy curtains ruffle, and Thibault came out of the backstage area through the side entrance, avoiding stepping on the stage.

I knew his rope act outfit included a button-up shirt, at least when he first stepped on stage, but he wasn't wearing it now, all his muscles oiled up and exposed. He probably had already warmed up, too, because his limp was gone and all the veins in his forearms were showing. His green eyes narrowed in on me, and from the look in them, I realised this was already part of the act. My boyfriend looked dark and dangerous as he strolled confidently past the tables and to my side. My nipples instantly pebbled, and I wondered if he could see them. I didn't dare look down, though.

When he finally got to me, his strong, rough hand wrapped around my nape, tilting my head back so he could catch my lips in a bruising kiss. It was a claiming, possessive move, forcing my mouth open as he massaged my tongue with his. I didn't dare touch him, not wanting to get oil on my hands, but eagerly let him do what he wanted with me. His other hand went to the base of my neck, thumb brushing my clavicle. I felt... owned, and I didn't mind it one bit.

He broke the kiss. I couldn't have done it; I had turned to putty in his hands. His lips hovered above mine for a moment, and he finally lowered them to my neck, delicately sucking my flesh between his teeth, enough to mark, but not enough for the hickey to stay for long.

"I never thought I would enjoy acting like a possessive boyfriend this much," he whispered against my ear, "but I didn't want any dickhead to get ideas, seeing such a sumptuous woman sitting alone in a cabaret, like this." I smiled. It was oddly thoughtful. He leaned back and huskily said, "Enjoy the show, Babe. Can you meet me backstage afterwards?" Babe? He never called me Babe.

"Sure, Honey, I can't wait," I teased back. He turned around with the same darkness in his eyes, the stage makeup only making it more intense. He took a moment to cast a warning look around as if to say, "Mine. Back off." Even if he had lipstick smeared all over his mouth, he looked every bit the part of the dangerous alpha-hole who would do anything to defend his woman.

In any other circumstance, I would have ripped him a new one for doing this. Now, my blood caught on fire as I ogled his ass while he walked back to the backstage area. Damn, my man was hot. I took my phone out of my bag and used the selfie function to reapply my lipstick like the queen I was supposed to be.

AERIAL

As Thibault had asked, I stood up to meet him backstage after the show.

The acts had all been amazing, but my favourite had undoubtedly been his rope one. My trapezist looked incredible when he was performing, and—unlike on the aerial chandelier—nobody was grinding on him. I liked and trusted Stephanie, but hell, nobody would want someone in such close proximity with their boyfriend. Especially dressed like that.

The aerial chandelier act wasn't the last one of the evening, so Thibault had already showered when I made my way to backstage. He put his arm around me and kissed my temple when I closed the distance between us, needing to be near him.

"Ready?" he asked.

"Yep!"

He took me to a cute bar that also served their appetisers on big, copious plates. We sat next to each other in a booth, and when we finally settled in, he asked, "So, what did you think of the show?"

"The aerial rope was a-fucking-mazing, Thib. How's that not your specialty? You're so good at it."

"A lot of the movements can be replicated on the trapeze, actually." I already knew that, but let him mansplain, anyway. "And since you don't need two fixation points, the rope is easier to install, so it's more convenient in places like Cabaret Rouge. I like trapeze better, though. I don't really know why." That made sense. With a shit-eating grin, he continued, "How about the chandelier? Did you like it?"

I winced and started fiddling around with the cutlery on the table as I said, "Yes, it was good."

"Puss, are you jealous?"

"No! I just liked the rope better!"

"So, you *are* jealous. You know it's not an issue, right?"

"Why?" I questioned. "It's not exactly a very healthy feeling."

"Are you going to prevent me from performing with Steph?"

"Of course not!"

He nuzzled my cheek. "Then, it's not a problem. I like it, Puss. It makes me feel... wanted." He sweetly kissed my cheek. "And you can't imagine what it does to me, seeing you dressed like this with that hunger in your eyes. Have I mentioned you look gorgeous? Are you even wearing anything under that blazer?"

"I heard the word sumptuous being mentioned, but I think you forgot gorgeous. And no, I am, in fact, not wearing anything under this blazer."

"I'm not sure I trust you, can I check?" His hand rose to my neck as if he was innocently cupping my cheek, but I could feel his little finger snaking in the direction of my very peaked nipple.

We were interrupted by the waitress coming to take our order, and I wasn't sure whether I wanted to thank her or strangle her. We asked for cocktails and two plates of appetisers to share, and the moment was effectively broken.

Thibault and I chatted about nothing and everything, and I discovered how much of a passionate and interesting person he was. Circus was his life, but he was interested in any and all forms of art, saying that you never knew from where your inspiration could come. He liked to go to museums but also the cinema, and he spent a lot of time on social media checking out other artists, from painters to photographers, without omitting musicians and makeup artists.

It was genuinely mesmerising; hearing about how a painting had once inspired a whole act that earned him the best grade in his class. Beyond the exposed muscles and strength acts he put together because they were easy, he was a complete artist and choreographer, capable of creating complex performances without forgetting a single detail.

I listened to him talk, drooling shamelessly. Metaphorically, of course.

He was also very passionate about teaching, and I interrupted what had been a monologue—not that I minded—to ask about Loup.

"He's doing good, Puss. Really, he's very driven, and before we started, I just wanted to try it out to see if it could work. Now, I'm confident it's possible. I can almost get to the flying trapeze platform without him panicking. The plan is to manage to do a couple of swings, which should happen next week, I think, and then meet together and start training."

"Are you sure I'll be able to do my part?"

He nodded. "It's not very different from what you already know. There's only one very crazy move, and I'm confident we can learn it in the weeks we have left."

"We? As in, you've never done it before?"

"I've never even seen it done before. I've asked Cody to draw up plans for the contraption that we'll use."

My stress level skyrocketed. The last time I had performed on a custom-made apparatus, it hadn't gone well.

"I know what you're thinking, Puss, so stop it." He poked my nose with his extended index finger, and I realised my eyebrows were gathered in a frown. "It'll all be fine. You have us, now."

He was right; I did. Acknowledging it warmed my chest.

We kept talking, eating, and drinking until the bar closed, and only when we were kicked out did we go home. I fell asleep almost instantly, curled up in the trapezist's big arms.

MANUELA ROUGET

Loup

Today was the day. I could feel it in my bones. My heart was in my throat, pounding mercilessly, but today would be the day.

I felt brave.

I watched in silence as Thibault climbed up the first part of the ladder. That had triggered me ten days ago, but it wasn't a problem anymore. I was amazed at how quickly I had improved. If I had known he'd be so helpful with my fear, I'd have searched for a trapezist lover long ago. Not that I truly was free of my phobia yet, or that trapezist lovers were easy to find. Even so, it was impressive.

Said lover was about five and a half metres up now, and my hands started shaking. It wasn't a problem, though. During a presentation, I would be too in control for it to happen, so I continued watching.

Six metres.

Seven.

He was finally standing on the platform, so high he seemed small.

"I'm okay," I shouted. It was a lie. A small one, though. I wasn't feeling terrible. His nod was almost imperceptible from down here.

Thibault removed the hook that held the trapeze bar to the platform and watched it swing back and forth. As soon as it came back to his side, he grabbed it with his right hand, his left one holding onto the vertical steel bars framing the platform.

"All good?" he asked, one final time. I nodded, briefly, but he seemed to see it anyway. His powerful shoulder pulled the bar up without letting it go, giving him the fraction of second he needed to let go of the platform, and put his hand on the steel rod without falling.

Suddenly, he was flying. His legs balanced rhythmically from front to back, to build up his momentum. He arrived at the extreme opposite where he had started, and pulled on his arms while propelling his legs upwards to gain more speed, more height. I felt like I was going to throw up, but I could still breathe. Thibault's back was getting closer to the platform. Instead of stepping back on it, he stilled his body in a position that resembled a seven, arms pushing the bar in front of him with his legs extended in the same direction, falling once more. This exercise probably was why his abs were this defined; they had to be tense as fuck.

About halfway through the swing, his body arched back, and using it as a spring, he let go of his hands and completed a backflip before landing safely, back first in the net.

My breathing came in rapid pants, shallow and hectic, but I hadn't wholly lost control yet. It was a win. I had done it.

Thibault walked awkwardly on the bouncing net, grabbed its edge when he reached it, and pushed his whole body over his head to get down, in a slower version of the backflip he had just done up high.

I probably looked like I had seen a ghost, but it was already a massive improvement from not being able to breathe at all, and he knew it.

"You did it! That was amazing, Wolfie. I'm so proud of you!" It was fucking ironic that the guy who had just done a backflip to get down a flying trapeze would congratulate me for sitting on my ass and breathing.

Thibault didn't care, though. He was happy for my progress and didn't hold it to anyone else's standards. That was probably what made him such a good teacher, too.

He straddled me, cupped my face in his hands—probably putting white chalk marks all over my face—and kissed me deeply. I kissed him back; it had become a very common occurrence as he helped me overcome my fear. His kisses were distracting enough to make me feel better.

He leaned back. "Do you want to call Fauve?"

"Yes, T-Bone, let's do that."

She arrived so quickly it was as if she had been waiting for the call. We told her about our idea, and that we knew now I could do it.

"I want to jump on the both of you so badly right now. Do you think it's possible to kiss two people at the same time? I don't want to pick."

"Then don't, Puss. Let's try it," Thibault teased.

Before I could say anything, I was caught in a triple kiss that was both curious and electrifying. Contrary to what one might think, our three mouths, together, they... fit. Just like soft, warm, wet puzzle pieces.

Our tongues danced together, and I lost myself in the sensations. Fauve was to my right, and both Thibault and I had leaned in to make our heights work. I tangled my hands in their hair, pulling slightly with my fingers while my palms encouraged them to get closer. They groaned. I didn't ever want to be kissed any other way. My dick was rock-hard in my sweatpants, but unfortunately, it would have to wait. We had more important things to do.

Fauve

The kiss destroyed me and built me back up instantly. It was a promise, hope, pleasure, all wrapped up in a sensual package.

Regretfully, I leaned back, creating a distance between our lips. I hated it, wanted to erase it and climb them like a tree, but that would come later.

"Can we start training, then?" I asked.

They nodded. Why did I always have to be the responsible one?

Chapter 25

Fauve

Four weeks before my final presentation, we started making the routine Thibault had created a reality.

We suspended the contraption above the foam pit first to make sure I didn't die stupidly while training. Just to be clear, I didn't.

I fell in the pit a lot, though, and it was exhausting. I got much better at getting out of it quickly, but it still took a big chunk of my energy every time.

During the second week, a tiny piece of foam got stuck in my left eye, and we lost four precious hours to go to the ophthalmologist to get it removed, and for the doctor to take care of the massive case of conjunctivitis it had given me. I went back to train right after. It didn't matter that my eye was swollen and itched like hell. The show had to go on.

Then, later that same week, I had to stop training for an entire day. I was getting a lot better at juggling and learning to do it with a partner. During one of the sessions, I wasn't quick enough to catch one of the clubs coming my way—I'll let you guess who had sent it—and it ended up giving me a black eye. On my good eye. So, I took twenty-four hours to rest because I couldn't rehearse with only a third of my vision. Or so Thibault and Loup said.

To get back at them for benching me, I made them do some flexibility exercises, telling them it was good for them—which was true. I drew a very sadistic kind of pleasure out of their whining, though. Especially Thibault's. Even if he hadn't shown his head this time, the Dragon wasn't truly forgiven yet.

So, I made sure that the trapezist warmed up his good leg well and his bad leg very well, then sat on his back until his hands touched his feet with his legs extended in front of him. Once this skill was mastered, I put him in the same position, pressed my chest against his back, and using my hands to press on his thighs so he couldn't bend his knees, pushed us both forward with my legs.

His howl of pain made my heart sing.

Eventually, he threatened to do the same for me, so I let him. He perceived how empty his threat was when I dropped in a front split and laid my belly flat on the floor, feet still pointed at the ceiling. He then stood up, mumbling inaudible insults, then he went to do some pull-ups. Loup watched the whole thing, giggling while working on his front splits. Thanks to the training plan I had put together years ago, his left side was as perfect as the right one.

Halfway through the fourth week, we decided to ask permission to do our presentation above the foam pit. We would have to rearrange the first part, and it might not look as perfect as if we were above an actual stage, but we were just not confident enough to risk me getting killed.

At least, the boys weren't. They hadn't even let me fall once in the time we'd been practicing the routine in its entirety, so it was completely illogical for me to risk failing due to a stupid fear, but they said it was either that or cancel the whole thing. Pussies, the lot of them.

I found a black sheet to cover the blue cubes and another white one to use as our background, so it didn't look as ugly as the bare foam pit. Due to the height, I had one option, and it was to have the white one custom-made. I was incredibly relieved when it arrived in time for the evaluation.

Finally, after an entire exhausting month where we spent every single spare minute rehearsing, Presentation Day came.

I was feeling experienced at this, and the nerves were improving each time I went on stage, but this time, I was grateful for the adrenaline. It was the only thing holding me up.

Our stage outfits were simple for this presentation. I was wearing black tight shorts that barely reached my thighs and a matching sports bra, while my men only had black leggings on. The objective was to go crazy on the makeup instead, so crazy we went.

Helped once more by Logan, we drew big stripes of glitter of varying colours on all our exposed body parts. He used eyelash glue to keep the sparkly particles in place, but overdid it in a way they rained down whenever we moved, creating a shimmering curtain around us. I had one big pink ring of glitter around my left forearm, another red one on my upper right one, a golden belt around my exposed waist, and several more going down my legs. Loup and Thibault both had a stripe that went diagonally across their torso, respectively blue and green—matching their eyes, Logan observed—and several others around their arms, like me.

We finished by doing our faces, Logan using the same material to create a band of gradually changing colour around our eyes and foundation to erase our lips completely.

We looked like futuristic glitter warriors, if that was even a thing.

I just hoped all the sparkle floating around wouldn't make my eye infection come back with a vengeance.

Wanting to get it over with, I had volunteered to go first. We listened to the chairs ruffle as our audience gathered in the gymnasium while we waited behind the white curtain. I finished strapping my wrists and ankles to make sure I didn't slip through the boys' fingers, then strapped their wrists to improve my own grip on them.

When the time to finish dousing myself in rosin came—we had rehearsed so much it never totally came off anymore—the drama happened. Since rosin made your hands sticky and powdery, I always waited for the last possible moment to apply the finishing layer that would make my grip perfect.

The little rosin bag that always hung from the wall of the gymnasium wasn't there.

"Thibault!" I called, "what did you do with the rosin? I need it now!"

He made his way over, palms open towards the ceiling.

"I don't know, last I saw it, it was hanging from that nai—Where is it?"

My adrenaline and stress level spiked, cold sweat running down my spine.

"Do you know if Loup took it?"

"Why would he? That stuff's been hanging there for a week!"

Seeing the expression on our faces, Loup quickly came closer. "What's going on?"

"The rosin's gone," I answered.

"Is there more in any of the other classrooms? I can run to get it!"

"The closest place is the small aerial studio—" The sound of Donna starting her opening speech cut me off. "There's no time."

"I'm not in the act when the music starts; I can go!" Thibault offered.

I shook my head. "You can't run with your leg, let alone before a performance where you'll need it!" Thibault threw his hands in the air, powerless, but didn't protest.

"We'll have to do without," Loup said. "We have the straps, and neither of us sweats much. Plus, I still have some on me after all of our rehearsals."

"Same," Thibault agreed.

They were right; that last rosin application before performing, helped my confidence more than it helped my grip. The situation was still nerve-wracking, and I had to breathe deeply to prevent my hands from shaking.

"Okay," I said with a shaky voice, a knot in my throat. "Let's do without."

I looked at the people gathering in the hall, pushing the curtain to the side. I spotted Nathalie, and our eyes met. She looked apologetic, almost, but still determined. She whispered something to one of the Adagio sisters sitting next to her, and they all laughed. Eva looked at me with a challenge in her eyes. Where the rosin had gone wasn't such a mystery, after all.

It hurt that they got along. Hadn't Nathalie said that friends were a distraction and she didn't want them?

When Donna finished her speech, feeling like I was about to throw up from both the stress and the betrayal, I stepped up on stage.

The first notes of "First Person on Earth" by Robert DeLong came out of the speakers, and Thibault's genius plan started unfolding. Muscle memory took over, and going through the steps became a barely conscious process; all our rehearsals having drilled the movements into our very bones.

The trapezist's idea was straightforward, beautiful, and complex, all at once. He wanted to tell our story.

Loup and I started the act on the floor, using the most complex bits of the performance we knew so well. After precisely fifty-three seconds, I turned towards Thibault and started the finale of the routine we had prepared for Cabaret Rouge. My acrobat boyfriend, on the ground, pretended to have a broken heart—dramatically holding his sternum—while our duet happened.

Then, after about two minutes, the last and most challenging part of our act started.

Cody had designed a trapeze with two levels. The first level, where we currently were, was lowering itself until it was about three metres high. The second level was now becoming apparent, precisely six and a half metres off the ground—fifty centimetres lower than the flying trapeze.

As I made myself comfortable on the side of the bar, Thibault used the other rope to climb on the upper level. He tangled his legs behind the bar and around the rope, in base position. I stood on the lower level, pulled on my arms, and threw my ankles up in the air, right into his arms, that he used to propel me even higher.

I stood on the highest bar, looking down at the audience eight metres under me. It was impressive; the height was vertiginous, the fall, deadly. It was exhilarating.

My partner and I started a series of figures, each more daring than the last. A diversion, really, while Loup got in position on the lowest level of the trapeze.

When the last notes of the music resonated in the gymnasium, Thibault threw me up after a swing. I forced my body into a backflip and extended my hand for him to catch me. He missed. An audible gasp came from the audience as I tumbled in the air, doing a second backflip in the process. The fall seemed endless, time suspended.

Our execution had been flawless, and instead of hitting the floor, my fall ended abruptly, the pull on my ankle telling me I had safely reached Loup's waiting hands.

My head hovered mere decimetres above the foam pit.

Loup let go of my right ankle for me to grab it and pull my feet to my head behind my back. I knew Thibault would be doing a back plank high above us.

Applause exploded all around me.

Take that, Nathalie.

Thibault

Fauve was a machine. There was no other explanation. How could this much energy fit into a body this small? She had spent a whole month rehearsing—only taking a twenty-four-hour break because both her eyes weren't functioning correctly and we *made* her—and passed her exams, did a routine that would scare even professionals—without rosin—and she was still standing to cheer on her friend.

Even I wanted to curl up in bed and sleep.

Mary's act was unique, though. Only curiosity kept my eyes open at this point. She had put her Cyr wheel on an inclined plane, which allowed for crazy accelerations and slow returns up the slope, giving the whole act different rhythms. It was super creative.

At some point, she even hula-hooped inside the wheel, which was something I had never seen before. I enjoyed the performance a lot. I just wanted my bed more. Possibly with a certain redhead in it. And maybe my best friend and another certain French person, too. We needed to convert our living room into a bedroom and put all our beds in it. Now, *that* was a genius idea.

As soon as Mary finished, I grabbed my three flatmates—Cody from his seat in the audience—and headed towards the exit. My girlfriend protested weakly, saying she wanted to see the remaining performances, but fuck that. People had smartphones; they would record them, she would see them next week.

We were silent the whole way back, the rush of adrenaline we had just experienced leaving us empty. Once in the flat, I gave them enough time to clean up—we had already left glitter all over the gymnasium and didn't need it in our sheets as well—and pulled them all to my room.

This time, the protests were more vehement. I grumbled I didn't care if my bed was too small. I needed them. Together, and with me. I felt like cuddling tonight.

Probably understanding that it was non-negotiable, Loup and Cody both laid by my side while Fauve splayed herself on top of the three of us. We were all asleep within minutes.

Fauve wasn't a machine, after all. She crashed and slept for fourteen hours straight, ate her weight in food, then went back to her room to nap.

When I woke her up to see the verdict announcement, she looked much better, a pretty pink colouring on her cheeks, and light returned to her eyes. She was stressed, though; I could feel it. I would have been, too, in her stead.

Since they were neither students nor teachers, Cody and Loup couldn't attend, and I was left as sole moral support if things went badly. I felt an odd pressure on my shoulders. It was a lot of responsibility to be the only one responsible for Fauve's wellbeing. I wasn't used to it, and I wasn't sure I liked it.

We headed to NICAM, and I tried to reassure her as best as I could. We had done a fantastic job at the performance. She was a great student. If they didn't keep her, it was their loss. I regretted that last sentence as soon as it left my lips.

Where was Loup when I—we—needed him? He was much better at this shit.

Thankfully, we had left home a little bit late, so we didn't have to wait at all for Dean Loewenberg to start announcing the ranking. We even missed the speech.

"In first place... Fauve Laurent!" Okay, well, at least we hadn't arrived after the dean called her name. That would have been embarrassing. I hugged her tight, whispering how amazing she was in her ear. I thought I felt wetness against my chest, but didn't dare look. She probably wouldn't want people to see her crying.

I was incredibly relieved. What would it have felt like for Fauve to fail because of my idea?

Donna Loewenberg continued announcing the names in rapid succession.

"In second place, Nathalie Roy! In third place, Mary Sue Shevchenko! In fourth place, Jonathan Young! In fifth place, Carlos Rodriguez! In sixth place, Clarissa Jones!

"To all the ones I haven't called, I am sorry, but you haven't been selected for this last phase. Thank you for your dedication, and I know you all have a great future in front of you. Do not give up on it because it didn't work out here.

"I will not tell you goodbye because I am confident we will see each other again. It is a small world, and a very small industry, after all.

"So, see you soon. To all the others, go rest because if you thought this phase was demanding, you've got a big surprise coming your way. I have three months left to shape you into the best possible artists, and you can trust that I'm going to make the most of it."

The audience dispersed after that. Fauve and Mary hugged, all emotional and tired. I ushered them towards the exit.

On the way out, Nathalie deliberately put herself in our path, flanked by two enraged-looking, eerily similar students.

"Fauve, can I talk to you for a second?" she asked.

"No." She successively tilted her head at the two other girls, clueing me in on their names. "Eva, Ana, I'm sorry you guys weren't called."

I had never seen my girlfriend refusing to talk like this, but I understood her. She had told me about her former friend's attempts at sabotaging her, and if Fauve hadn't forbidden me to do it, I would have gone to see the dean on her behalf by now.

Eva opened her mouth to speak, but Ana laid her palm on the other girl's arm, effectively cutting her off.

"Thanks, Fauve," Ana said. "We're proud we've come so far, and won't give up now. The world will see more of the Adagio sisters, this I guarantee." The corner of Fauve's lips tilted up, as she nodded her agreement.

I laid my hand on her back as she turned it on Nathalie, changing sides to put my body between them.

"Do you want to come home with us, Mary?" I offered, ignoring the three of them.

She shook her head. "Thanks, Thibault, but I told Liam I'd meet him at his apartment. Take care of her for me, will you?" She kissed Fauve on both cheeks and headed towards the metro, while we went back home, my arm wrapped around Fauve's shoulder the entire time.

We lived to fight another day.

Chapter 26

Fauve

IT WAS ALL WE waited for, now; the decrease in pace that came after the evaluation presentations were done. This time, there was no celebration of any kind, the entirety of students being utterly exhausted. We just wanted to rest, sleep, and lick our wounds.

Classes started again, though, and way too soon. We still had a massive amount of things to learn, it seemed. I knew it sounded pretentious of me to say after only six months of studying, but the rhythm had been so fast-paced it seemed like the stream of information that was continuously fed to us would die down, at some point. It didn't.

The stream changed into rapids, and to stop rowing would send us crashing on rocks.

One of our new common classes this term was the wheels, where Mary excelled. She was better at Cyr wheels than at the

German one, obviously, with the former being her speciality, but she had already practiced on the latter, too, and I loved watching her on both.

I, on the other hand... let's just say that my first tries weren't mind-blowing. With her tutoring, I managed to not hurt myself and do some tricks on the German wheel. I still had no idea how the Cyr wheel worked.

It was a strange feeling, being among the six finalists. I was experiencing a severe case of imposter syndrome. Did I deserve to be here? I couldn't possibly be within the top circus artists in the world, it was impossible. I had probably only earned my spot, thanks to Loup and Thibault's help. I wouldn't have made it alone, which meant I shouldn't be here. I hadn't even been training full-time for that long!

The guys helped me—a lot—with those thoughts. But they couldn't erase them altogether.

The Saturday after the presentation, I called my parents, and my mother didn't help either, asking me if I would give up circus at the pinnacle of my career just like gymnastics, or if I would persevere when things got hard, this time. I had never told her how close to anorexia I had been when I was a kid. She never knew how bad I felt about my body or the exact reason I quit training. One day, out of the blue, I had told her I couldn't do it anymore, and she still resented me for it.

Mava and Mapa knew, though. Years after the fact and encouraged by how supportive their son and they were, I had told them. They had become even more encouraging of every single one of my endeavours—if that was even possible—and participating in their calls with their son was an absolute pleasure.

A few days after our performance, Loup found a job as a waiter, which relaxed him a lot; he didn't have to worry as much about his finances anymore. Mava and Mapa still helped him financially, but it wasn't as much.

The direct consequence of his new job was that he was now absent on Friday nights, too, meaning that Cody and I had them all to ourselves.

During the first weeks after the presentation, my body was still recovering from the intense training rhythm I had put it through in March, so we stayed home after I came back from NICAM. We started watching *The Office* again, from the beginning. With all the drama, rehearsals and classes starting again, I had forgotten the first few seasons and didn't want to watch the last one without having them all fresh in my mind.

So, we ordered food, I curled up in Cody's arms, and we watched the show until we fell asleep on the couch. He usually caressed any and all surfaces of my body he could reach, and I discovered on this occasion that I liked his hands—a lot. I had always wanted his touch on me, but I was only now understanding why.

His hands were soft. Unlike Thibault's that were always full of calluses and scratches or Loup's whose skin had dried up because of the chalk, or mine that were callused, hurt *and* dry, Cody's skin was smooth, delicate almost. His long, agile fingers were made for typing on a computer or clicking on a mouse. His nails were always clean and neatly manicured. He didn't let any dead skin accumulate, and I was positive he used cuticle oil.

His hands felt a lot better on my skin than mine.

He had noticed how I looked at them, too, knew how watching him study got me all hot and bothered because of the speed he switched from mouse to keyboard, back and forth, relentlessly.

During one of our Friday nights, he even gestured for me to sit on the couch between his legs, and when I questioned him, he only declared, "I wanna know how many times I can make you come in one episode." I practically leapt from my spot on the sofa to where he was gesturing. He spread my legs above and around his thighs and got to work, pleasuring me with both hands as my body relaxed against his.

Six. The answer to his question was six. In twenty minutes.

Cody had magical hands.

After those first few weeks had passed, he started taking me out on Friday nights. It became our thing, discovering the hidden gems of Montréal together. Some places he knew, some places we just spotted online and went to explore.

I liked how Cody was invariably well-dressed, too. I always got all dolled up on Friday nights, just to match his level of elegance. He always said I didn't have to. I answered that it was precisely why I did it.

One of those nights, he took me to the docks on the Saint-Laurent River, and by pressing a button on a nondescript door, transported me into what looked like a parallel universe.

The speakeasy bar was so packed we had no choice but to be practically glued to each other. They served bourbon and whisky cocktails in gaudy glassware, while a jazz band played in a corner. It was literally underground, with exposed beams on the ceilings and heavy wooden tables.

The sounds of both chatter and the music made it all too loud to talk, so we just sat there in companionable silence, exchanging chaste kisses and very cheesy smiles, sipping our drinks. Mine had been served in a porcelain mug that looked like a panda, while his was in a fish head, with a little umbrella on top. The bartenders had decorated it with fresh fruit and a lot of crushed ice, which prevented the fish head from being too disturbing.

It wouldn't have been a great first date. Fortunately, it was nowhere near our first.

That night, we came back home slightly tipsy, laughing and teasing each other like smitten teenagers in the subway.

The keys hung up on the apartment wall told us Loup and Thibault were already there when we arrived home, and suspicious sounds came from the former's bedroom. Loup groaning and Thibault moaning could be identified. I headed towards the room's door, but Cody stopped me, putting his hand on my upper arm.

"Wait," he said, "I have a better idea," he explained it to me with a mischievous grin, and I started giggling uncontrollably. The sexy noises were growing louder by the second, so they probably hadn't heard us.

Still dressed, we sat side by side, demurely, on Cody's bed, and started putting on a porn-star-worthy vocal show. We knew it was only a matter of time before Thibault and Loup erupted into the bedroom. I had bet on five minutes. Cody had bet on three. In our defence, we were a bit inebriated.

I moaned, softly, because I couldn't do it too loud, or else, they would come soon, and Cody would win. That wasn't to my boyfriend's taste, though, and he slapped my thigh, hard. I was already in character, so instead of yelling that it hurt, what left my lips was, "Oh yeah, Cody, spank me!" We were ridiculous. It was hilarious, though.

He started shaking his ass from left to right to make the headboard hit the wall that was conveniently shared with Thibault's room. He looked like a duck waddling outside of its pond, arms gathered to his chest to help with the momentum. I giggled; he scowled at me, and I started moaning again, louder this time.

Three minutes came and went, and he accelerated his wiggling to make it sound like we were getting close. Four minutes after we'd started acting like idiots, Loup and Thibault barged in the room, wearing only boxer shorts. Loup's cock was rocklike and straining through the thin material, while Thibault's was soft but quickly hardening again.

Their faces when they took us in, sitting side by side on the bed, hands chaste in our laps, were epic. Disappointment, curiosity, and arousal all mixed up in a whirlwind of expressions.

Cody and I got caught in a fit of laughter.

Thibault scratched his head. "I knew she never sounded like that when I fucked her, in the beginning of the year. Want to get back to my room, Wolfie? I think we should finish what we started."

"No!" I yelled. They were delicious, almost naked, and I didn't want them out of my sight. Despite having three boyfriends, I hadn't had sex in more than a month. A lot of foreplay and delicious orgasms, yes, but actual intercourse, no. I had been too tired, too busy, too preoccupied, and for a second, I felt guilty for not properly taking care of them. Then, my desire came back in full force and erased the guilt completely.

"Well, Plume, I think this room is way too unequal, clothing-wise, at the moment," Loup teased. "I'd rather go back to a nude-only place."

I ripped my clothes off before attacking Cody's.

Chapter 27

Loup

"No," Plume protested, butt-naked. "Stay, please." She threw me a look she knew I couldn't resist, full of longing, love, and mischief.

Fortunately, I had come prepared and bearing gifts. Her eyes narrowed in on my right hand, which carried a case she knew well. Black and simple, it was about the size of a small pillow. It also contained all the sex toys we both owned.

Her eyes went wide, and she squirmed on the bed. I wanted her, but I also wanted to make her work for it. She and Cody had interrupted us, after all.

"What's in the case, Loup?" the latter asked.

I threw it his way. He opened it, and his eyes went wide, matching Fauve's.

"Man, how much do you spend on sex toys each month?"

"Probably a lot less than you spend on shoes." Thibault and Fauve tilted their heads in unison, cheeks straining to contain their laughs. "The world would be a better place if more people bought sex toys instead of guns, or drugs, or even alcohol. They're definitely not something I will be ashamed of.

"Plus, only two of those were really expensive, and I built up this collection over years. I promise I'm not a sex toy addict." Loup winked.

Like the good engineer he almost was, Cody quickly became more focused on understanding how the silicon devices worked than reading the room's energy.

"There's no remote?" he asked.

"I have an app on my phone. There are also buttons on most of them."

"Interesting." He was captivated. Weirdo. "Can we try this one?"

He held up the one I had given to Fauve for Christmas.

"What do you think, Plume?" She nodded enthusiastically. I had taken the toy out of the box, cleaned it up, and paired it in case of such an occasion. I ran out of the room to get my phone and wasn't surprised when I came back to find Cody sucking on Fauve's nipple while she moaned, eyes half-opened.

A devious smile graced my lips.

I had an idea.

Erasing the distance between Thibault and me, I hooked a finger in the waistband of his underwear and pulled, releasing it only to hear a satisfying snap when it met his skin.

"Naked, now," I ordered.

I pushed down my own boxer briefs, stepped out of them once they touched the floor, and knelt on the bed, straddling Cody's leg, probably giving the trapezist a lovely view of my ass and balls.

I seductively crawled up the engineer's body without letting our skin touch and stopped to look at his face when my lips were level with his very erect cock. I let my mouth hover so close over his taut skin that it twitched under my breaths, and Cody diverted his attention from Fauve's breast to look at me.

"Is this okay?" I asked.

He nodded slowly, lips parted, breathless. The sight made my abs clench, and I couldn't resist the urge that took over my body.

I licked him from balls to tip, fast and hard, pressing my tongue against his dick, then caught him in my mouth and sucked him in as far as it could go. Cody moaned, low and deep, hands clutching the back of my head. As fast as I had gone down, I pulled back, the movement almost brutal, pushing back against his palm. He groaned in protest, but making him want more was exactly what I meant to do, so I just grinned again.

I pushed myself up and forward, barely letting Cody breathe before ensnaring his lips in a scorching kiss. Beside us, I heard Thibault move, his broad shoulders coming in contact with my thighs, and Fauve moaned breathily.

Only then did I let my body lie on Cody's, growling low in my throat when our hard dicks touched. Our tongues were still tangled together in a slow, wet dance, caressing and teasing and exploring. It was the first time we kissed like this, and I would make sure it wasn't the last.

Without letting go of his mouth, I bent my knees to kneel above him. Breaking our kiss, I grabbed my case, of which the contents had mostly spilled on his chest, searching with my eyes until I found the sex toy he had picked.

The sight before my eyes was decadent, and it took all of my self-control not to forget my idea and just start fucking them all.

Having spread her legs wide, Thibault was going down on Fauve, whose right knee was halfway across Cody's torso. The trapezist's cock was completely hard again, even if I had finished sucking him off right before we entered the room. One of Cody's hands was on Fauve's breast, the other stroking his dick slowly, sensually.

And his grey eyes were focused right on me.

Add to that the colourful silicone toys that littered the bed, and my lovers became a sight to behold.

Finally spotting the Christmas toy, I grabbed it and palmed Thibault's ass, initially to push him gently off Fauve, but getting distracted in the process. The scene was a feast, and I felt like a starving man. So much skin to touch, lick, stroke, so much pleasure to be felt, all readily available. I didn't know where to start.

My hand slowly snaked up and down Thibault's backside, progressively getting closer to his crack. His ass was delicious. Round, plump, and firm, it was proof of all the hours he spent in the gym. Closely watching his reaction, I let my hand go lower until my middle finger met his puckered hole and pushed. The moan that came out of his mouth, directly into Fauve's pussy, was pure debauchery.

I couldn't get enough.

But I really wanted to play the game I had come up with, so I removed my hand, letting it slap down hard once on the trapezist's ass for good measure.

I laid down on my side next to Cody, whispering close against his neck, "I have an idea, let's watch them finish, and I'll tell you guys after." He shivered, eyes half-open, goosebumps appearing on his forearm. I kissed his shoulder softly and leaned my head on it, focusing back on our lovers.

"See how gorgeous they look together?" I breathed low enough that only Cody could hear me. "How beautiful their bodies are, how close they are to their release? Look, Cody, and tell me what you see, what you want them to do, what you want to do with them." His eyes snapped open.

"They're amazing. I want... everything," he said, echoing my thoughts from earlier, eyes riveted on our friend pleasuring our girlfriend next to us. "I want to watch Thibault fuck Fauve as she sucks you off. I want to fuck you while you fuck her, and I suck Thibault. I want the three of us to fuck each other as she watches. I thought about it, Loup, and there are so many options, so many possible combinations, and I want them all."

When I heard Fauve's whimpers accelerating, her hand grasping the sheets, I propped myself up again and kissed the shit out of him. Still watching from the corner of my eyes, I saw Thibault get ready to fuck her and put my hand flat on his chest, pushing him back.

"Wait, I have an idea," I said again.

"Oh, are we feeling naughty today, Wolfie?"

"Very." I bit my lower lip, eyes navigating the scene. "Cody, T-Bone, stand up. Plume, on your hands and knees at the edge of the bed."

They eagerly obeyed, and I stood up, too, hand still clutching the toy I had found.

"How do you feel about a little game, Plume?" I asked once she was in position, "You face forward and with the toy in place, have to guess who's fucking you. If you're right, you'll win a reward, whatever *you* want. If you're wrong, you'll get a punishment, whatever *we* want."

"What do you mean the toy in pl—" I cut her off by slowly, carefully inserting the already vibrating toy in her exposed pussy. She was so wet from Thibault's ministrations it slid right in, her body barely offering any resistance. "Oh, Loup, this feels so *good*," she immediately moaned.

Fauve

This was the best Christmas present anyone had ever given me. Loup had turned on both the internal and external vibrations, and it felt incredible. It was almost a struggle to remain on all fours, the pleasure in my body making me feel like a puddle of goo on the floor.

"So, Plume, do you want to play?" Loup asked. At this stage, I didn't want to play; I *needed* to play. I needed to feel their bodies against mine, their cocks in me, their balls slapping my clit.

"Yes," I groaned, frustration making me impatient.

"Are you sure this won't hurt her?" Cody asked.

Loup chuckled. "With how wet and turned-on she is, I'm telling you, it'll feel incredible."

I heard movement behind me and felt the blunt tip of a dick rubbing on my clit, between my legs, before pulling back and finally entering me in one powerful stroke.

This would be a hard game to play—no pun intended. None of them had an incredibly wide or long dick. The three of them were average-sized, perfect to fuck me but would be very difficult to differentiate.

As soon as soft hands took hold of my hips, I knew, though.

"Cody!" I shouted.

"Well, done, Plume," Loup praised me. "Such a good girl, recognising her lovers by the way they fuck. What will your reward be?"

"I want—I want you to increase the vibrations," I panted. Ever since he entered me, Cody hadn't stopped his long, powerful strokes, and I was feeling them everywhere. As I demanded so, the toy's rhythm increased suddenly, both stimulating my clit and front wall.

"*Fuck*," Cody moaned, his dick pressed against the toy. I felt so full, so good, that it wouldn't take long until I came again. Or so

I thought until Cody withdrew, the toy's vibration returning to a minimum. I let out a pained growl.

Loup taunted me, "Uh-huh, Plume, we're still playing, remember?"

I arched my back and squeezed my legs together like a cat in heat, trying everything for the pressure between my legs to increase, to finally come.

I felt another dick against my entrance, but the hands on either of my hips were different this time. They didn't belong to the same men. Were they trying to trick me?

"Who is it now, Plume?"

"Thibault!" I exclaimed. With everyone's state of arousal, there was no way they would let Cody go twice.

"Well done," Loup confirmed again. "And what do you want, now?"

"I want to come," I said without hesitation. In that instant, there was nothing I desired more in the entire universe. If someone offered me millions to just delay my orgasm a bit more, I would say no.

The vibrations were turned up to their maximum, and my men all moved. Loup laid down to kiss me while Thibault fucked me in earnest, and Cody nipped at my nipples from under me. In a handful of my trapezist's thrusts, I was gone, shouting my release against my acrobat's lips while my other boyfriends held me up, and the toy was switched off as my clit became painfully sensitive.

Loup rose back up again, nodding to Cody so he'd do the same, and I was left tragically empty. It didn't last, though. Someone pushed inside me once more, the silicon vibrating again.

"Who is it?"

"Loup!" I was sure of it, those were his hands, and he was the last one to go.

He had planned for my reasoning because a slap landed on my ass, and he exclaimed, "Wrong, Plume!" I looked back. Loup was at Cody's side, and he was holding me while my engineer fucked me. I couldn't stop a moan from leaving my lips. I had never done anything this erotic before.

Cody's thrusts started getting slower, and I felt a second cock rubbing against my clit, then its head pressed on my entrance. There was no way it would all fit in there, but I trusted them. They weren't going to hurt me by trying this.

From the angle, I could tell Cody and the second mystery boyfriend started alternating their thrusts, one filling me halfway while the other rested between my ass cheeks and then switching again. They were so close their cocks sometimes rubbed against each other before penetrating me, and I could hear trios of moans coming from behind me.

I felt another orgasm creep up on me, powered by how erotic what we were doing was.

"Who is it, now, Plume?" a breathless Loup asked. I had no idea. There were no hands on my hips to help me, just the torturous feeling of their dicks alternating inside me.

"Loup," I declared again. Was he restrained enough to pass up on his turn twice in a row?

"Wrong again! Now, you get two punishments, Plume. What will it be, guys?" I whimpered. I wasn't afraid of them taking things too far. Not so long ago, I literally had let one of them throw me from the height of a three-storey building, another's arms preventing me from crashing on the ground. I trusted them implicitly.

Thibault had stayed relatively silent so far, only moaning, groaning, and playing along with Loup's game. For the first time, he spoke up, talking to Loup, "First punishment, she's going to suck Cody's dick until he comes in her mouth. Second punishment is while that happens, you're going to fuck her, I'll take your ass, and she won't be allowed to watch."

I whimpered, both in frustration and need. I wanted that to happen so badly, but I also wanted to *see*. The way I was positioned,

I could barely glimpse what they were doing. With Cody in my mouth, my view would be completely cut off.

"Get in position, man, so she stops making those noises. Otherwise, I won't last long," Loup ordered.

Cody sat against the wall in front of me, and I immediately took his dick in my mouth, dying to feel full again. I sucked and nipped and rolled him on my tongue, fondling his balls with one hand.

"Guys, you need to get on with it; otherwise, this foursome is going to be over before it starts!" Cody panted.

Loup's hands on my hips were joined by Thibault's, who laced their fingers together. The acrobat groaned as his hips pressed against mine.

"You feel so good, Wolfie," Thibault soothed, "so tight and warm around my cock. Does it feel as good for you as it feels for me?"

I let go of Cody's balls to reach between my legs, lining up Loup's dick and my pussy. Thibault's next thrust triggered a chain reaction, and suddenly, we were all joined like kinky Lego pieces. It was deviously beautiful.

Thibault dictated all our rhythms, pushing Loup against me and me against Cody but as planned, nobody lasted very long.

My acrobat came first, laying heavily on my back and pressing the toy still inside me on my sensitive clit. Thibault and I came next, both our releases triggered by Loup's. Cody waited for me to catch my breath before I felt his hot cum spill in my mouth.

I crawled on the bed and curled up at Cody's side, utterly exhausted. He palmed my cheek and tilted my head towards his, laying a feather-light kiss on my lips.

"You're amazing, Fauve. This was incredible, and I lo—"

"Wow, that was fun!" Thibault interrupted. Both he and Loup had gone to the bathroom before laying down because they knew that once they collapsed, they would be done for.

What was Cody about to say, though? That he'd loved it? The trapezist joined us on the bed and plastered himself against my back, spooning me from behind.

Loup joined us shortly after, laying down on Cody's other side, his head on our lover's chest. He caught my wrist and laid a soft kiss on my palm.

"Love you, Plume."

"Love you, too."

And I immediately fell asleep, unsure of how many people I said that to.

Chapter 28

Cody

I HAD FEARED FAUVE and Loup leaving us before, but after Friday night, it had turned into pure, undiluted terror. I had almost told Fauve I loved her, although if left to chance, the odds of her staying in Canada at the end of the year were one in six. This wasn't particularly high, but after watching the videos of the last presentation for the five people that remained, I didn't think all of them were indeed threats.

Clarissa, for instance, was really good at what she did, but she hadn't truly evolved. She and her partner had done quick-change numbers since the beginning. Creative and funny, sure, but repetitive. Stacy had got stuck in an outfit during their last evaluation performance, resulting in her elimination.

The four others, well, they were threats.

One in five, then. Not good.

I couldn't let Loup and Fauve leave; I just couldn't.

First of all, because she was a brilliant, hard-working person. The fact she wanted to go back to finish business school—even though she didn't like it—was proof enough. Her parents should trust her, believe in her, and have confidence that if she told them she would make it without a degree, she could. Hell, she had three boyfriends; we could provide for her while she found another gig. She would never let us, though.

Fauve ate, slept, breathed, and lived circus. She didn't deserve to get trapped in an office job she didn't want in the first place. After all her hard work, even if she came in second, third, fourth, or fifth, both she and Loup had a right to live their passion. They would be in at least, what? The top fifty best circus artists of their generation? Surely, there were jobs in the industry for people like them.

Finally, because it would break my heart. It would break Thibault's heart, too. I wanted to believe they would be selected, that they would get the job. But my stupid pragmatic brain kept reminding me of those odds. And worse, there was nothing I could do to influence them.

Fauve

If April had taught me something, it was that I hated Canadian spring. Nature came back to life, the flowers grew, the birds sang, and all that bullshit, but there was mud every-fucking-where. I abhorred the mud. It was ugly, dirty, spongy, and I had a tough time adapting to it. I was so ready for summer. Couldn't we skip to May already? I wanted the weather to be warm again.

I was walking towards NICAM, grumbling that my shoes had been stained for what felt like the millionth time when Thibault caught up to me with an air of the cat that got the cream.

"Hey, Thib, what happened?" I asked. He didn't look like this when I left home this morning.

"I have a plan."

Uh-oh. Not good. Or, very good. With him, everything was possible. I teased, "Another one?"

"Yep. How do you feel about doing flying trapeze for your final presentation?"

"Mmh. Terrified. Bad. Worried. Scared. What made you think it was a good idea?" I asked. I was inquisitive. This hit me as a terrible idea, but he seemed genuinely proud of it, and Thibault usually didn't joke about that stuff.

"Because no one else is going to do it! The judges expect us to come up with something really impressive since it's the final round. What's more impressive than flying trapeze, honestly?" I could have given him several answers to that. Flying trapeze was far from the most dangerous thing circus artists did. Crazy people, all of us.

I kept my mouth shut. "Puss, your class has no aerialists. Nobody is going to expect a flying trapeze act! That's your shot! In two months, if you train every day, you have time to learn some pretty impressive figures."

I wasn't convinced. I could give it a go, though. What was the worst that could happen?

Actually, forget I ever asked.

MANUELA ROUGET

Yawning so hard my jaw felt like it was going to detach, I entered the gymnasium. It was the one where our second presentation had been. Thibault had insisted we meet at dawn so that no one knew what we were preparing.

I was surprised to find Stephanie with him. I raised an eyebrow at her, and she must have understood the question in my eyes because she immediately said, "Hey girl! Are you excited? You're going to learn what flying truly feels like today! Thibault asked me to help because there's no way anyone can safely teach this stuff alone. Besides, I owe you for what you did for me in December." She was way too energetic this early in the morning. I appreciated what she was doing; I truly did. But the part of me that still needed half a litre of coffee to fully wake up wanted to be annoyed. Badly.

I yawned again. Thibault was almost dancing from one foot to the other, grinning.

"Puss, let's begin. We don't have much time before people start piling in. I need to teach you how to fall safely in the net, first."

Why did I always start by falling?

My boyfriend was right, though; it was the best place to start. It turned out nothing I had trained for before had truly prepared me for the safe flying trapeze landing position. To be sure that your fingers or toes wouldn't stay stuck in the net and broken by a rebound, you had to land on your back, with your arms and legs up in the air, like a turtle stuck on its shell. It was totally counterintuitive, and the catlike movements you had to do in the air to ensure your back touched the net first were challenging.

The lunge belt that Thibault had secured tightly around my hips prevented me more than once from acquiring diamond-shaped bruises on my face. The trapezist held the other side of the rope it was attached to, and using his hands protected by heavy leather gloves, he stopped me whenever I was dropping too fast, or in the wrong direction, or in the wrong position. I had never thought I would one day struggle to just fall.

Yet, here I was, failing at falling.

Stephanie helped me take off from the platform, holding the bar for me until I was ready to take that terrifying step into the air.

Once satisfied with how I was falling, Thibault taught me how to properly give impulses with my legs so my pendulum didn't lose momentum. He even compared it to a child going back and forth on a swing. I sassed that I would be seven metres high, suspended by my arms, and therefore, it had nothing in common with a swing. He retorted that the physical principles were the same and to not fear it.

Right. Easier said than done.

Since I had no idea of what to do, Thibault yelled instructions at me from the ground on how to swing my legs to the exact rhythm of the flying trapeze.

"Back, front, back," he screamed as I reached the other side of the pendulum. "Front, back, seven!" A bang resounded in the gymnasium. The goddamn seven position got me every single time.

Its objective was to prevent my calves from being hit by the platform on the backward extremity of the swing. I hadn't looked at them, but I was pretty sure the back of my legs was already black and blue.

When my boyfriend signalled, I let go of the trapeze and fell safely into the net. The worst part of getting hit was this; even if your legs were hurting, you couldn't just give up. You had to get safely down first, then you could complain to your heart's desire. I didn't like it. I liked my reactions to be loud and immediate.

"Puss, you need to contract your abs sooner. That's the only way for you not to get hurt."

I grumbled. These two months were going to be fun.

"Very good, Fauve, now pass your leg to the front, split and, wait... wait... wait... Hup!!" Thibault commanded. I let go, contorted like a cat so that my back touched the net first, tensed my body, waited for the rebound, and finally stood in the net to go to his side.

We had been training for a week, and even though my entire body was bruised—falling in the net hurt a lot more than it seemed—I was making tremendous progress. The palms of my hands were one big blister that begged to be burst, but I was understanding the appeal of it all. The sensations were exhilarating.

"Puss, that was so good; I'm so proud of you!" He wrapped me in his arms. "The progress you've made is very impressive, and I think we'll be ready to start catches next time."

I winced. Falling after posing had already been hard. What would it take for me to stay airborne?

"Thibault, about that," said Stephanie, having just landed graciously in the net, "who's going to be her catcher?"

"I will," he declared.

"And who will man the lunge, then?"

"You can do that."

"And what about the platform? Who will help her? Daniel?"

"No, what we're doing here has to stay a secret. People can't know," Thibault protested. "Even if he's in our year, and we've trained together a couple of times, I'm not sure I trust Daniel with this. We need to teach her how to do a one-handed departure; that way, she can manage alone."

Stephanie frowned. "I don't like it, Thib. You know that move is dangerous for beginners. I know several people who dislocated their shoulder because they tried it too soon." She turned towards me, then. "What do you think? It's your evaluation, after all."

I hesitated. Apparently, my answer didn't come quick enough for our friend because she continued, words aimed at my boyfriend this time, "See? She's not comfortable doing it, and I'm sorry, but I won't help you get her hurt."

"She didn't say anything."

"Yeah, because she probably doesn't want to upset you. But if she'd wanted to learn it, she would have jumped on the occasion."

She wasn't wrong. I wasn't feeling overly at ease with the whole flying trapeze situation. Was that even something that needed to be said? Only a crazy person would feel cosy up there. And Stephanie and Thibault, apparently.

Now that she had spoken up, I was starting to listen to the little voice in the back of my head that told me that this wasn't a good idea. It had been drowned in my boyfriend's enthusiastic words but quickly became louder, and I wasn't so sure this was the way to securing my spot at Cirque des Etoiles anymore.

"Thibault, I think Stephanie might be right; I don't know about this anymore. I'm sorry, but we need another idea." I looked resolutely at the ground. I didn't want to see the disappointed look in his eyes.

He approached me and cupped my cheeks. "It's okay, Puss. Steph is right. It's your presentation. Whatever it is, I'll respect your choices. And you've already learned so much. I'm proud of you." I didn't say it, but I was proud of him, too. He had grown a lot. Old him would have at least tried to convince me his idea was best.

"Woohoo," Stephanie cheered. "And come on, girl, better to lose because of your idea than win, thanks to someone else's."

"I actually don't agree at all with that statement," I deadpanned, smiling to soften the blow of my words.

"Yeah, I know. It sounded much better in my head, though. I think I spent way too much time on that life coaching website last night." I chuckled at Stephanie's words. "Let's go; it will be amazing to not wake up at dawn tomorrow."

At that time, she didn't know how right she was.

Because the next day, when the first student came in to train, he didn't notice the loose screw that barely held the cable. He didn't see that it wasn't fitted in its hole, its threading sticking out. He didn't check if that giant structure would hold him before launching himself in the air. He just executed a perfect one-handed departure, flawless and mastered to the perfection, jumping up to gain more momentum.

The screw holding the cable fell down to the ground. The bar, unbalanced, swung to the side then tipped, making it impossible to hold on to.

The trajectory was deadly, throwing the trapezist out of the safety net.

The sabotage had been executed to perfection.

And in the fall, Daniel broke both of his legs.

Chapter 29

Fauve

"WE HAVE A SABOTEUR in our midst!" the dean yelled.

During our first classes of the morning, we were asked to gather in the hall at the interval. When the lesson ended, awareness of Daniel's accident had spread throughout the student body, and my mind was reeling.

If Stephanie hadn't put an end to my flying trapezist velleities, it would have been me. It was evident that, if ranking first after being selected last had made me a threat, winning twice had now made me a target. I would have to be especially careful when I practiced from now on.

Donna Loewenberg stood tall in front of the six of us. Her pantsuit was blood-red today, covering a white Lavalliere shirt. Her grey hair was pulled back in a high ponytail, blue eyes scanning her students, analysing our souls.

"This is not a novel, and you are not bickering children competing against each other for a petty reward. You are all professionals, and I'm extremely disappointed in you." Wow. That hurt.

Although—as she had just emphasised—we weren't children, all our eyes fixed on the floor, and they stayed that way.

"While disappointed, I am not surprised," she continued more softly, but still with steel in her voice. "Sabotages happen every year, and even if we do everything we can to prevent and punish them—our security team is already checking the cameras, by the way—we have unfortunately come to expect this type of occurrence. It is the first time that someone almost got killed, though, and I can promise you I will do everything in my power to see the culprit brought to justice.

"Also, I guess it is time for my being-a-cheat-will-get-you-nowhere speech. Although they are near, you still have time before your last exams, and I don't want someone else to get any ideas.

"Each and every one of you is an amazing artist. At this point, it's just something you'll have to accept about yourselves because it is the truth. You all have the capacity, perseverance, and creativity it takes to make it in this business." Back straight, her posture regal, she met all our eyes, one after the other, as if she could read right through us.

"But do you want to just make it, like a shooting star, or do you want to have a long, productive career? Because putting obstacles in the way of others will not get you very far. There are thousands of amazing artists out there who will become better than you if you don't use your time wisely. Taking them all down would take an entire lifetime. The only option you have to make a living from this is to always improve. Stay innovative, keep thinking outside the box, experimenting, creating. Because it doesn't matter if you're doing something a little harder or in a cleaner way. What's important is doing something different. Something that no one's ever seen before. And this takes time and hard work, time you will not have if you spend it all sabotaging other artists' material!" She almost shouted that last part, hitting the podium with the side of her closed fist as her voice became louder. After taking two deep breaths, she continued, "So, that was the first part of the speech. The second part is very simple, if I find you tampering—or if I find in the future that you did—with anyone's material, you're out. Or fired, if you made it to Cirque des Etoiles. I don't care why; I don't care when. Our profession is already dangerous enough not to tolerate idiotic behaviour. I won't, and you shouldn't, either. If your material is not exactly the way you left it, come to me, and we'll investigate."

Should I turn Nathalie in? She *had* made me fall during the aerial silk class, thrown a juggling club in my face before making it look like an accident, and I was almost sure she had stolen the rosin before our presentation... Was she responsible for the flying trapeze, too?

I decided against it for the time being. I had no proof. And she had done those other things out of a desire to protect her sister. Would she badly hurt me to do so? It didn't sound like the friend I knew at all. Then again, neither did the club and rosin episodes.

Donna pressed her lips together and sighed. "But honestly, I have other things to do, so whoever's being an ass, please just stop. Better even, come forward, and I'll consider not torpedoing your entire future as a circus artist when I find out who you are, because I will. Trust me, you don't want to be on my bad side. You all know how well connected I am, that's why you're here, after all.

"And in case someone's thinking of being very stupid, I have a team of lawyers at my back, and you've all signed an agreement not to cheat—however dull that may sound. We're not playing in the same league, so do not behave as if we were.

"Just be smart, bold, and—particularly in this case—know your limits."

I looked around, trying to decipher my competitors' faces, checking if someone looked suspicious, guilty. The saboteur had almost killed one of our fellow students, after all.

My eyes met Nathalie's, but she promptly looked away, leaving the room to go to her next class.

We dispersed after that, Mary and I going back to an empty classroom to study.

"Who do you think did it?" she asked.

"Girl, I don't know. I'm not sure I want to. Was it aimed at Daniel, or me? I mean, not many people knew I was learning flying trapeze. We've asked the administration for permission, but that's it."

"Yeah, but I don't see who would benefit from hurting Daniel. After all, the Cirque des Etoile job reward is only for our program. The other students' positions are more secure and less cutthroat. You, on the other hand... Someone's taking down the competition." She lowered her voice saying the last part of the sentence. We hunched over the table.

I nodded. "Yeah, I think so, too."

"You know it's not me, right?"

Our heads snapped towards the source of the voice. Captivated by our conversation, we didn't hear Nathalie entering the classroom, which door we had left open.

Mary slowly leaned back in her chair and crossed her arms. "And how would we know that?" she questioned.

"Because I would never hurt you, I—"

My eyes snapped to our former friend as I cut her off, "You almost made me crash on the ground during the aerial silk class, but okay, I'll buy that maybe it wasn't on purpose. You did throw a juggling club in my face, though. *That* was on purpose. And how about the rosin disappearing on Presentation Day? I could have gotten seriously hurt that day!"

Nathalie's shoulders slumped. "I did do all that. But my goal was to throw you off your game, not kill you!" she protested. "And it didn't even work, but I'm in the final phase anyway, which was all I needed to secure my sister's situation, so I don't care anymore. I told you I was only in the program to take care of my sister, and now it's done!" She spread her arms at her side. "Plus, you heard Donna. She's going to destroy whoever did this, and I've heard she's done it in the past. The person—or people—who tampered with the trapeze have nothing left to lose, so I don't think they're in the competition anymore.

"I also don't believe any of the remaining ones are capable of it. Mary is your friend; if she wanted to take you out, she'd just put a laxative in your food the day of the final performance, and that would be it."

Mary pursed her lips. "Eww, gross!"

Nathalie continued, unbothered by the interruption, "She wouldn't try to kill you! Jonathan is dating your flatmate. I don't thin—"

"Jonathan is what?!" I blurted. Loudly this time, because this conversation was just too much to take in calmly. "What flatmate?" I didn't picture Cody or Thibault cheating on me—us, really.

"You know, the one whose head is almost shaved, with the tattoos." It took me a minute to understand who she was talking about. Then I raised a brow, trying to remember if I had told Nathalie that Logan wasn't actually my flatmate. She had seen him at our flat one of the times she'd come over, so maybe she had jumped to conclusions.

"Jonathan is dating Logan?!" I exclaimed. Why the fuck hadn't he told us? Because he was my competition?

"Yep, since December, I believe." Nathalie sounded smug as hell, and I wanted to slap the bitch. Screw diplomacy. I had reached my limit.

Mary intervened, "So, you think whoever tampered with the trapeze is not in the running for the Cirque des Etoiles job anymore?" Right. The saboteur. Life-threatening stuff was more important than Logan's dating life. Or so, I told myself.

"Yes, I do believe the saboteur's already been eliminated," Nathalie said, articulating exaggeratedly, as if we were intentionally being slow.

"Nobody still in the running will risk getting on Donna's bad side. Even the five who'll lose, if they're still on her good side, they'll still gain exposure from having been part of the top six in the program. As she said, we're all some of the best in the world at our specialties, so we have options!" Nathalie threw her hands in the air. "Now, if we cheat and she finds out, our careers are done. Over. Finished. *Terminée. Acabada*. Taking that risk is stupid. Desperate, really. That's why I think it's someone that's already lost." I could see her point. I didn't like it, wanting her to be the villain she had acted like these past few months. But it made sense.

"But what can they expect to gain by this?" Mary asked.

"Getting called back, maybe? Some people did pretty similar routines to Fauve's; they might think they'll be called back if they remove the only hand-to-hand act. Or not, I don't know; maybe it's just that you're the easiest target since you depend more on your material than the rest of us." She was right, and the thought was scary.

I wasn't even close to forgiving Nathalie for what she had done. Even understanding where they came from, I thought her decisions were the wrong ones. Time had proven me right; despite the odds, the three of us were now in the final phase.

But I didn't think she was responsible for the sabotage of the flying trapeze anymore. It wasn't a nice thought. Before, I only had to look out for her. Now? It could be anyone. The coming weeks would be nerve-wracking.

An awkward silence ensued, only disturbed by the rhythmic noise of Mary tapping her finger on the table on which our books were open.

Nathalie very pointedly looked at her phone. "Well, it's getting late; I promised Keira I would meet her new boyfriend over lunch." I nodded, a knot in my shoulders relaxing. She took three steps away from the door, her shoes squeaking in the silent hallway, then seemed to change her mind and came back. "Girls?"

"Yes?" Mary asked.

"For what it's worth, I'm sorry for what I've done, I took things too far with you. Please be careful. Whoever wants to hurt you is still out there." With those ominous words, she left and didn't come back this time.

I sighed. "Well, that was tense."

"You know," Mary said tentatively, "we could investigate." She seemed way too excited by the idea.

"Mary, this is not a movie," I scolded. "We have better things to do than investigate. The administration is on it; let them do their job."

She lowered her eyes back to the sheet of paper she was writing on before we were interrupted. "Yeah, you're right." Then, she looked at me again with a roguish grin. "Not even a little?"

"Mary!" She just chuckled and went back to studying.

Chapter 30

Fauve

The following weeks were exhausting. Our class schedule was as intense as ever. I was surprised there were still enough general subjects to occupy our mornings after almost eight months of classes.

The aerial silk classes with Donna were my absolute favourites. She was amazing, simultaneously strong, flexible, and incredibly creative. She never let anything limit her or her students, always finding something people were good at. I started practicing hard to impress her, and my body gradually became covered in burn marks.

During one of those practices, Stephanie walked in on me, trapped in the silk after trying a snippet of a routine we had learnt earlier that day. I usually always made sure that someone was close by for that exact reason, but it seemed the students in the neighbouring classroom had left during my practice, and I hadn't noticed.

After scolding me for not paying attention, Stephanie helped me get down and offered to practice together thereafter. She had her exams coming up too, and didn't want me to get hurt right after she'd saved my life—her words. We started coordinating our schedules, and it got more productive and fun than when I was practicing alone or with Thibault. He was an incredible aerialist, but Steph was better at silk than he was. I preened when Donna finally noticed how fast I was improving.

In the afternoons, we still worked on our specialties with a tutor; and I divided my time between aerials with Thibault, and Adagio with another teacher.

Since we were only six, it had become impossible to hide in the back of the classroom and not participate. You had to come in, be on top of the subject if the teacher asked anything, then repeat it for the next class.

I was becoming increasingly tired, and it worried me, since with exhaustion came sloppiness and, with it, injuries.

A few weeks after Donna's speech on cheating, we started rehearsing my final presentation. I was worried because it felt like we had started late. However, a part of my brain liked to remind me that I had thought of same thing every single time, and it had worked out just fine.

I had decided we would perform the same act as we had done for the third presentation, but with several twists. After all, there was no rule stating all of our evaluation acts had to be different, and I liked the one Thibault had put together. I liked it a lot.

Thibault, Loup, and I had started staying late at NICAM to rehearse. We had created a checklist to verify our material was precisely how we had left it, and only started training after ensuring everything was in order. It was us being ridiculously paranoid, although necessary, unfortunately.

AERIAL

The saving grace in this stressful environment was the people around me. Mary and I still got along fantastically, always hanging out or studying together. The atmosphere at the flat was saccharine sweet, and the guys were growing increasingly comfortable with PDA between themselves, even outside of a sexual context. My heart rejoiced in my chest whenever I caught Cody kissing one of the other two. Embraces between Thibault and Loup made me happy, too, but they happened way more often, so I had more time to get used to them.

On the nights when the three of us stayed late at NICAM to train, I usually took my time to change back into my regular clothes, knowing full well they would probably be in each other's arms when I arrived.

In the frenzy of the presentation rehearsals, I never got a chance to speak with Logan about him dating Jonathan. I wasn't mad; I had no right to be. I'd never even asked who his boyfriend was and what he did, after all. My friend often mentioned a "Jon," but that was all I knew. I should have cared more.

The last week before the show, classes were cancelled, allowing us to rehearse full time, and on the morning of the evaluation, Logan came to the flat to do our makeup. What we had planned would easily take all day since it was a full-body makeup. We were doing it at home, and I was so happy summer was finally here because it meant I could just wear a thin dress over my white bra and bikini briefs on the way to NICAM. Still, I hoped it wouldn't smudge it. Thibault and Loup would throw on beach shorts over their white trunks and call it a day. We only hoped we wouldn't be stopped by the police for walking around half-naked. Or worse, the makeup wouldn't drip everywhere because of the heat. It was supposed to be waterproof, sweat-proof, smudge-proof, but you never truly knew.

Logan started out on my legs, painting them integrally before moving up. Once we'd finished joking around and catching up on the events of the last few weeks, I led the subject towards what I wanted to know.

"Will you be helping Jonathan do his makeup later today?"

He threw me a sly look, as if to tell me he knew full well what I was doing.

"No. He's been doing drag since he was twelve. He's much better at doing his face than I am. He would probably crucify me for even offering." He chuckled. "Who told you? Not even the guys know."

"Nathalie. You know her, she's been at the flat a few times."

"Oh, right, she saw us…once. We were hanging out in a bar. Jon saw her, waved at her, and that was it. I didn't think she remembered me; she barely even said 'hello.' Now, how do you feel about it?" Our eyes met in the mirror.

"I'm not sure, honestly. I don't like it, but I would probably have done the same thing if I were you. You must have been in a shitty position all these months, caught between your friend and your boyfriend."

He rubbed his head with the hand that wasn't holding the paintbrush. "Yeah, I wanted to tell you guys, but in December, it was all very new, then the drama happened with Nathalie, and I thought you wouldn't be thrilled to learn I was dating another one of your competitors."

"Well, now you guys have been together for months, so if you trust him, I trust you, and I understand I wasn't emotionally available. I'm sorry." I winced.

"It's fine. I understand, too. And we're happy together, so it's cool, really. I'm relieved it's out in the open now, though. It felt like I was back in the closet and had to come out all over again." He chuckled. "A weight has been lifted off my shoulders."

"Well, you guys don't have to hide anymore. You should come to dinner sometime. We haven't really talked much, Jonathan and I, but he's never given me a reason not to like him." His eyes met mine, a soft smile growing over his features.

"I would love that."

Chapter 31

Fauve

THE FINAL PRESENTATION HAD to take place in NICAM's amphitheatre. It was one of the conditions of the assignment. My reaction to this had been immediate, blurting, "What amphitheatre?!" as I read the email.

Thibault had laughed, telling me I hadn't explored nearly enough of the possibilities the institute offered. I was inclined to agree.

The major consequence of this new venue was we wouldn't be performing above the foam pit, and if I fell, only mattresses would cushion my fall. The secondary consequence was we had to move a lot of equipment out of the gymnasium, and I was scared shitless of the saboteur using this to his or her advantage.

The benefit of it all was that we would perform in an impressive venue, in front of a beautiful background, which I was really excited about. Maybe stupid, but one hundred per cent true. The huge venue also allowed us to invite our friends, and I was so excited that Cody and Logan were going to be there.

The moving of the material had happened throughout the week, so everything was already set up when we arrived at NICAM.

We checked the installations thoroughly, though, using our list to ensure everything was in the right spot. Every rope, solidly attached. Every screw, tightened. We also managed a quick makeup check, and except for retouches here and there, it was intact.

Showtime.

This time, the order of performances had been defined randomly. Nathalie went first, and, of course, she and her sister had put together a fire juggling act. Our relationship had become less tense since we had spoken, but it was difficult to admit out loud that she was amazing. Even if she was. Fire juggling was badass.

Then went Jonathan. Or Alisja Adore, since they were in full drag. Once again, they had been incredibly creative in their act, and instead of heels, they were using ballet pointes as their shoes. When the music started, they also fixed knives under the pointes, strapping the handle around their foot and balancing on the blades and tips. It was marvellous. They then threw the other knives at moving targets while dancing and lip-syncing. My mind was divided between wanting to push Alisja to the side so they wouldn't steal my place as number one, and wanting to be their best friend. They had excellent ideas.

Clarissa and her partner, Stacy—the quick-changing Barbies once again reunited—stepped on stage next. She had required her friend's help, the same way I had with Loup and Thibault's. They were good, but weren't really doing anything different from what they had done for their first, second, or third presentation. Cody and I had talked about it, trying to identify who was the true competition, and who were the people I could easily beat. It turned out his analysis that they were good but not evolving had been spot-on.

The atmosphere, backstage, was tense. Everyone was painfully conscious of how many people had already been eliminated, and that the saboteur still hadn't been caught. People were silent, both before and after their performances.

Suddenly, we were next. Before climbing onstage, I did one last stretching and warming up round, trotting around the backstage area to elevate my heart rate. I was barefoot, but didn't care. The soles of my feet were black with dirt most of the time, anyway.

I was finishing my round when I spotted a silhouette perched high above the stage, in the area where we stored our material. It was a metal bridge, right above where we would perform, where riggers installed our material, and electric motors made it go up and down. And since we were the only aerial performers, no one had any business being up there.

I didn't dare move, not wanting to be spotted, but at the same time, I couldn't exactly wait for the drama to unfold. Something was happening, of this I was sure. I stayed frozen in my spot as the volume of the music coming from the stage decreased.

Could I stop the show without consequences? I was expected on stage any minute now. I was sure something had happened up there and didn't want to risk the saboteur escaping. It was dangerous for me to perform on an apparatus that had been tampered with. I was out of options, and time was running out.

As the quiet returned, I heard sounds coming from outside the building. Shouting and then ruffling, as if someone was running wearing heavy equipment. People armed with tasers and dressed in black swarmed the building, coming in from all the directions. My surprise made it seem like there were fifty of them, but there couldn't have been more than a dozen. Without hesitation, they climbed the stairs to the fly space, and I saw one of them seize the silhouette. I stayed there, too dumbstruck to move.

"Fauve, thank fuck you're here," Thibault said, wrapping me in his big arms. "You were gone for a while. We were scared when we didn't see you come back, and we thought something had happened to you."

I hugged him back, then watched silently as the policemen took Eva, one of the Adagio sisters, out of the building.

Nathalie had been right, after all. The saboteur had been eliminated from the competition and was hoping to get back in.

I heard heels clicking down the corridor, getting closer.

"Fauve, my dear, how are you?" Donna Loewenberg asked, laying her palm on my upper arm. "I'm so sorry you were so close to the action; it wasn't supposed to happen this way." She continued walking towards the direction the guys in black had gone.

Extricating myself from Thibault's arms, I trotted behind her. "What do you mean, 'wasn't supposed to happen this way'? This was supposed to happen?"

She threw me a sideways glance. "Yes, we knew someone was tampering with our material. I am no stranger to rivalry, and I knew it was only a matter of time before somebody ended up being hurt. Again. So, I got in touch with the security team NICAM hires for occasions like this and set up a trap."

Donna arrived next to the guy in black that seemed to be in charge. He was about her age, with dark hair and light brown eyes. Just as she had done with me, she palmed his upper arm.

"Where is she?" she asked him.

"We're keeping her outside; we've called your attorney, and the police will be here soon. I got this, Donnie. You can go back and take care of your students." Donnie? How close were these two?

"Thanks, Lincoln, I owe you one." She tilted her chin and turned to me.

"She had the time to mess with our trapeze, though," I stated.

"It was a decoy. After the flying trapeze episode, I guessed you were the target and had a copy of your material made. I have had the original one under key in my office since the performances started. The staff is changing it back as we speak." Nobody had even noticed her come and go. Who was this woman? "Let's go back to the others. Do you feel well enough to perform?" she continued. "Or would you like to take a minute?"

"Are we certain it was my stuff she was trying to sabotage?"

She nodded.

"Is it possible that I go last, maybe? To catch my breath?"

"Sure. Let me check if Carlos is ready to go, otherwise we'll take a break as he prepares, and resume after."

I didn't want to think about everything that had happened so far. Not now. I still needed a breather, though.

Donna nodded. "Okay, then. See you out there."

The adrenaline was quickly replaced by bone-deep exhaustion. I barely caught a glimpse of Carlos's act.

Mary's, though, I watched from the beginning to the end, remobilising my strength.

She and Liam had built a Cyra, hybrid between a Lyra—the other name of the aerial hoop—and a Cyr wheel. They used it on the ground first, somehow fitting both their bodies into the thin structure.

After a moment, an almost invisible cable descended from the ceiling, and they passed it through a hole at the top of their contraption.

Then they took flight, twirling in the air as if carried by a tornado. It was amazing and crazy poetic, and I couldn't take my eyes off them.

Which was scary as fuck.

I did some breathing exercises, applied a ton of rosin on my hands, wrists, and ankles, and stretched until I felt like myself again. It didn't take too long; I would take time to process that someone tried to kill me—twice—later.

I returned to our backstage spot, grabbed Thibault and Loup's hands, and kissed them softly.

"We're ready when you are," Thibault offered.

"I'm ready, let's do this."

The music started as we stepped onstage. "Wise Enough" by Lamb blasted from the loudspeakers. Cody had helped me discover the song. It was one of his favourites, and I had immediately fallen in love with it. He didn't know we had picked it for tonight, though. It would be a surprise.

Like three months ago, Loup and I first performed the Adagio routine we knew so well, dancing and spinning around each other.

We had filmed ourselves multiple times while rehearsing. The big trick of our act was that, in normal lighting, our makeup was invisible. The beginning of the performance seemed naked, with us only in our white underwear under the plain projectors, without any colour in sight.

The exact setting continued as I did the duo trapeze part of the act with Thibault.

The difference between our third and fourth performance came about halfway through when the normal lighting switched off, and black light revealed the swirling colors painted on our skin and clothes. We had also painted both bars of the trapeze—to see them—but not the ropes. Thibault climbed first to the highest stage. He looked like he was flying, suspended in the air.

I climbed next, while Loup settled on the lower level of the trapeze. In our planning, my boyfriends and I had added another tweak. At this point in our performance, Thibault threw down a rope and pulled me to the higher level of the trapeze with the sole force of his arms. I looked as if I was levitating, floating, magically suspended.

Aerial.

I performed a series of backflips, Thibault throwing me back and forth, high above the ground, while Loup waited.

Just like last time, we pretended to fail a catch for me to fall into Loup's waiting hands.

And same as before, a gasp emanated from the audience.

I guess an impressive enough trick is still impressive the second time.

Especially knowing that this time, we didn't have the foam pit to catch us in case of failure.

It was okay, though. We hadn't failed, and I had never planned to.

The music ended, and Thibault joined us on the ground. The three of us saluted, holding hands.

We had just finished our last show of the year, the last time we would perform in front of these teachers, the last time we would defend my spot here. The feeling was bittersweet, indeed.

We went back home, and the agonizing wait before the results began.

Even though my body was exhausted, I almost hadn't slept all night, instead tossing and turning in Thibault's bed. At one point, he got upset and started massaging my muscles until I fell asleep. I should upset him more often.

In the late afternoon, we all headed to NICAM. For these final results, families and friends were allowed to attend. Mava and Mapa were watching it all via video chat, having insisted we call them when the ceremony would happen. My own family decided not to attend, though. My genius cousin had an event at her university, and my mom had preferred to go there.

As chic as ever, Donna Loewenberg waited on a stage that had been erected for the occasion in the hall, with a podium and a microphone on it. She looked incredible, as always, in a navy-blue pantsuit and a black button-up shirt, hair pulled back. Her piercing blue eyes scanned the audience, and seemingly satisfied, she started her last speech of the program.

"Hello, dear students, parents, friends, and welcome to NICAM. I am so glad you are here today to celebrate with us the six finalists of the intensive circus program and the crowning of our best student.

"For once, I will not start from the top. I'm sorry, everyone, but since it is my last time announcing your results, we will start by the sixth position and gradually make our way up. Today, I'm feeling dramatic.

"Out of the fifty who started this year with us, our sixth-best is..." Cue drum rolls. "Clarissa Jones!"

"Our fifth best is..." *Not me, not me, not me.* The words swirled around in my mind relentlessly. I needed to at least be in the top four. "Carlos Rodriguez!" He stayed in the same spot since the last ranking. I wasn't surprised.

Forget the top four; I needed the top three.

"Our fourth best student is..." I had finished biting all my nails off and was now getting started on my lips. Loup grabbed my right hand and Cody my left. "Jonathan Young!" I threw a glance at Logan, sitting next to him. The knife-thrower seemed disappointed, but was saving face.

"For the top three, I would like to call them on stage. You are outstanding artists, and I want you to come next to me. You don't have stage fright, right?" The audience chuckled. There were around forty people in the hall: students with their families and friends, for the most part.

My heart was jumping in my throat. I felt like I was about to pass out. I looked around, spotting Nathalie and Mary pushing through the crowd. It would end almost as it had started, with the three of us.

We walked to the stage and stood together at Donna's side. Thibault and Stephanie gave me an encouraging nod as I passed them.

What was I going to do if I got called first? Shake their hands, and tell them I was happy for them? It would be a lie.

"Now, in the third position," Donna started again, "Nathalie Roy!" It would be insulting to celebrate noisily, but it took all my self-control to prevent myself from doing it.

Only Mary and I were left, and she grabbed my hand, holding it tight. In mere moments, one of us would have our heart broken. I selfishly hoped it would be her. I wasn't going to lie; I didn't feel like a hero. I felt hopeful, though, my dream within my reach.

"I will now announce the winner. The artist whose act we liked best, whose performance has been judged worthy of performing at the Cirque des Etoiles this year is..." I was going to pass out. My breaths were shallow, palms wet. My blood had turned to ice, and my vision blurry. "Mary Sue Shevchenko! Congratulations, my dear. I look forward to working with you! Our invitation extends to your partner too, of course." They hugged. I wasn't functioning anymore. I was seeing the audience applaud, but all I could hear was white noise, and my heart pounding in my ear. All my strength was used to not collapse. I had failed.

At Donna's words, a part of me withered and died.

"Fauve," Donna started, "your performance was incredible. All the teachers, tutors, and I loved it. I do not doubt that you will have a brilliant career in this business, and I wish you the best of luck." She shook my right hand, putting her left one on top of mine. "Thank you for participating, you did great, really." I wouldn't cry, I wouldn't cry, I wouldn't cry.

My heart felt like it was being ripped out of my chest. I avoided looking at the audience. I didn't want to see the look on Cody's face, the disappointment in it. He had been right from the beginning; I was going to leave.

I forced my limbs to move to congratulate Mary. I hugged her tight, and she whispered in my ear, "I'm sorry." Her words almost broke me, but I held on.

"Enjoy every second of it, girl. You deserve it," I whispered back. "Text me when the Cirque des Etoiles is in Europe, so I can come to see you."

It was a fight to get the words out. My throat had constricted painfully, and I couldn't hold in my tears for much longer.

"Go to your men," she ordered, "we'll talk later."

Except we wouldn't.

Because I'd be gone.

I walked to them through the audience, staring at the floor. Loup grabbed me as soon as I was within reach and hugged me close against his chest, shielding me from interrogating looks. A few tears escaped at that moment.

"Let's go home, Plume." He ushered me out, Cody and Thibault probably following us. I didn't look up; I couldn't. I should have done more, trained more, created more—anything, to change that verdict. But I couldn't, no longer.

And the home we were going back to wasn't home anymore.

Chapter 32

Fauve

I WAS TRYING AND failing not to collapse when we arrived at the flat. I was exhausted, devastated. My dreams were turning to dust when they had been within my reach, mere moments ago.

Opening the door, I went directly to my room to pack. I was going to ask my parents to get me on the earliest flight back to Paris. There was no need to drag this out, after all.

Loup didn't let me, though. His strong arms wrapped around me, and he lifted me to sit on our bed, with me in his lap.

"What are you doing, Plume?"

"Packing. If we stay longer, leaving will feel even worse. I want to go back to France next week, at the latest." There, I would see my friends from college, and my heart would slowly heal. If I spent the summer here, hanging out with Cody and Thibault, going back in August would be excruciating. I immediately stood back up.

Rummaging through my things, I started looking for my passport. I kept it in my bedside table, always, underneath a pile of more or less useful documents. My eyes were already puffy from crying in the subway, and my vision blurred again, making it impossible to see correctly, so I just took out the drawer and flipped it on my bed, creating a sea of paperwork on my grey sheets.

Underneath it all, my phone started ringing. Finally finding my passport, I ignored the annoying sound and searched for my wallet, to put away the very important document in my hand. When I looked up, Loup had found my phone and held it flat in his palm. It rang again.

With a supplicating gaze, he oriented the screen so I could see who was calling, and said, "If you don't answer, she's gonna keep calling."

My mother.

All my hurt, disappointment, sadness, and regrets swirled and merged in my chest as I stared at the blinking screen. They grew and grew, until I couldn't take it anymore, and all that remained was a black mass of pure, unadulterated anger.

I grabbed the phone from my boyfriend's hand, and bringing it to my ear, I simultaneously pressed the green button and barked, "What?!"

I immediately started pacing like a caged lion in the small room.

"Fauve," my mom greeted me, warm as a glacier. "I take it you didn't get the job, then. Your father and I are checking the flights as we speak. Is next Monday okay?" It was typical of her. No "How are you feeling?" or "You made the top six of the best circus school in the world, it's already great," let alone an "I'm proud of you."

Even though I was packing to leave when she called, I snapped.

I didn't want to leave. I was twenty-two, for fuck's sake, I wasn't a child she could boss around anymore. The performance at Cabaret Rouge had proven some venues would pay to have me perform. Since then, I had trained and improved so much there was a good possibility I could get smaller gigs, until getting cast by one of the major companies. I had ranked first in my class not once, but twice, only to be second the third time.

I was good at what I did, and it was past time my mom realised it.

It was past time I stood up for myself.

"No," I deadpanned. "Next week is not okay, and neither is next month. I'm staying, Mom." My tone left no place for debate. "Aren't you even a bit interested in my results this time around? I came in second place, *Maman*. Second! And the four people I just beat are some of the most talented, creative people I know! And guess what? Their parents support them!

"So, you know what, Mom? This time, second best is going to have to be good enough, because I'm staying!" I was yelling by the time I finished, my phone pressed against my cheek, covering itself in sweat.

Silence stretched between us. Would she finally understand that this wasn't a fluke, that I was determined and I wouldn't stop now that I had made it this far?

I heard a sigh as if she was making a difficult decision. "You know we'll stop sending you money, right? You shouldn't break your promises, Fauve. The deal was that you would come back. We trusted you."

I saw red. "Well, since I was a kid, I have trusted that you wanted to see me happy, and look how that keeps turning out! I don't care about your money, I have everything I need here. I have two months of visa left and I bet I can find a job in that length of time! I'm good enough for a lot of people, and as your daughter, I should be good enough for you, too!" I took a deep breath before saying, "I do not need you anymore, Mother." This felt like I had finally said everything that had been festering in my mind for years.

It felt... amazing. As if I had taken the weight on my shoulders, thrown it on my mom, and squished her with it. Only if it was Mario Kart style, though. She would walk around squished in 2D for a while, then pop back in 3D. Even if she annoyed the crap out of me, I didn't want her to die.

I had just squished my mom with the boulder that was on my shoulders, and it felt amazing. Powerful.

She wasn't done with me, though.

"You know, Loup will have to come back to France eventually, right?" she pried, as if talking to a petulant child. I interrupted my pacing to look at him, and he met my eyes unflinchingly. He was close enough to have heard my mom's question; and I drew strength from the steel in his eyes. He tipped his head in a way that would have been imperceptible if I didn't know him as well as I did, but in our case, it could as well have been a shout of encouragement. He had my back, and always would. Behind him, Cody and Thibault also stood tall, grey and green eyes watching me intently.

Then, Cody silently mouthed, "I love you," and it took all I had to focus on finishing my call.

"By the end of Loup's visa, we'll have a job, and he'll only spend a holiday in France, then come back here. Or we'll get married if we have to. The only thing you have to understand is that I'm not leaving!"

I had never heard my mother sound more smug and condescending than when she said, "Fauve, you and Loup getting married will solve none of your visa problems."

After this conversation, it became quite obvious my mother was only interested in judging me, and nothing I did could make it any better. So I'd make it worse, but at least I'd revel in taking that condescendence down a notch, for a minute.

"Mom, we fell in love. The both of us. We're with two Canadians guys—my flatmates, you know? I told you about them. It's in a very happy foursome, and marrying them would definitely guarantee us a visa."

"Fauve!" My mother protested. "I—"

I cut her off, finished hearing what she had to say. "No, Mom, whatever it is, I'm done listening. I know you won't accept our relationship, so I won't even try. Yes, the four of us have been together. As in *together*, together, for months, and it still feels amazing. I'm not leaving them, I'm not leaving my career, and especially not because of a bullshit pact I should never have made in the first place. With you, of all people.

"So," I said more calmly, my tone final, "goodbye, Mom. I wish you all the happiness in the world, but I don't think you would recognise happiness if it bit you on the ass. Despite it all, I love you and Dad, so please call me when you calm down." And I hung up.

In six months, I'd made a dragon my pet, and a harpy, my bitch.

Not bad for an acrobat.

Cody

"No," Fauve told her mother. "Next week is not okay, and neither is next month. I'm staying, Mom."

My heart stopped. It completely stopped, then a warm feeling took place in my chest, and it restarted at a frantic, accelerated pace.

After all of her bullshit excuses, she was finally standing up for herself. For us.

I watched her verbally battle against her mother, and could make out that she was standing her ground, without understanding the words. I was fully bilingual, the language wasn't an issue. I just had trouble focusing, words didn't make sense anymore.

She was staying.

The fight lasted for a moment, then her mother said something that had her looking around, seeming insecure for the first time since the beginning of their call.

Loup nodded, and I finally put words on the feeling that made me feel like I was both flying and sick at the same time. "I love you," I silently mouthed.

With renewed strength, Fauve started shouting on the phone again. When she mentioned a foursome and a marriage, I smirked.

She was really staying.

I almost didn't want to believe it, but this wasn't the type of conversation you came back from. It made me sad, that it had been necessary, but also incredibly happy.

She was truly, definitively staying. And Loup, too.

We were going to be together.

We needed a bigger bed.

What? Someone in the group had to be the pragmatic one.

"That," Thibault started, effectively making me snap out of it, "was almost as hot as when you threatened to cut off my balls, Puss."

Loup turned to look at him incredulously. "She did what?"

"Yeah, before you arrived, I was an ass to her. She made me believe we were going to have sex, so I made her come on my fingers. Then, instead of sucking me off, she took my balls in her hands and threatened to emasculate me if I ever behaved like a jerk again. That was super hot. Well, this was hotter."

Loup's eyes bounced from Thibault to Fauve, and I saw my opening.

I took two big steps, caught Fauve, and wrapped my arms tight around her, nuzzling her neck. "So, now we're all in love with each other, huh?"

Fauve looked like a deer caught in headlights. She leaned back so she could see my face. My extremely thrilled face. That seemed to relax her, tension visibly leaving her shoulders.

"Yeah, I probably should have told you before I told my mom. I'm sorry, Cody." She tilted her head back, and whispered right against my lips, "I love you."

The sound went straight to my cock, that instantly went hard as a rock. I grabbed a handful of Fauve's ass and pressed her tight against me. "I love you, too, Fauvette." I nipped at her ear, then breathed against her neck. "We're going to celebrate, now. Tell Thibault and Loup whatever you have to tell them, then get them naked in my room; your bed is a mess."

I released her abruptly, stomping out of the room like a man on a mission.

I had a surprise for her, too.

Chapter 33

Fauve

MY EYES LINGERED ON Cody's ass as he walked out the door, then I immediately obeyed him, getting closer to Thibault. Looking him right in the eyes, I said, "I love you."

"I know," he replied with a shit-eating grin, which earned him a hit on the shoulder. "Ouch!" he exclaimed. "Cody, get the ropes, she's getting violent again!" I scowled at him.

"You deserved it. I just stood up to my mom for you and you're making fun of me," I accused, making sure my voice was as playful as I felt. I never thought that fighting with my mom could feel so good. I was on fire, there was no other way to describe it. That, added to the fact the noose had slipped from my neck, was making me horny as hell.

So, I just started undressing right in front of them. "Let's go, and get naked. Cody's waiting for us." I'd torture Thibault into saying it back later.

I sauntered out of the room without checking if they were following me, to find Cody standing next to his bed in all his naked glory.

All of my men's bodies were works of art, but in different ways. Cody's was very literally sprinkled with artwork. His right leg was covered in such intricate designs almost no skin was visible. On his left leg, the tattoos were not as close together, but still covered most of thigh. His lower abs were entirely inked in planets and constellations, the lowest black moon dangerously close to his dick...now standing at attention.

How had Logan focused while tattooing all of this?

My eyes made their way up Cody's body, slowly reaching his soft hands in which his long fingers held a Polaroid camera.

"Like what you see?" he teased.

"Very much." Why deny it? At this point, there probably was a puddle of drool all around me on the floor.

At that moment, Loup and Thibault entered the room, naked, panting, cheeks flushed, and rock-hard dicks bobbing against their abs as they walked.

"Did you get started without us?" Cody teased again. It seemed that my conversation with my mom had put him in a good mood, too.

"Just having an important conversation," Loup answered seriously. Then, he took two big steps towards Cody, grabbed his hip to press their bodies together and quickly said, "I love you," before kissing the other man, as if he was the air he needed to live, the polaroid camera ending up trapped between their writhing bodies. I wanted to be that camera.

I cleared my throat. "Cody, what was your idea?"

They stopped kissing, and in the softest possible way, Cody palmed Loup's cheek, ignoring me completely. I didn't mind, the scene before my eyes was too cute to interrupt. Even if I was jealous of the camera's position.

"I love you, too," Cody whispered to Loup. Then, he turned towards me and declared, "I bought this so we could make memories before you went away. You're not going anymore, but I think we can still take a few pictures. What do you guys think?"

Thibault was immediately on board. "I think the best picture deserves a reward. I say we reward hotness with hotness; whoever's in the hottest photo wins an orgasm."

"What if all three of us are in it?" I inquired.

"Then, I hope Cody can multitask." The trapezist winked, his smile bright like the rays of the sun.

Then, it all became competitive. And heated. The three of us were known for sexy-as-sin performances, and it was our job to know what our limbs would look like in a determined position. Cody took shot after shot of our naked bodies tangling together in elaborate poses, and I wanted to keep all the pictures coming out of the camera. It was decided; I wasn't giving them away. Mine.

I was comfortable leaving them with the guys because I trusted them with my life. Plus, even if they got leaked, none of them had my face showing, and I didn't have tattoos.

Suddenly, Thibault weirdly twisted his upper body to look directly at Loup's... crotch? He very pointedly did the same for Cody and said, "Okay, good, I thought I was the only perv who was getting excited in here, but now, I can tell I'm not." I chuckled, then kissed him.

Apart from the fact that we were naked—the situation wasn't at all PG13—we hadn't done any real sexual poses. It was closer to sensual and suggestive, instead of explicit.

Thibault's comment changed that. He continued, "How about you, Puss? How's your pussy feeling? And the rest of you?" I rolled my eyes.

"Why don't you find out?" I taunted.

"Come here. I want you to sit on my face."

He sat on the bed with his thighs slightly apart, erect cock twitching against his stomach. I couldn't resist and gave it a big lick as I passed.

"Say it, first," I ordered, caressing his balls with one finger and watching them immediately retreat against his body.

"Make me."

I then proceeded to drive him crazy with soft, unsatisfying, but very arousing touches.

Click, churrr.

"Puss, please," he moaned. I enjoyed having that much power over this man.

"No. Say it or I'll bite," I threatened, softly grazing my teeth against the sensitive head of his cock.

He relented, "I love you, Puss, I do! But please stop this, or it'll all be over before it starts."

Click, churrr.

The camera's printing sound echoed in the room. I went to stand on the bed, putting a foot on each side of his face so that I faced Cody. And I slowly lowered myself—without bending my knees—until my nether lips hovered just above Thibault's mouth, just like I had done with Loup all those months ago. Except this time, I faced his dick. I arched my back and pointed my toes, doing a perfect split over the trapezist's face.

Click, churrr.

Half of me wanted to see the pictures, and the other half wanted to remain exactly where I was. Thibault's tongue had started its dance between my thighs, his big hands grabbing my ass cheeks to spread me even wider than I already was. I bent my legs, my thighs starting to burn, and lowered my torso on my trapezist to take him in my mouth. I teased the head of his cock with my tongue first, just the tip, then blew on him, and finally took him in my mouth, my lipstick painting red circles around his girth.

Click, churrr. Click, churrr. Click, churrr.

I sucked him relentlessly, massaging the base of his cock with my hand while his tip hit the back of my throat.

His wicked tongue teased my clit mercilessly, and he had taken advantage of how wet the photoshoot had made me, to spear two fingers into my pussy. I heard Cody circle the bed so that he was to my right.

"Arch your back, Fauve." *Click, churrr.* "Yeah, oh wow, this one is incredible."

The camera's noise and Cody's praises seemed to increase my arousal tenfold, and I came embarrassingly fast. I took a moment to catch my breath, resting my cheek on Thibault's muscled thigh, still giving his cock slow pumps with my hand.

Click, churrr.

"Your turn, now."

I swallowed him, my head bobbing up and down as fast as I could, hollowing my cheeks on the way up. My hair was everywhere, getting in my face and around Thibault's cock.

Click, churrr.

His balls tightened, and I eagerly swallowed his cum when he emptied himself in my mouth.

"Let's switch," he exclaimed. "Cody, you're up."

I grinned. This was pure torture. Focusing on the beauty of the images made it impossible to have proper, satisfying sex, while making me wet as fuck.

Loup let all the photos he had gathered in his hands fall on Cody's desk before coming closer. I stood up to meet him halfway while Cody pressed himself against me, his rock-hard dick grinding against my lower back.

My boyfriend leaned in to whisper in my ear, "You look amazing in these, Plume. I'm so glad it wasn't me with you because I got to watch the most erotic thing I have ever seen. And now I get to ravage every centimetre of this gorgeous body." He kissed me deeply, making me open my mouth wide for him. "You still taste like him. Delicious." He captured my mouth again, and curled my leg behind my knee, shoving his dick deep inside of me.

He pushed my right leg up until I was once again doing a split vertically along his body.

"I have an idea," I said. "Loup, hold my legs." I bent my back at an impossible angle and took Cody in my mouth with my head upside-down, laying my hands on his knees for balance. He moaned, pinching my nipples.

Click, churrr. "Holy shit, that's hot," Thibault admired. "Loup, pull back a little. That's it." *Click, churrr. Click, churrr.* I heard Loup's head turn. "What? I want one of these, too. You three can fight for the other one." Loup's hips had started moving, and feeling him in me like this was incredible.

I had nearly forgotten about the camera, and I almost orgasmed again, then and there, the mechanical sounds playing deliciously to my exhibitionist streak. Loup groaned appreciatively. "Come back to a normal position, Plume. I want to fuck you until you see stars." I chuckled as much as I was able to with Cody's dick in my mouth. Was any threesome position ever considered "normal"?

I gestured for Cody to sit on the bed and started sucking him with my ass in the air. Taking it for the invitation it was, Loup entered me from behind, at the same time fucking me and making Cody mouth-fuck me.

Click, churrr.

I snaked my hand in between my legs and made myself come around them at the exact time Loup's orgasm hit. He collapsed on the bed.

Two down, one to go.

"Can I do some tied-up ones?" Cody asked. I nodded enthusiastically. He grabbed a soft rope from his bedside table and gestured for me to join my hands behind my back. He started securing my elbows and tied a series of complex knots that went down to my wrists. He then separated the two strands on each side of my waist and tied a loose knot on my belly. When he passed the rope between my legs and around my thighs, I realised it would press exactly on my clit, and if I tensed my arms or thighs, I could increase the pressure. Cody kept tying knots around my legs until he reached my ankles. If it was possible, I got slicker than before, pondering about my plight.

"Someone has been studying," I noted. We needed a hook in the ceiling. Badly. Two and a half aerial artists live in this apartment, after all. We could use it to train.

Among other things.

The knots were tight but neither hurting me nor cutting my blood flow. I was immobilised but didn't feel restrained or blocked. I felt held, comforted, cared for, even exposed in such a vulnerable position, cum started to run down my thighs.

I felt loved.

Cody entered me from behind in a drawn-out stroke, and I screamed, his curved dick rubbing on all the nerve endings inside me.

"I won't last long, Fauvette; you look incredible like this," Cody breathed. I felt his back arch, his hips pressing harder against my ass.

Click, churrr.

I squirmed, making the rope rub against my clit, but it wasn't quite enough.

"Let me help, Puss. Wolfie, take this." Thibault handed the camera to Loup and snaked a hand between my legs, pressing on the knot hard. His other hand came to pinch my nipple, and I shattered, pulling and pushing against the rope that genuinely felt like a restraint, now.

Click, churrr.

Cody came a couple of strokes later, my pussy still clamping around him. He groaned as he did, low and dangerous.

He paused with his hips pressing hard against my ass and only then, gradually withdrew, reaching for the rope and untying me. That had been amazing.

We all laid down on the bed, tangling our limbs together. Thibault stole the camera from Loup's hands, pointed it at all of our sweaty chests, and blindly took the last shot.

Click, churrr.

Looking at and distributing the pictures almost made us go for round three. We were all too tired, though, both by the emotions of the day and our lovemaking. I fell asleep in a warm pile of limbs, my mind full of beautiful images.

And in the morning, my phone was bursting with emails filled with job offers.

Our photos also gained a permanent place in my wallet.

Epilogue

Fauve

"*ALL THE GREAT STORIES ended with food,*" I thought as I took in our very full, very noisy living room. We didn't have a table big enough for everyone to sit around, so we had taken off the doors of both Thibault's and Cody's bedroom and put them on the trestles we usually used for our desks. We had thrown clean linens over them because we didn't have a table cloth big enough, and decorated it with flowers, marking very carefully where the gap between the two doors was, as well as the holes where Cody had disassembled the doorknobs.

We didn't want anything to fall *through* the table. Even if the scene would be funny, the clean-up wouldn't.

Cody had guaranteed me he could put the doors back in place. I had told him that if we lost part of our deposit, it would be on him. He'd just winked in response.

We had invited all our friends to the flat to celebrate the signing of our work contract.

I had met with Nathaniel Lavoie—head of the Cirque Edouard—on Monday. During the previous weekend, Cody and I had gone through all the offers I had received, picking the best possible offer. It turned out NICAM published our rankings on their website after the intensive program was over, and since the best student was already taken by the Cirque des Etoiles, I was the best student available for hire.

Half of the offers were from foreign companies, or to work on tours, and since Cody and Thibault couldn't leave Montréal yet due to their schooling, refusing them had been a no-brainer. A bunch of them were to teach classes, and I didn't see myself doing that just yet. There was so much I still needed to learn.

But the Cirque Edouard seemed like a good-sized, interesting, dynamic company, and the first I had met with. The meeting had gone so well it also ended up being the only one. Nathaniel even wanted to hire Thibault and Loup.

I negotiated our salaries—thank you, Business School Negotiations Class—and the conditions so that we were comfortable in our new lives. We wouldn't make a fortune, but a living, yes, without a shadow of a doubt.

I had also negotiated work hours compatible with business school classes. Without my parents' support, I'd need a student loan, but I was getting that degree. For me, this time, not because I had to.

Nathaniel was an older man—probably in his sixties—with soft brown eyes and a mischievous smile, and I instantly liked him. He was a former juggler and was passionate about circus, which had created an instant bond between us.

Thibault, Loup, and I had gone back today to sign the paperwork. I would start the work visa procedures next week. There was no emergency, after all.

Tonight was for celebrating.

I looked at our friends, gathered around the makeshift banquet table. Everyone important to me had come, and my heart was all swollen and warm with happiness.

Logan and Cody had their back to the living room door. The tattoo artist was making goo-goo eyes at his boyfriend, who had come as Jonathan, dressed elegantly enough to rival Cody in terms of style.

Next to Logan were Loup and Thibault, obviously plotting something, whispering together in low voices, then laughing before looking at me. I wasn't sure I wanted to know, either.

My trapezist boyfriend had invited Steph, who sat between him and Mary, creating a stronghold of estrogen in a testosterone-dominated room—her words, obviously. My girlfriends seemed to be hitting it off, and that worried me a bit. I wasn't sure the world would survive Mary and Stephanie being friends.

My bestie had asked me if she could bring her new beau, Liam—a request I had immediately granted—absolutely forbidding me from calling him her boyfriend. I hadn't decided yet if I was going to do it just to tease her.

I went to sit directly across from Loup, between Jonathan and Liam. I wanted to grill them on what they expected from my friends and decide if I approved the relationships. Not that it would do much if I didn't.

Still, I felt protective. Logan and Mary were chosen family, after all.

I hadn't invited Nathalie. Although I hoped she was well, I wouldn't take the first step and talk to her. Her betrayal and sabotaging of my performances still hurt. Plus, I knew she was friends with the Adagio sisters at some point. Had they been plotting my demise together, then Nathalie bailed on Eva, and possibly Ana, when things escalated? The police investigation was still ongoing, and I couldn't wait to finally have some answers.

I felt sad when I thought about everything that could have been, but my living room was proof I had enough friends as it was.

We ate, we drank, and we laughed, and I didn't think it was possible for me to feel any happier. Every time my eyes met Loup's, he silently mouthed, "I love you," or some equally sappy shit. I was sure the smile I had plastered on my face was just as mushy. My cheek muscles were starting to cramp from the amount of sheer happiness bursting through my very seams.

Everyone had brought their favourite dishes, which meant there was no harmony, whatsoever, in the menu apart from the joy you could taste in them. Loup and Thibault had taken care of the desert, cutting a myriad of fruits and gathering a mountain of treats to dip into a melted chocolate fondue. Logan had even borrowed his parents' fountain that now stood proudly in the middle of the table. We'd had to put another wood board across the two doors because we were scared the device would fall in the gap, and having it closer to one side of the table had almost started World War III. No one wanted to be far from the melted chocolate-y goodness. Obviously.

It was close to one in the morning when our guests left. For the last few hours, we had just let the chocolate fountain run on the table, clearing out the rest and lazily dipping fruits in it while we drank sparkling wine. Nobody was really hungry anymore, but did you need to be to eat chocolate-covered fruit?

We accompanied Stephanie, Mary, Liam, Logan, and Jonathan to the door and went back to the living room to finish cleaning up. The day had been rich in emotions, and my bed was calling me.

My plans were thwarted when Thibault caught me, lifting me and depositing me on the table. "Don't do that," I protested, "I'm not sure the doors will hold."

"They will," said Cody, who had come closer, watching us with hunger in his eyes. "We tried." That relaxed me a little.

Loup had come back from the kitchen. He closed the distance between him and Thibault and dipped his fingers in the still running, melted chocolate. Without missing a beat, he swiftly spread it on my neck with a mischievous grin.

"Loup, please don't; I'm exhausted. I planned to crash," I said with a gentle smile.

"What if you let us do *all* the work, Puss?" Thibault proposed, readjusting himself in his pants. "Plus, you're dirty, now. We need to clean you up, anyway." Illustrating his words, he licked the chocolate right off my neck. I shivered, my nipples hardening and peeking through my t-shirt. At home, I rarely wore bras, and I wasn't changing that new tradition for some dinner guests.

Loup came to my side and took off my t-shirt while pushing me to lay down on the table. "Relax, Plume, we just want some more dessert."

While Thibault took off my pants, my panties coming off with them, Cody pulled me so that my legs were on the table, too. I ended up splayed down completely naked, the three of them towering over me, devouring me with their eyes. Suddenly, I didn't feel so tired anymore.

"Relax, Plume," Loup repeated. "Let us feast on you." I nodded my consent, and they descended on me like starving wild beasts.

Cody captured my mouth with his, tangling his tongue with mine and cupping my face in his hands. In the meantime, Loup had spread chocolate all over my lower stomach.

"The doors are going to be disgusting if we continue like this," I protested feebly, temporarily breaking the kiss.

Thibault snorted. "Not if we're very thorough in our cleaning." Both he and Loup started licking off the chocolate around my belly button, then. I could feel their tongues sometimes tangle together on my skin.

Cody whispered in my ear, "I think you're overthinking this, Fauvette. I can see it in your eyes. What if I blindfold you? Will it help you relax?" He seemed to consider it for a minute. "I think so." He took off his t-shirt—the first piece of clothing that came off any of the guys' bodies—and tied it around my head. "Now, you have no choice but to focus on the sensations running over your skin."

He was right; it felt as if my sensitivity had increased tenfold. I felt a cold liquid being dripped on my right nipple while warm chocolate was applied on the other one.

"What is it?" I asked.

Cody released the breast he'd started sucking on with a pop. "Wine, Fauvette. Don't worry, trust us, let go." I truly relaxed then, slackening my muscles.

I could feel Thibault's tongue descending on my stomach, licking off chocolate. I whimpered; none of them had touched me where I truly wanted to be touched yet, and the need was starting to become unbearable.

Suddenly, his tongue disappeared from my skin and I moaned in protest.

"Shhh, Fauvette," Cody soothed. "He's coming back." His hand snaked on my inner thigh, and without any warning, he pushed two digits inside my dripping core. I moaned, again, in pleasure this time.

Cold pieces of fruit were being placed on my skin, warm chocolate filling the space between them. The contrast between the temperatures made me hyper-aware of the pleasure coursing through me, thanks to Cody's magical hands.

When Thibault and Loup finished decorating my body, they abandoned all restraint and devoured me like wild animals. Another hand joined Cody's between my legs, dipping in my wetness first, then rubbing my clit. Three mouths licked, bit, and sucked every centimetre of my body, and I detonated with a shout, pussy clamping on Cody's fingers.

"One..." he counted.

They made me come four more times, with their hands, tongues, teeth, and lips. When they were done with me, my legs were truly and completely useless, so they carried me to our room, tucking me in and kissing me goodnight.

All the great stories ended with food, indeed.

But this didn't feel like an ending.

It felt like a beginning.

Acknowledgment

If anyone had told me a year ago that I would now be a published author, I'd have called them insane. We all know a lot changed in this past year, and those changes somehow made this book come to life. Still, it wouldn't have been possible without all the amazing people that helped me stay on track, that kicked my ass when I second-guessed myself, and that pushed me through it all.

My alpha readers, the Eggplanter Ladies, made this book possible. If you liked it, thank them. Without them, it wouldn't exist. It is not a figure of speech or exaggeration, it's a fact. I think that at least a third of the book has been changed for the better after you gave me ideas. Mila, Mary, Sam, Sami, Kim, Ashley, and Marissa, even if we've never met in person, our conversations make my days better. Also, thank you for making me go to the supermarket, even if it's boring, and takes time, and I hate it. Writing is a lot harder on an empty stomach.

To my beta readers, thank you for not letting me become complacent. I had a good story before you read it, and you helped me make it into something I am truly proud of.

Z, please never change. You're a great editor and your comments made me giggle even through the final round of edits, when the mere sight of the words I'd written gave me nausea.

To Marie, Marie, Clarisse, Clarisse, Léa, Salomé, and Shirley, thank you for being the most heteroclite, unpredictable group of friends. We've known each other for almost ten years now and I can't wait to see what you become. Your unconditional support—even when you learned I was writing a smutty book—means the world to me. One thing has to be clear, though. Your parents are *never* reading this.

Speaking of, Mom, Dad, Seb, I hope you never read these words or, if you do, please *do not talk to me about it*. They come after way to many orgies for me to be comfortable with that conversation. Still, thank you for being an amazing family. You have taught me to chase what I want and to be proud of what I accomplish, even if it's not exactly what's expected of me. You've been there to celebrate every single one of my wins (even the ones that took you halfway across the globe) and now, look! We get to celebrate the release of my super-spicy book! I can't wait.

Last but not least, Fer, thank you for being an amazing boyfriend and all-around human being. For always supporting my crazy plans and making them sound sane. For loving me when I don't.

I hope we see each other soon, I love you.

About the author

Manuela Rouget is a globe trotter and a polyglot who uses her experiences around the globe to build stories in her head.

She studied mechanical engineering and product design but has always been a bookworm and dreamt of writing her own stories.

In 2020, she fell in love with the reverse harem sub-genre and self-published her debut book in 2021, hopefully, the first of many.

If you like her work, join her reader group, Manu's Circus Monkeys!

To find out more:

www.manuelarouget.com

And of course, if you loved my book, consider following me and leaving me a review!

MANUELA ROUGET

Amazon

Goodreads

Bookbub

Facebook

Tiktok

Also by Manuela Rouget

Flying High Duet

Aerial – Book 1

Stellar – Book 2

Of Blood & Skin Series

Playing It By Ear – Book 1 (2023)

The Cleanup Universe (Co-write with Mila Sin)

The Meetup - MF Novella

The Cleanup - Contemporary Why Choose

MANUELA ROUGET

The Payback - Contemporary Why Choose (2023)

Made in the USA
Las Vegas, NV
24 November 2024